WOLVES

SIMON INGS

GOLLANCZ
LONDON

The right of Simon Ings to be identified as the author of this
work has been asserted by him in accordance with the
Copyright, Designs and Patents Act 1988.

First published in Great Britain in 2014 by Gollancz
An imprint of the Orion Publishing Group
Orion House, 5 Upper St Martin's Lane, London WC2H 9EA
An Hachette UK Company

A CIP catalogue record for this book
is available from the British Library

ISBN 978 0 575 11973 4

1 3 5 7 9 10 8 6 4 2

Typeset by Deltatype Ltd, Birkenhead, Merseyside

Printed in Great Britain by Clays Ltd, St Ives plc

The Orion Publishing Group's policy is to use papers that
are natural, renewable and recyclable products and made
from wood grown in sustainable forests. The logging and
manufacturing processes are expected to conform to the
environmental regulations of the country of origin.

www.simonings.com
www.orionbooks.co.uk
www.gollancz.co.uk

for Mark and John,
and for my brother Richard:
the truth will out.

ONE

His phone call had to come, of course, hard on the heels of the accident and Mandy's maiming, and a life reduced to routines around special cleansers and prophylactic socks. 'How the devil are you?' he says, very hail-fellow-well-met.

Michel and I were best friends at school, and I have swapped desultory messages with him over the years. I have said 'Call me when you're in town.' (But he says he has a horror of cities.) The last time we talked I was still living in the old locomotive factory. Kicking rubbish out the way of my front door each evening. Ringing in food. Working into the night, rocked to sleep at last by sirens and breaking glass.

I fall back, sprawling across the sofa, trying to parse what he is saying. The line is clear enough but for some reason I am finding it hard to work out where one word leaves off and the next begins.

What would he make of this place, I wonder? The floorboards are warm and smoothly waxed. The rug is so thick it needs mowing. The coffee table is a sheet of reinforced glass balanced on four gigantic marbles. The television is part of the wall. Explaining all this to Michel – explaining that this is all Mandy's, not mine – would involve us in a series of nod-and-wink, good-on-you-mate exchanges wholly at odds with the real tenor of my life. The sleepless nights. Feelings of impotence. The smell.

Michel's sending video with his call. He's sitting in virtual darkness, and the gain's boosted into the uncanny in an attempt to render his face. It shines out of the glass in my hand like an amber traffic beacon.

I don't reciprocate. Imagine the picture I would make: my death's-head, can't-complain rictus; and behind me, unnoticed, Mandy walks by on her way to the kitchen, swinging her big clown hands. Her raggy face.

Where is he, exactly? The setting is unreadable: a mass of shadows and angles. The devil in his smithy. 'Can't complain,' he grins. His teeth are in shadow – a crackling grey lightning in the maw of his mouth.

Caught between two worlds, I find it difficult to carry communication between them.

Not difficult. Impossible.

'We wondered if you'd like to come up.'

Come up. Come up?

'We've a cottage. And – get this. A boat.'

Who's "we"? 'The thing is …'

'Yes?'

'The thing is, Michel, I'm a little bit fucked.'

Laughter. Of course. He doesn't know.

'Mick, I've been in an accident.'

A pause. 'Bloody hell. What happened? Are you all right?'

Well. I don't know what to say.

Am I all right?

'Who was that on the phone?'

'An old friend.'

'Yes?'

'From work, Mandy. No one important.'

'I'm going to bed,' she says.

'All right. Do you want me—'

'No, I'll do it myself.'

'Well. Okay.' I lever myself up from the sofa and walk out onto the rear terrace. 'I'll be through in a minute.'

Mandy's house is set among tall white mansions, on a crescent with a private park. A canal runs at the back of her house, and rowing boats varnished the colour of honey are secured with exotic bike locks to the poles of private jetties. Sometimes young women with expensive feathery haircuts pass by, girls really, sculling the narrow water in boats as sharp and thin as slivers of bone.

Of course at this time of night there's no one around at all.

I've been living at Mandy's for nearly a year. I knew from the start it was a mistake. I was quite happy where I was, in my little conversion flat high in the eaves of the old locomotive works, on the other side of the city.

Mandy hated the place. After climbing all those heavy stairs, 'Is this all there is?' A view of brick-paved courtyards, fly-tipped mattresses, an occasional bicycle.

3

This was not snobbery, I realise now, but a failure of the imagination.

'Conrad.'

Mandy writes. She performs her own poetry on a women's magazine programme on the radio, rubbing up against some horrendous scoop about clitoriclectomy, perhaps; an interview with an upcoming singer-songwriter; witty pieces about vests and soup.

'Conrad, come and help me.'

Most of the things from my old flat are in storage. We don't need them here. I should have just thrown my chipboard furniture away; it would have been cheaper than paying storage every month.

'Help me get undone.'

One piece of mine has made it as far as Mandy's bedroom. My mother's mirrored dressing table was the first item my parents bought for themselves after their wedding. They came across it on their honeymoon in the mountains. Goodness only knows how it had fetched up there. The drawer fronts, the table-top, even the legs are scaled with glass. Mounted on the back and sides of the table are three large cantilevered mirrors. The central mirror has a white-painted wooden frame studded with light sockets. I can't imagine what Dad expected me to do with it in my tiny flat. He must have thought I would sell it.

How could I possibly sell it?

'I need some help with these,' says Mandy, holding up her arms.

When we fall in love with someone, we fall in love first with their world. Sometimes love for the person follows.

Sometimes not.

Mandy and I used to drive out through the forest in search of up-market boot fairs. Every time we rode over a steep bridge, or round a sharp bend, or through a tunnel, Mandy tooted her horn 'to warn oncoming traffic'. It was charming at first. Toot toot. Alongside gorges, over high saddles. 'Toot toot.'

'It's what the horn is for,' she insisted. She was so frantic to be in the right, she would make up things to be right about. We pulled up at a T-junction. 'Well?'

'Well, what?'

'Are you going to tell me if it's clear on that side?'

'Just drive.'

'I can't see.'

'Learn. How do you manage when I'm not in the car?'

'When you're not in the car I can see out of the window.'

'Oh, fuck off. Drive. Actually, don't. Stop. Stop the car.'

'Don't be so childish.'

I tugged at the door. She had put the child lock on. She gunned the engine and we kangarooed into the road.

It went dark. The air shot out of my lungs. It froze into glass and washed over my face. There was a single, sharp retort – one steel rod striking another. The engine found its voice and started to warble. The car spun and rolled over. A scaffolding rod shot through the cabin of the car. I rested my head against it. The metal was cold and rough against the back of my head. There was another, more complex impact – a plastic eggbox crushed slowly under a heel. Mandy sang along with the engine. I opened my mouth to join in and a piece of glass embedded itself in my tongue.

This, when at last they cut us out, is what they found to say about me:

'Contusions. Bleeding from the mouth.'

Mandy's notes – I have seen them – are stored in a binder as thick as my fist. Mandy being Mandy, she read them cover to cover, policing her care. I turned the pages for her. 'You missed one.'

'I didn't.'

'You turned two over. There.'

'Right.'

'You see?'

'Yes.'

'Now get your hands away.'

My hands are always getting in the way. My hands are a necessary nuisance for her, now she has lost her own.

The straps around her arms are wet. She has been trying to unbuckle them with her teeth. This is what she is supposed to do; why, indeed, the straps are made of a flexible raw leather. But she needs practice – the hands are heavy, and she has not yet worked out how to cradle their weight while she undoes the straps. There is an art to this. This is what the physiotherapist said to Mandy at last week's appointment. An 'art'.

Mum's old mirrored dressing table is unexpectedly useful to Mandy, now that she has to shed and reload limbs twice, sometimes three times a day. Whatever happens between us, I can see I'm never going to get the table back.

'Hold still.'

'Yes. Thanks, Conrad.'

The hands, electrically warm, more or less flexible,

more or less intelligent, give and shift in my grip like freshly killed rabbits. I am very careful not to show any revulsion as I lay them on the table. 'You want fresh socks?'

After a few hours' wear, no matter how carefully she washes, the socks around the stumps of her wrists begin to smell. She uses all the gels. They lie across the mirrored surface of my mother's table in bitter, medicalised parody of past times.

'Shit.'

'What?'

'I haven't done my face.'

I look into the mirror, see her china-white and staring. The fillers smoothing her scars require a special cleanser to loosen the collagen. The rest is routine enough. I know how to do this. 'Let me help.'

Mum used to test her make-up on me in front of this mirror. On its bright glass surface, thumb-sized pots containing micas and gels were laid out like the controls of a starship. I can remember the feel of my mother's fingers, the heat of her breath on my neck as she ran her brushes over me. Her laughter, and her head beside mine in the mirror, her eyes the same colour as mine. You could not tell us apart.

TWO

I had grown up in a big, overblown red-brick inn built originally for commercial travellers plying the coastal resorts of the north-east. Mum and Dad had bought the business for well below the market rate when the bypass was announced. They had imagined that, with the road relieved and an uninterrupted view of water meadows under low chalk hills, city people would come and visit them for a bit of easily-accessed rural quiet. But even with the bulk of the traffic drawn away, the road was always too noisy to be ignored, and only a few years after their purchase the water meadows were grubbed up to make a housing estate.

When I was a child, I used to pretend to myself that I was growing up in the country. Once the water meadows were sold to developers, I had to come to terms with the fact that we lived in this weird, free-floating, light-industrial suburbia, unable to guess which of several nearby towns would swallow us first.

I never liked the housing estate. I tried to avoid it. I tried to avoid even looking at it. I rehearsed constantly the look and feel of how things *had* been. Buttercup games. Nettle stings. Mum's impatience ('You should have had a drink before we came out.'). The roil and bark of dogs someone had let off the lead to go snuffling after water rats. Sometimes there had been horses, their paddocks marked out with lazy fences – a couple of strings of barbed wire on rickety grey posts jammed in the ground. Mum would wrap a bit of old fruitcake in silver foil and let me feed the horses. When I closed my eyes, screwed them up tight, concentrated, these memories would parade past, always in the same order, as though, rather than naturally remembering, I was tuning into the same reassuring story, again and again.

Whenever I had to walk through the estate, I could feel my childhood recollections falling away from me, the way dreams fall away on waking.

My mum, whose name was Sara, poured everything she had inherited from her family into the hotel, then spent her whole life struggling to 'recover her financial independence'. She had no idea – none – how to make money. I remember one spring I kept catching colds because I had to keep my bedroom window open all the time to get rid of the stench of clary sage – one of the more obnoxious essential oils she had convinced herself she could sell in industrial quantities to her friends. She even included that muck in her food sometimes – self-medicating again.

Fancy bathroom goods. Headscarves. Distressed furniture. Modern antiques. She set up business after business. She had cards printed. Often these featured figures from the Tarot. The hotel paid for all this, of course. Materials she never unwrapped, solvents and pigments she never used, brushes she never cleaned. Though she never made money, an entire self-contained apartment on the hotel's top floor was given over to her experiments in commerce. There was a room for dress-making, a room with a sink where she made her own cosmetics and toiletries, and a room you could barely get into, piled with hand-made paper, stacked with boxes of ribbon, easels, unopened acrylic paints and business cards by the boxful. Days went by and Dad and I did not see her. She had a little kitchen up there. A sofa bed. She spent weeks at a time designing and making her own clothing. The sweet roast scent of her coconut, honey and beeswax facial scrub wafted every so often through the corridors of the hotel, down the stairs, sometimes as far as the dining room and the bar.

Each of her businesses followed the same arc. Each began with a market research trip to her preferred department store, reached the top of its curve with the arrival of a box of business cards, and came to earth with the rearrangement and further filling of the glass-fronted cabinet next to the check-in desk. The cabinet was not so much a point-of-sale as a small museum of wasted effort. Once in the middle of the night I came downstairs to find her trying to wrestle it off the wall.

'Help me.'

'Mum. There are guests.'

'Help me get rid of this stupid thing.'

'Mum, you need to put some clothes on.'

I remember, near the end, Mum turned the whole of her apartment into a Bedouin marquee, every straight line softened with a piece of hanging fabric as she chopped her way through hundreds of pounds-worth of silk and brocade for home-designed wedding dresses. She had me come upstairs to model them. I was her maquette.

In the room she kept for dress-making, and opposite her little sofa bed, sat the mirrored dressing table. She'd dress me up and turn me this way and that in front of the mirrors, asking me what I thought. I said to her, 'I think you need to clean the mirrors.'

Bit by bit she made that apartment her private world. She painted everything white. She got rid of the sturdy red carpeting that ran through the rest of the hotel and left the floorboards bare and unvarnished. Come the evening, when we were doing our own thing and not just eating from the hotel kitchen, I had to go and stand at the foot of the stairs and call her down for meals.

'I think I'll eat up here.'

'You could have said before. It's chops.'

'I'm fine up here.'

'Do you want a glass of wine?'

'I'm fine.'

For all Dad and I knew she had bottles of her own up there.

In vain the doctors explained to us that she was not going to get any better; her highs were only going to get higher, her lows more abyssal. Mum had a horror of what she called, with aplomb, 'iatrogenic medicine'. She had, in other words, a terror of pills. She wouldn't even take aspirin for a headache. When required, she self-medicated with alcohol and cigarettes and managed to disguise her despair very well, right up until the time I found her in the boot of our car with a plastic bag over her head.

THREE

The last time we tried to have sex, Mandy wore her hands. It was all right at first, giving myself to their sheen, their industry. She even touched herself for me. Her robotic fingers hummed a little, and she brought herself to a small climax against their vibration.

Then we turned off the light and all I could see were her big white plastic clown hands turning in the dusk.

'What?'

'I'm sorry.'

'What is it?'

She flopped onto me, and her big white hands crashed into the pillow either side of my face like bludgeons, like hammers.

She had begun to adjust. She stroked me with her feet. She wanted me to like her feet. She wanted me to accept them in their new, exalted role, as she accepted them – as second hands. All I could think about, when she touched me with her feet, was the woman, the friend of my dad's, to whom I had more or less lost my virginity. This was not a particularly happy memory.

She ran the soles of her feet along my penis. She wanted me to join in. She pressed my foot to her sex. My toes scrunched her hair as though it were a carpet. Her hand kept me from pulling away.

'What's wrong?'

I touched her clitoris with my toe. It was wet there. It felt all wrong – wine spilt on a carpet. 'I can't do this,' I said.

My company aside, Mandy spends much of her time alone. Her father is in a home and can no longer be relied upon to recognise her. Her mother remarried over twenty years ago and lives and works abroad. She has no brothers or sisters.

Mandy is learning who her real friends are, and it's been a steep learning curve. One of them sent her flowers and a card that told her to 'Get better'. There are much kinder women in her life, but they are older than her, and by now they have their own responsibilities: jobs, young children.

Mandy's life has been comprehensively locked down since the accident. Until she's restored enough and confident enough to leave the house, I am all she's got.

'You should leave the house,' I tell her. 'We should go for a walk.'

She holds up her big white hands: evidence for the prosecution. 'Go for a walk,' she says.

'Yes.'

'Go where you like,' she says. 'I'm not keeping you here.'

In the kitchen I neck a couple of tablets. Spending so much of my time indoors, in Mandy's overheated rooms, and breathing the recycled air of the hospital, has given me one head-cold after another. 'I could take you for lunch.'

Mandy says nothing.

'In town. I could take you for lunch.'

'How am I supposed to eat lunch?'

'The way you usually eat lunch. With your hands. And I can help you. If you get into real difficulties we can ask for a trough.'

Mandy bursts into tears. 'Why do you have to be such a cunt?'

So I take her to lunch, and that's when I learn that there are two kinds of people in the world: those who still enjoy playing in puddles and those who never did.

When high water overcomes the Middle, it rises through the pavements everywhere at once. Mandy and I teeter along duckboards down flooded alleys – pausing distracted at this church or that, this bookshop, that stand-up patisserie – and slip, the pair of us, like a couple of drunks, on stone footbridges, their steps edged in marble slick as soap. The water in the city's culverts is always the same colour, regardless of season, weather, or time of day: the blue-green of plastic garden furniture.

Again and again I crash against the rocks of her resentment.

'Do you have to keep bumping into me like that?'

'Do you have to keep pawing me?'

This after she asked me to take her arm. ('Please. I'm afraid to fall.')

The water is gone by lunchtime. From the window of the first-floor restaurant I watch as a clear foot of it drains away through tiny sink-holes between the flagstones. The damage done.

Mandy is playing her 'Come here, go away' game with the staff. She wants the waiter to dry her shoes. She wants the waiter to bring her shoes back. She wants the waiter to bring her some dry shoes.

In the centre of the square, a man and a woman in smart-casual clothes trot in circles, round and round. Every so often they point at random into the air, as though firing imaginary weapons.

Mandy wants a drink. Mandy wants the waiter to know, me to know, the world to know, that she cannot be expected to sit down to five courses with wet feet and no drink.

Out the window, I watch them playing. The couple's gestures are ungainly and unpractised. I lean back in my chair, and now I see that I have been watching them through a flaw in the glass; that they are smaller and nearer than I thought. That they are children.

Mandy stands up suddenly. 'You can have my starter if you want.'

'What is it?'

'I'm going.'

'Why?'

'All your sniffing and snotting,' she says. 'I feel sick.'

It is beginning to dawn on me that Mandy is not actually depressed. She is grumpy. There is a difference, morally.

'Why can't you use a handkerchief?' she says.

It's after midnight by the time I get home. She's left everything on, as usual – the television, the fan in the downstairs bathroom. I go around the house, stepping softly, switching off the lights.

Upstairs, I look in on Mandy. She is already asleep. I pull the covers around her and shut her door.

On the terrace, I take out my phone. The air is still, and the canal running past the end of the garden might be a mirror; the lights reflected there are still and absolutely solid. If only the water were closer I might be tempted to throw this useless slab in, just to break the tension.

Dad's number has been ringing all week, unanswered. Now it comes up unobtainable. I stare at the screen, the number illuminated there, as though it's the technology that's betraying me.

More likely Dad, hearing of the accident, has shaken me off at last. Since I texted him from the hospital, six weeks ago, I have heard nothing from him. My emails bounce. My messages vanish into the aether. I can make any number of excuses for him, and that's exactly what I have been doing, for months now. For years. Maybe his phone was stolen. Maybe he lost my number. After years of widening separation, maybe he is struggling to contact me, just as much as I have been struggling to contact him.

The thing is, I can no longer fool myself. I remember this feeling too well, from our last days at the hotel—

The phone rings. An unfamiliar number. I swipe the call open. 'Hello.'

'Conrad.'

17

I lean back against the wall. 'Michel.'

'How are you?'

Still fucked.

Of course, if he knew my real circumstances, if I told him everything, he would know how impossible it is for me to accept his offer. As it is, he cannot understand my reluctance. 'A couple of weeks, longer if you like, though it's very cramped here – you'd probably do your nut.'

He has his camera turned off this time. I try to picture him from his first phone call. His orange face aglow. The shapes and shadows round him. He might have been sitting in a toolshed.

'That's very generous.'

'So you'll come?'

The company I work for is tiny, vigorous and volatile. I've been on compassionate leave since the accident. My job is hanging by a thread. I can't explain this to Michel now, because I've already spun him a line about how free-spirited my life is. I can't turn down his invitation without seeming unfriendly. Though, of course, I can't go.

'Hanna would love to meet you,' he says. 'Have I told you about Hanna?'

I make the right noises, letting him talk himself out. Behind the sardonic delivery that is his signature, he sounds the happiest I've known him. 'She has this plan for survival. We're going to live happily ever after.'

'That's nice.'

I should tell him about Mandy. Why don't I tell him? But after all this time – we left school, what, ten years ago? – it feels wrong to burden him with my present horror. I shared too much with him before: things he should

18

never have had to hear. No wonder we've hardly spoken since.

'We have this boat,' he says.

A boat. Christ. I had had it in my head, until the accident, that I had done pretty well for myself. A place in a pretty, watery, wedding cake-y part of town. Michel's woman has a *boat*?

'We're going to sail around the world.'

That sort of boat. A working boat that you sail. That's all right, then. I had visions of them sunbathing in public view in exclusive marinas.

'We'd love you to see it,' he says. 'It's a bit of a wreck.'

Which reminds me.

'I've not been going out much,' I say, without thinking. 'Since the crash.' I should have said I was back at work. I should have said I was working all hours, trying to catch up on myself.

Stupid. Stupid. *Now* how am I going to get out of visiting them? Given that I have told him I'm my own master, alone and fancy-free, and on the sick? Of course I cannot go. Shall I tell him that *I* am incapacitated? That *I* have lost my face, my hands?

'Well, how about just for a week, at least?' he says.

'I can't,' I tell him, increasingly desperate. 'I can't.'

Mandy has a touching belief in mornings; in her mind, for a little while at least, they have the power to set all things to rights. 'Come on in,' she says. 'The door's not locked.'

She's in the bath. The water's heat has flushed her scars: her face is edged and crazed, more shattered than torn.

'I'll wash your back.'

She's put on weight, slumped here, undone, day after day in these white rooms. Slim pads of fat give under my fingers as I work soap along her spine.

'That's nice.'

'I'll do your hair.'

She turns, her face sliced up into a smile. 'You do too much for me.'

She slides deeper into the water, raises her legs out of the water, and fetches me the shampoo from the shelf behind the bath. I take the pink bottle from between her clamped feet, my throat in spasm, and she shimmies herself upright again. While I work the shampoo through her hair she raises her knees and rubs her stumps against them, washing them. A smell rises. Soap and roses.

'Who was it on the phone last night?'

Falling in love with a person is hard. Falling in love with a world is easy. Confusing the two loves is easier still. I spend the day wandering round the house in mourning for it all. Mandy's kitchen. Mandy's underwear. Mandy's pillows and shoes. I love her scarves and her seven different kinds of toothpaste (a flavour for each day of the week). I love those little blue bottles of essential oils gathering dust on her bathroom shelf. I was always a sucker for Mandy's world. Her visits to out-of-the-way antique shops. Her cutlery drawer, every knife and fork a 'piece'. Wine glasses from an arcade near the Palace of Sports. Cushions from a woman who lives on one of the old lime tree avenues in the Turkish quarter. In Mandy's world, everything has an aesthetic value. The humblest objects acquire a small but telling erotic charge.

Packing is the work of a moment. Laptop and charger, a couple of jumpers, underwear, jeans. Mandy has a hospital appointment this morning. She's back from her fitting at two. I haven't got long. Every time a taxi passes outside the window, my heart gives a tiny jolt.

It's all right. There is time. I wonder if Mandy's hands are dexterous enough yet to allow her to unlock her front door? They must be. She managed all right the day she walked out on me in the restaurant. Only that was a Tuesday. Maybe the cleaner was in.

I don't know.

Anyway, I should phone her, if only to warn her, to tell her I'm gone.

FOUR

A t its grandest, the north-coast highway is a monster. Its four-lane carriageways are barely enough to feed and relieve the half-dozen ferry and container ports that have spread – a slow and steady flood of glass and steel – to fill the mouths of every valley, making islands of a dozen basalt hills.

To the east, the landscape is economically unimportant and much less dramatic, and the road, having expended its strength on valley-spanning ribcage viaducts and swooping white-tiled tunnels, withers at last to a tiny, chicaned, suburban memory of itself. A main road. A high street. A bus route. At each junction, mini-roundabouts form pronounced bulges.

There is not much else to see. A shingle bank blocks my view of the waves. There are some shops – an uneasy mix of tourist services and struggling convenience stores. Hair Trendz. Raz the Newsagent. Artisanal Fruit Beer & Cheese for that 'Tasty Gift'.

This is as far as the national rail network will take me. The regular railway loops south from here, its banked-up rail bed forcing the narrow-gauge local service into a weed-choked alley, embankments on the landward side and a sloping sea-wall on the other. Dead turfs and twigs poke up through its concrete honeycomb. A solitary string of barbed wire makes a notional boundary between the two railways, the big and the small.

There is a café at the station, its chunky pine furniture slathered over with a glassy, polyurethane varnish. At the back of the café is a flight of stairs leading to a model railway exhibition. A 00 gauge layout runs round three walls. In the centre, vitrines display larger, stripped-down engines and mechanical toys. Not all of them are very old. Some I recognise from my childhood. I pause to study a model circus, with cages for the lions, and slop buckets hung on little hooks outside the cages, and caravans with washing lines strung between them, and a make-up tent. The flaps are tied back and there is light inside. I hunker down to see in. A female clown is preparing her face in front of a mirrored make-up table. Her frown is illuminated by light thrown from tiny bulbs embedded in the frame of her mirror.

I stand up quickly, self-conscious, the butt of an obscure cosmic joke.

Wooden steps and boxes bring small children up to the height of the railway's lower reaches, where a variety of goods trains, car transporters, tanker trucks and passenger locomotives weave in and out of sidings and through plaster-of-Paris tunnels, braking and accelerating with an unnatural facility. Clear panels protect the exhibit from curious fingers. Here and there, where the light hits it at an angle, you can see, printed on the glass, the handprint of a child.

The railway crosses a rugged, stepped landscape, rising in one place almost to the bobbly-papered ceiling. (In one out-of-the-way corner, small figures hung on thread simulate the plight of climbers attempting a dangerous, off-width chimney on lichenous rock.)

The trains weave around each other, stop at red signals, go at green. (The abrupt physics of this miniature world is its only unavoidable shortcoming.) The choreography is complex and contingent, signals responding to signals. I wonder if the pattern ever repeats itself. The exhibit may be self-organising, not operating according to some master timetable but to regular readings of its own internal state. Anyway it runs so seamlessly, the eye tires of it in the end. The trains will run and stop and run again as the stars will rise and set, interminably. The rest of the diorama is, by contrast, steeped in incident and drama. True, its occupants – people, road vehicles and animals – are frozen in place. But this actually heightens the drama, bringing to mind scenes glimpsed from a speeding train carriage.

A car has crashed into a safety barrier on a narrow mountain switchback. Witnesses are running up the hill, around the blind bend, to warn on-coming drivers and prevent more collisions.

In the valley below, a lorry driver rests his arm on the sill of his side window as he waits for a flock of sheep to cross a ford. The livery on his truck is written in Cyrillic.

He has driven a long way – is he going to fall asleep at the wheel?

At the entrance of a small rural station, a man and a woman are embracing a child. She stands beside a small leather trunk, and wears a daypack, from which merges the head of a teddy bear (or it might be a rabbit). The parents are not so encumbered; they have come to wave the child off. Where is she going? To school? To stay with a grumpy lone relative, high in the papier maché mountains?

Outside, a steam whistle blows. I glance at my watch and hurry down the stairs, out of the cafe and down the concrete ramp to the platforms of the narrow-gauge service. A train is pulling out of the station. The locomotive is serious enough: its jet-black body is as long and sleek as a classic sports car. It is not a toy. Still, it only comes up as high as my chest. The top of the driver's head is just visible above a polished cowling as he passes by. He is sitting on a padded leather or vinyl bench seat directly behind the boiler. Steam tickles my ankles. Crisp clouds of water vapour obscure the platform for a split second, boiling into the air even as they form. Coaches rumble by. These are taller and wider than the locomotive. It is possible to sit two abreast in them. Some coaches are open, others are fully fitted, with brass-handled doors and sliding windows. A baggage car passes, stuffed with bicycles. In their off-scale compartment, the bicycles look gigantic.

Children wave at me as their coach trundles by. I grin back at them but I keep my hands in my pockets, reluctant to commit myself to the game. The train clears the station and there is Michel, on the platform opposite, looking – in his donkey jacket and cracked DMs – as though he has just stepped out of a protest march. He's studying another locomotive, on the other side of the far platform. This one is bottle green, with polished pipes and spoked iron wheels, whose rims and details are picked out in red enamel. It is prettier than the engine that just left, and its lines are less muscular. An engineer is polishing its controls with a rag.

Michel straightens up, turns and sees me. He has lost his runner's poise. He has put on muscle. An all-weather tan has darkened his already dark complexion – he looks like a Romany gypsy in an old print. At the same time, he has acquired a new brightness. A thin beard softens the mournful line of his mouth. His hairline is already receding; and he is smiling. He never used to smile so readily. God help me, he's happy. He shines with it.

I look for a way to cross over. There is a footbridge, back near the café, but there are no trains at the moment, no squeals of wheel on rail, and the platforms themselves are toy things; they stand barely a foot above the rail beds. Michel waves me over. The engineer behind him frowns but says nothing, just carries on rubbing. I cross the rail bed and step up onto the opposite platform.

'It's good to see you.' He embraces me. 'Bloody hell.' He finds us an empty carriage. We sit opposite each other, my kit bag perched on end in the seat next to me.

We sit and we talk; we say the things people usually say, but these pleasantries – 'Smooth journey?' 'How are you?' – leave less of a mental trace on me than the fact of our proximity. Michel's presence is like a scent. It presses against me, heavy with memory, as we wait for this pretty green engine to pull us east, towards the shingle banks and the sea.

FIVE

Dad had expected Mum to take charge of the look of the hotel, and fill it with the things she made. Curtains, cushions, hand-printed wallpapers, framed pieces. Mum couldn't sell for toffee, but she had skill, a good eye. Instead she spent her whole time looking after me. I have no memory of her doing anything for the hotel beyond a bit of absenteeism cover here and there. She ran into town for supplies if an order fell through. She handled the bookings when our manager went to pick up his daughter Gabby from school. She served at the bar, but only when Dad wasn't around. (Meeting her for the first time, you wouldn't say she was a friendly person.)

So the whole weight of running and furnishing and maintaining the hotel fell to Dad. It was done out in his style, not hers. Not that he really had a style. He had interests. Hobbies.

He collected soldiers. Some were made of glue and sawdust. The others were lead, hollowcast, slush aluminium. There were army men too: generic green plastic, lightweight and homogenous, fitted out for abstract war.

Soldiers skirmished along the edges of shelves, and over the deep, white-gloss windowsills at the back of the house. They sidled along door frames and dadoes and square-cut skirting boards. They balanced precariously on the tops of framed prints. Once a room was freshly made up, Dad would go in and prop a soldier up under the desk lamps, hide another among the stalks of dead flower arrangements. He imagined he was creating witty arrangements – talking points. Really he was playing with them. A mortar with a two-man crew. A despatch rider on a motorcycle. A motorcycle with a sidecar. A scout car with a mounted machine gun.

The hotel couldn't drum up sufficient clientele on its own, and relied instead on referrals from the local veterans' hospital. The concussed, the confused, the psychogenically deaf. Dad took special care of soldiers blinded in the field by anti-personnel weapons.

I remember one in particular, because of his hair. It was albino-white and well past regulation length. He was one of a party of four blinded by 'friendly light' – a misdirected anti-sensor laser fired from a forward position. He used to compensate for his handicap by hunkering through space, unwilling to acknowledge any collision, any trip, any act of clumsiness. His eyes were hidden behind opaque goggles. Where they left off, crow's foot wrinkles leant him an anxious air, as though he were wincing against light he could no longer see. He would turn his head back and forth, back and forth, scanning the space before him with his big black glasses. Beneath his service shirt, khaki and colours, his visual vest click-clacked like the shutter of an old-fashioned camera. Equipped with crude, Braille-like vision, he was not altogether blind, but details escaped him. He was in the wrong corridor, but how was he to know this? Every corridor looked alike to him.

I'd been playing with Dad's soldiers. Two hollow-cast iron infantrymen vanished under the albino's rubber-soled boots. I could see by his face that he felt them under his foot. He tried very hard not to vary his pace. He moved on, implacable, nothing-the-matter, in the wrong direction. He fetched up eventually in the plating-up area. The kitchen staff patiently and courteously turned him around.

The blind soldiers – I noticed this early on – had two personalities. There was the barefoot personality, and the booted one. Barefoot, they were sensitive, depressed. In their fatigues and boots they were very different – clumsy, and garrulous. Sometimes, when the soldiers put their boots on, they lost their balance. They leant against walls. Sometimes they fell over.

The hotel had a large garden. Mum and Dad never did much with it: a lawn that slewed downhill, dotted here and there with shrubs, each in its island of mulched earth.

Servicemen pecked their way across the lawn like crows. I suppose they imagined they were on one of the gentler stretches of the gorselands: landscapes dimly remembered from basic training. One raised to the sky a face mostly hidden by big black goggles. He stood sniffing the air like an animal in a zoo. Aware of his captivity but unable to fathom it, he scanned the sky for clues.

When I was very young I had been given a set of brightly coloured skittles, painted like soldiers. I rolled a wooden ball and knocked them down. Years later, watching the servicemen from my bedroom window, I found a way to play the game with real soldiers. I remember the feel of Dad's remote control unit, slippy in my fingers. I remember the soft black nubbin under my thumb. I pressed: outside, servicemen toppled and sprawled over the dewy grass. They lay there, checked themselves, then, as one, they picked themselves up. They said nothing. They turned their heads slowly, vests click-clacking like cameras, orienting themselves against a Braille of shrubs and bracken and flowerbeds. Soon they were moving about the garden again, set on their slow, hesitant courses, their soft green fatigues speckled with lawn clippings. Army men.

'It's important we toughen our feet,' Michel said, stuffing his lurid blue rugby socks into his boots. 'Footwear doesn't last forever.' Michel was using the school's weekly cross-country run to prepare me for a world without consumer goods. We tied the laces of our rugby boots together and slung them around our necks.

Rhododendrons, stabbing and spiteful, massed along the edge of the millrace. Michel shuffled along the top of the wall, holding on to their branches. I followed him. White water rushed beneath us.

'We'll wait here.'

The bushes screened us from the path our games teacher, Mr Hill, would take as he caught up with his runners. Of course anyone inside the mill house would have had a clear view of us hiding there – but there was never anyone in.

I heard Hill running past. I rose and palmed the foliage aside and watched him go. I didn't like cheating him, but I liked Michel more.

Michel was quiet, lugubrious, self-contained. For me, at any rate, he had extraordinary presence. A glamour. If he understood my feelings for him, he never let on. He showed very little tenderness for me. He wasn't interested in my weaknesses. He wanted me to be strong. He cared for me as you would care for your side-kick, your familiar, for the man you had chosen to watch your back. He said we had to toughen up.

There was a narrow path of flattened grass beyond the bushes. After about fifty metres, even this petered out among bogs and fallen birches. Nothing here grew above a sapling's height before it keeled over in the soft earth. The ground was so soft you could sink to your waist in it.

'My feet hurt.'

'Put your boots back on, then. We have to do this gradually. No point in getting cut.'

I found myself a seat – a damp cradle of tree roots – and wrestled damp socks over my wet feet. Balanced, comfortably barefoot, on a fallen log, Michel looked more strange than beautiful. I dithered, hoping he'd help me up. But as soon as he saw I was ready he moved off through the undergrowth, and suddenly a ridiculous fear took hold of me: that here, minutes away from school and everything familiar, Michel would abandon me and I would never find my way home.

We teetered on logs. We picked our way. Just under the

31

surface of the mud were roots tough enough to sprain an ankle. Ferns towered over our heads. Even in this tiny corridor of untended green, even with the river to guide us, we sometimes lost our way. Nothing grew straight. Nothing held. Trees clung to life amid stands of nettle, oily-looking brambles and, at last, Michel's centre of operations: a circle of abandoned refrigerators.

Michel drew a stick through the earth, sketching his ideas for me. Earthworks. Palisades. Curving paths that drew assaults ineluctably to one easily defended chokepoint. Here, where the fridges made a sarsen ring, he planned to dig down, roofing his redoubt with turf and leaf litter. The earthworks too he would camouflage, hiding them behind stands of blackthorn, its barbs as vicious as razor wire.

The river, swollen by recent rains, babbled against the trunks and roots of trees. 'One stiff rain and you'll be living in a mud-pool.'

Michel surveyed the ground – a golfer lining up for a putt. 'I don't think so.'

'Besides, all these defences – how are you going to come and go?'

He rehearsed for me the construction of his artful runs: traps he would safely crawl over, but which would stick an unwary intruder stone dead.

'Just don't mistake your entrance and your exit.' What I meant was, 'Don't talk shit.'

Michel, deep in his dream of Millennium, missed the joke. 'Now there's the truth.'

'I promise I'll come visit you during the End Times.'

Michel laughed. 'Come the End Times, it'll be every man for himself.'

*

Cadet training at our school started when we were fif-
teen. The terms of the school's foundation had gifted
it military pretentions which it didn't particularly
deserve. Some came from service families and took being
a cadet very seriously. Most of us regarded the whole
carry-on as a tiresome cousin of our regular Wednesday
afternoon games. There were trips here and there. Now
and again you got to fire a gun. Most of the time you
spent square-bashing or listening to well-meaning guest
lectures. These revealed rather less of military life than
the news bulletins and debate programmes to which we
were already addicted.

There was a lot of fuss made over various military
traditions, and slightly desperate attempts were made to
foster a friendly rivalry between the services. There were
rivalries, but they were local, accidental, and very short
lived. They absolutely refused to take on an ideological
aspect. Particular groups of friends joined particular
services. Their preferences and animosities became the
preferences and animosities of their service. Dress us as
they would in scratchy serge and ill-fitting plastic boots,
we were still schoolchildren, and our ordinary loyalties
and friendships survived their every experiment.

It didn't help, of course, that 'they' were our teachers.
Uniform did not transform them, though some took it as
a licence to behave less well towards us. In crabfat blue
or khaki, they were no less themselves than we were.
They looked ridiculous. The captain of the navy cadets
was our school chaplain, a five-foot tall martinet whose
crisp whites had to be ordered specially because the real
service had no uniforms that small.

33

The cadet experience was entirely without glamour. There was an almost wilful shoddiness to it all. The air cadets played tug-o-war, heaving on their elastic rope. Once the rope was extended, a lever was let go, sending the school's glider rolling across the sports fields. Sometimes it ended up in the long-jump pit. It never flew. Navy cadets kicked their heels indoors, staring at charts. Once a year they visited the coast and wetted and stained their heavy blue serge trousers in the sumps of a smelly, decommissioned frigate. I had imagined Michel, my closest friend, would join me in the army; they at least took us on night exercises every half-term.

I knew that Michel came from an Army family. He showed no interest in discussing the connection. He certainly wasn't bound, through family loyalty, for a service career, as some were. All the same, it came as a surprise and a disappointment when he told me he wasn't joining me in the Army cadets.

'Well, what are you going to do?'

'Community service.'

I burst out laughing.

'What?'

There were a handful of peaceniks and loners among us, and the school catered for these aberrant consciences by sending them off on shopping errands for the local elderly and infirm.

Michel was too much of a loner to suffer a parade ground – this I understood. But try as I might I couldn't picture Michel helping the weak and needy. 'You're kidding.'

'It's a way of getting to know people,' Michel said – a prospector describing a geological expedition; there was no warmth in his vision. 'It's good to see how people manage.'

I imagined him casing every joint.

Our school cross-country route began with a circuit of the sports fields, then led us along a street lined with ostentatious wooden houses as far as the Margrave, its lead-roofed porch smothered in lilac. Here we turned down a bridleway – tarmac at the beginning, cinders at the end – that took us past an old mill. Though it had been converted long before to an ordinary dwelling, the millhouse was genuine. There was a pond and a race, and a pale scar of stonework in the brick wall marked where the axle of the wheel had spun. For me, the house marked the psychological boundary between town and country. Whenever I passed over the stile and crossed the plank bridge over water canalised between walls of aging, moss-felted brick, a weight lifted inside me. I felt free.

Michel was a runner. He represented the school in regional competitions. He won cups and shields. The rest of the time he wasted strength and athletic talent on muddy scrambles through farmers' fields and break-neck, shit-strewn verges. The rumour was our games instructor was making our cross-country courses as unpleasant as possible so as to persuade Michel onto the playing field, where his speed was desperately needed. If this was true, he may as well not have bothered – Michel never had and never would see the point in team games.

Each Wednesday afternoon we left the other cross-country runners to their muddy zig-zag and slipped away to assault courses of Michel's own devising. No one knew about this. At least, no one said anything. Hill, our games teacher, had his suspicions. He once asked me why I 'of all people' had signed up for cross-country in the summer term. 'I was counting on you for the cricket.'

'I'll come to evening practice,' I offered. 'I want to do something to stretch my legs.'

Michel counted cadence as we worked through the exercises his father had taught him. Press-ups. Squat-thrusts. We pulled ourselves up on low-hanging branches. We climbed trees. Passing a patch of scrub, we set ourselves at the undergrowth. Sometimes the route was obvious and clean enough – a sheep run, a fox-scrape. Otherwise I sat this particular game out, waiting for Michel to pick and tear a path through to me, pace by pace, inch by inch, through thorns and briars. He emerged at last, scratched, bleeding, grinning, riding a strange, flagellant high.

Past Michel's 'redoubt' of abandoned fridges the ground got easier, littered with tissues and condoms, crushed cans, charred fire circles. The bark-chip track, come upon so suddenly, the feel of it through my boots, was baffling. 'But this is my way home.'

'Yes.'

'The hotel's down that way.'

'Yes. There you are. Jesus, Conrad, have you never tried to follow the river before?'

I looked back the way we had come. There was no sign of where we had emerged from the undergrowth. No path, no break, no clue.

I had gathered, in my usual vague way, that Michel's father was an Army man and that he was no longer around. What I didn't know was that, a few months before Michel had arrived at the school, his father had returned home, or most of him had, on a military plane.

I can't remember who first told me the story. It wasn't Michel. He assumed I already knew. How could I not have known? The kids haunting the streets where his father was ambushed had used his head as a football. The video had been pulled, but a couple of boys claimed to have seen it. (They never said so to Michel's face.)

Michel's dad's death and repatriation occurred before he came to the school; they were, indeed, *why* he moved here, his education paid for by the pension the military gave his mother. Michel and I attended different classes, and it took a while for our orbits to cross. By then the gossip must already have stalled.

The point is, once I knew about his father, Michel came into focus for me. His loneliness. His cult of self-reliance. These were scabs over a psychological wound. I understood that he was hurt, and I imagined I might be able to help him. At the very least, I could keep him company as he healed. I wanted to do that for him. I wanted to be with him. The truth is, I wanted him, and it pleased me to couch my desire as care.

And all the while Michel went on preparing me for our civilisation's collapse. The Fall, he called it. He was very convincing. It was just around the corner now, he said: the battle of all against all.

SIX

At full pelt – we can't be doing more than thirty miles an hour – the train makes too much racket for Michel and me to talk. It is awkward to sit like this, pressed against a past I am afraid will swamp me. I smile, and with some dumb-show to acknowledge my awkwardness, I open the window and lean out to watch the fields skid by.

The road, fag-end of the famous north coast highway, tails off near here. Clogged with caravans and mobile homes, it turns wearily inland to feed holiday parks, resort camps, an army firing range, a summer water sports school, a private airfield and, off on an eerie shingle limb of its own, an old power station.

The carriage rocks across a set of points. The fields are planted with cereals. In front of them, in a broad, bright band coming right up to the edge of the rail bed, poppies tremble beneath a cloud of moths. The moths are tiny, white-winged, light as ashes from a bonfire. The gust of our passing catches them and choreographs them, and for a moment they abandon their zig-zag trajectories and give themselves up to the slipstream's swirl.

Abruptly, the train is canalised again; it rushes along a weedy, rackety corridor made of fences, wickets, head-high breeze-block walls and here and there, in the more open stretches, flagpoles, greenhouses, gazebos, weath-ered trampolines and bleached-pink plastic pedal cars. To travel at speed between these back gardens is to glimpse the collective unconscious of the region – its lonely pride and thin hope.

'We're doing up a boat.' Michel, weary of our silence, has decided to compete with the racket of the train. 'Did I tell you?' he bawls. 'Hanna and me.'

'Yes.'

'We're doing up a boat.'

The train slows to running pace and we emerge from between back gardens, through weedy fields and bare gravel lots marked out by chicken-wire, into the apparent chaos of the coastal banks – a vast, near-barren shingle expanse that edges year by year, bizarre and unmap-pable, further into the sea. The train brakes again, easing its way over uncertain ground.

It dawns on me that we are still running through gar-dens. But these are big, barren gardens, without fences, without walls. To say that nothing grows on the shingle would be unfair. A few local specialists thrive among the pebbles. Their geometrically simple flowers and cactus-like leaves suggest an occupation of dry land by pioneering seaweeds.

A roll of rusted wire lies across the pebbles, as sculptural in its way as the column of a ruined temple. Even this is not right, because the mind should not have to strain so hard for its metaphors. Better to say that this abandoned concrete pill has shape and mass of its own; and that tar-paper shack embodies the theory of its own construction. Things here are themselves. They are too few to gather into categories.

Paint sticks arranged in a pretend flower bed. An arch made from the planks of an old boat. A rabbit skull perched on a rock. Rows of pebbles, set more or less upright. A half-buried tyre. Old fishing net, pooled in a perfect circle. Buoys. Rusted cans. I would lay odds that some of the subtler effects aren't even deliberate, and what seem to be gardens are simply happy accidents: artefacts of the starved eye's hankering for pattern. But this, I suppose, is the gardener's art around here: to set the eye right to the landscape, so that, from the hulks of derelict fishing boats on the horizon to the cracked concrete kerbs marking the road to the railway station, everything comes into focus – one giant garden.

The railway runs unfenced over the shingle. At our current crawl, you could safely jump from the carriage and head off in any direction, towards any landmark. The tar-paper houses. The lighthouse. On the horizon, black hulks of old boats, upturned, make fishermen's shelters.

'We're fixing up this boat,' Michel says. It's the third time he's mentioned this in as many minutes, and already there is a pall of futility about the enterprise, especially here, where year by year, inch by inch, the shingle piles up on itself, making new land.

'Hanna wants us to sail around the world.'

Here the land gathers itself and rises to meet your footfall. What need of boats, round here?

She looks like an urchin spilled from the chorus of an old musical. Hanna. A five-foot-nothing shit-eating grin above a threadbare green jumper and holed, varnish-spattered jeans.

These, she tells me, are the clothes she wears while she works on the boat. Already with the boat. No sooner are we out through the ticket-hall-cum-giftshop than she has her arm through mine, as though we are old friends, and she is telling me about the dryness of the summer and how her skin, rashed with glass dust spilling from the sander, has tightened across her bones.

I glance at her arm in mine – blonde hairs, strong tendons – checking her out in spite of myself, my reserve, my embarrassment. Christ, her skin! It glows.

She asks, 'Has Michel told you about the boat?'

This is why I am here. This, by now, is obvious. They want someone they can show it off to.

Together we walk to their house along what, round here, passes for a street. It takes me a few minutes to see it as that. There are no walls, no fences, not even ditches worth the name. Just a few little gullies that may be property boundaries, but could just as likely have been scooped out year by year by the rain.

The houses, tar-paper shacks, cluster in unnecessarily tight groups that, for some reason, sit several minutes apart from each other. The road connecting them is

41

made of cracked cement, reduced by infrequent traffic to parallel tracks. Between the tracks, bluish grass struggles to grow.

Not all the houses are fisherman's shacks of tar-paper, sticks and prayer. One, made of concrete, apes the epic slab-work of the power station, visible in the distance. Less convincing are a handful of barn-buildings, painted black to 'blend in' with the locals. Their long, floor-to-roof windows and sliding patio doors are a reckless extravagance round here.

Hanna and Michel's house is easy to spot – there is a thirty-eight foot ketch sat out in front of it on trestles. 'Come and see.'

They escort me, Michel on my right, Hanna on my left. Their every anecdote, remark, gesture and glance is rooted to or through this boat of theirs.

I'm more interested in the house. It's an old one. A tar-paper roof and plank walls – materials chosen to be easily mended and replaced. How much is left of the original structure? Round here, under a salt, corrosive rain, I imagine houses get by the way bodies do, by being constantly repaired and replenished.

It looks too small, too flimsy to be an all-year place. It is not black, unlike so many of its neighbours. Once upon a time it was green. Paint has peeled from the wood and hangs in fronds. The walls and window frames are smothered in this mineral, yellow-grey creeper.

Mick and Hanna crowd me, anxious, trying to fix my attention on the boat. The house, as though aware of their slight, rustles its lifeless foliage.

The boat, then, since there is no avoiding it.

They have parked it in front of their living room

42

window to block their view – or, rather, so that they are confronted, morning, noon and night, with their beloved boat. They have knocked together those hefty trestles themselves. The boat sits upright, head-height above the ground. They've been working on the hull. 'The hull is a mess!' They stand either side of me, pointing out to me, in exhaustive detail, all that they've taken on. There's a hole in the stern. The deck laminate crackles and pops when you walk on it. The fittings are corroded. The electrics are impenetrable. 'The tiller and the forestay are sound.'

It's a shell.

'We figure it'll be as easy for us to tear out the old bulkheads and begin again.'

'Yes.'

'If we're going to live on the thing.'

'Yes?'

'We owe it to ourselves to make it comfortable.'

'I suppose.' What is it that they want me to say?

Michel struggles with the tarpaulins covering the cabin. He wants to show me their work. All through the summer, they have laboured on this hulk, chamfering and filling. The masks and goggles they've been wearing while they sand off the old gel coat are lying on the table in the cabin. 'Still, the dust creeps in under your mask. Into the pores of your hands. Look.' Michel shows me his hands. He tells me that he hardly recognises himself in the mirror any more.

'And Hanna's skin comes out in a rash. Look – like paint over wet putty.'

'Maybe it's not the fibreglass at all,' she says, running her small brown hands over her arms. She sees me look- ing. 'It could be the sand blowing in from the dunes,' she says. She rubs her hands against her jeans, cleaning off imaginary grit.

Michel tells me that to wake sore and stiff from working long hours on the boat, to discuss practical things over a breakfast of coffee and processed bread, to come home sun-dazzled, their skins buzzing, and to work at their books silently and together – all this has added up to a life so clear-cut and so pure, it has begun to resemble a religious retreat.

Hanna reminisces, 'The deck was so waterlogged we had to strip it back to the ply in places. Whoever had it last drilled straight into the deck. Every hole is a sponge.'

A stage laugh from Michel. 'Thank God they never got around to resecuring the bulkheads! They'd have drilled straight through the hull.'

We go indoors at last. We try to. The front door sticks; salt has swollen the wood. Tough grey grasses have taken root in the sand collecting under the porch. The blades are sticky and scaly, as though coated with powdered glass. While Hanna struggles to open the door, I bend to pluck a stem. It won't give, and my fingers come away bloody.

There is mould around the doorframe, damp in the corners of the ceiling, a mealy smell everywhere. The rooms have fibreboard walls. They give slightly if you lean on them. There are three rooms: bathroom, bedroom, living room. You step into the living room straight from the front door and at the back of the room is the kitchen. A thin brown carpet covers the living room floor. It peters out near the kitchen, where cork-effect vinyl floor tiles have begun to lift at the edges.

'Would you like a drink?' There is no shortage of drink. There are several kinds of gin. There is tonic, kept in the fridge, but no ice.

'That's fine.' I take the G&T from her hand. 'Terrific.' It tastes disgusting, an extract of hedge clippings.

Michel cracks open a can of lager and sits beside me on the sofa. I move over for him, my palms chilling on the nylon-mix fleece they've thrown over it. I'm cold at the core in here. I'm not shivering. My hands and feet are fine. This cold begins on the inside, deep in the pit of the lungs. A tubercular chill.

Hanna sits opposite us on a seat made of cardboard boxes and polystyrene packing. Everything here is reused. Everything is repurposed. Gear fills their living room. Clothing in plastic storage tubs. Boots and waterproofs. Damp-bulged books and curling maps are piled on every flat surface. In this room as cramped as a cabin, heavy with gear, carefully organised yet still tipping into an unavoidable chaos, where the stowage succumbs to sheer weight and numbers, it is possible, I suppose, that they are conducting a dress-rehearsal for their voyage.

'It's American-built.' Hanna fetches me yachting magazines from a pile on top of the fridge. Michel gets up and clatters about, 'fixing some more drinks'. Hanna moves me to her chair made of boxes ('the light is better here') and drops the magazines into my lap. She hunkers down beside me and flicks from one dog-eared page to another, showing me pictures of boats similar to theirs, each with a slightly different rigging. We might be choosing shoes or handbags, except that the choices she makes now may make the difference between life and death. 'This, you see; it's a very heavy system.'

Michel comes back with full glasses. He wriggles into the sofa's damp and Hanna joins him there. They tuck the felty orange throw around themselves. Their hands dance and couple in the gloom. They've learned to compensate for their discomfort; they've made it cosy, made it theirs. They're living through a little Fall here, 'saving on bills', taking baby steps in readiness for when the lights go off for real, forever, and the telephones stop ringing, and the pipes go cold and brittle, and the only water's rain which they must boil.

I should not have come. I seem to be gathering all the living room's dampness into myself, pooling it behind my breast-bone – a big wet bag of phlegm I cannot even bring up. 'I just need— Just a moment.'

I fumble with the door knob, trying and failing to suppress the welling inside my chest. I have to get out. I have to get out *now*. The door squeals against the frame, and I stumble out of the shack, into the shadow of the ketch.

Beneath the hull, on a shipping pallet and under clear shrink-wrap, there are sheets of marine ply. Next to them there's a stack of tins and plastic gallon buckets – gelcoat varnish, stripper, paint. Unopened bags of chopped glass fibre ripple and crackle in the wind. This itself is a sort of garden, I suppose, its boundaries marked by shadows that develop even as I watch.

The evening sun is still strong enough to burn through the haze. I move out of the shadows, into the light. Still I am trapped. There are no lines for me to cross, no boundaries to leap. This garden goes on forever. I keep walking. The distant houses are black and soft, sculptures of burnt sugar, without doors, without windows, silhouetted against the setting sun. The upturned hulls of the fishing boats might have been sculpted from blocks by winds howling off the sea. Their shapes are natural, circumstantial – no need to infer a human agency at all. Even the road, what's left of it, might have been scoured by rain, a line as contingent as any runnel in the stones.

'Conrad?'

I half-expected Michel to come running out after me. Not Hanna. I am glad it is her, and embarrassed. What has Michel said about me, that she is so easy with me, so friendly, so concerned?

She falls into step beside me – her errant house guest, bolting off. She does not question me. I don't know where I'm going; round here there doesn't seem to be anywhere to go. She isn't bothered. She does not try to stop me. I am glad of that. After a minute's pointless ambling, gently, she slips her small, hard arm through mine. After Mandy, the feel of Hanna's arm against the edge of my ribcage, the heat of it, is deliciously cruel. I should never have come. I squeeze her arm hard against me as though staunching a wound.

Two lighthouses guard the point. Swirling round the modern, automatic one, a concrete ramp leads to a door half way up the tower. Why a ramp? As though the people who built this, for all their aptitude in cast concrete, never got around to inventing stairs.

The old lighthouse is taller, massier, painted black. A board painted with opening times is screwed to its only door. This has already been padlocked shut for the night. 'Oh,' says Hanna. 'Bugger.' As though this lonely tourist attraction had always been our quarry. It is impressive, how Hanna is nudging me, gently, gently, back into the

47

ordinary. 'Come on,' she says, 'let's go see the keeper's house.'

'Going to see' anything round here is really just a form of words. To see anything from anywhere here requires no more than a shift of one's attention. The house is behind and a little to the left of us. It is the biggest structure on the shingle. It is perfectly circular – a mansion bent round upon itself to form a perfect 'O'. In the centre, where the back gardens should be twisted round to nothing, there is a greenish glass cupola. To bring so much expensive stone to such an out-of-the-way place, never mind pile it up and dress it in this radical form, suggests a level of self-belief the present age could not muster. The building's big blocks of dressed honey-coloured stone are fitted together with a neatness that reminds me of Mandy's townhouse with its bridges and canals, its traffic of exotic hybrid bicycles and semi-electric executive cars.

I had better call her, after all.

When Mandy speaks, she instinctively tries to wave her hands. She has not yet become accustomed to their weight. Her white plastic hands carve the air, lugubrious and slow, a knife in one, a fork in the other. I have phoned her in the middle of her dinner.

She shrugs my sudden departure off, refusing to show the hit. She knows what my unannounced excursion signifies. She wants me to know that she is going to make this easy for me. She says, 'You're too young to commit, I suppose.' Her formulation – that, being a few years her junior, I am too immature for her – is a generous one. It raises the kindly spectre of 'irreconcilable differences'. She is, in fact, handing me an alibi.

Even over this stuttery video link, I can see how hard she is working to deal with our sudden break-up. Her scars are red with the effort, and her face has screwed itself up in that odd, lopsided way that it falls into so easily now. It looks as though it has been stitched together out of rags. Which, I suppose, it has been.

We discuss bills, forwarding arrangements, practicalities. (No mention of my mother's table.) Already she is talking about when, not if, I should move out. That she despises me for running away is a given. Still, I expected this conversation to be much more difficult and, if I'm honest, to be a deal more flattering to my ego. Anyone would think that it was Mandy throwing *me* over.

Then – at the very end – she says, 'I don't suppose you have to make a final decision yet.' Her face, glassed and reconfigured, trembles over a forked mouthful of celeriac salad, and for a second the illusion – that her face might simply slide off the bone – acquires a ghastly realism. It is all I can do not to reach out to hold it in place.

SEVEN

Mum's depressions were more or less regular, and always straightforward. In some ghastly way I looked forward to them. They made life simple. Mum in a slump was a loved object, someone to be taken care of, fed, read to, made comfortable, encouraged to wash and dress. She became my doll, as I became hers – once she was free of her black dog and rushing about designing wedding dresses or cooking up new kinds of make-up.

'Sit up, Mum.' 'Mum, do you want to watch a movie with me?' 'What do you fancy to eat tonight, Mum?'

She would take to her bed – not for long, a few days – and it was up to Dad and me to keep the house running. Life was rugged and clear – a set of operations to ensure our fitness and the hotel's hygiene.

'I'll take the first shower.' 'Call and see if George can cover the bar tonight.' 'Bin bags. Tea. Eggs.'

Mum's manias were much more difficult. It is one thing to be brought low by a warring world, and the assured mutuality of destruction. It's another thing to think that you can do anything about it.

Mum's political convictions, her financial ineptitude and her frequent mood-swings were mutually reinforcing. I remember how, in her euphoria, it would occur to her, as if for the first time, that she had never been 'depressed'. She had been *oppressed*.

Patiently, she would explain to me exactly how I oppressed her. Dropping her guard, she would then expand upon her theme, describing all the many ways – some of them wincingly intimate – in which Bill, my dad, oppressed her. Her chief oppressor, however, was money. Among the aisles of the supermarket ('Marmalade (big tins)/Bleach/Serviettes') I remember how she once attempted to anatomise for me the structural iniquities of a market-led economy.

I was less entranced by her philosophy than by her shopping. Ignoring the list Dad had given her, she was gathering all manner of unfamiliar stuff: dried fruit, porridge, soya meals, packet soups. It took Dad and me a couple of days to decipher this. It turned out that Mum, in her escalating mania, was preparing to abandon us for a protest camp that had grown up around a nearby military airbase. She would make friends there, she told us. She would meet like-minded women. She believed that friendships struck up around late night tea-brewing sessions were the soil in which her full potential would bloom, after so many false starts and wrong turnings.

She explained all this to us with a strange mixture of assertiveness, enthusiasm and sullenness, drawing us in and locking us out in the same breath. The camp. Its emergent structure. Its spontaneous spirituality. Its rejection of paternalistic hierarchies.

The camp became the site of an annual pilgrimage.

Dad was never able to visit Mum at the camp. Men were not welcome. The women of the camp believed that patriarchy was imbued with violence – that all men were rapists. These were the kind of things Mum would say to Dad as she packed for the camp – in the weeks of her euphoria, before the next bite of her dog.

Was it for better or for worse that Dad and I were forbidden to witness her first flame-outs, and the hours of her descent? Dad waited for her call. Her confused directions ('I'm in a phone box.'). Her declarations of defiance and need. He would tell me to 'look after the fort' while he drove over and gathered up the wreckage. The camp wasn't far. An hour by car. Two hours on train and bus, if you were clever with the connections.

At last, provoked and frustrated by Mum's accounts of the camp, concerned for her and jealous of this other life she hankered after so much – though it had yet to do her any good – I decided I would visit her. I would do it without Dad's knowledge, or the camp's, or Mum's for that matter. It would be, I told myself, a surprise for her.

Because of his work with blinded servicemen, Dad was invited to speak at conferences. These sometimes required an overnight stay. The next time I was on my own over the weekend, I put my plan into action.

Mum's rooms smelled close and sweet. In the corner opposite her daybed was the mirror-clad make-up table. I turned on the lights framing the central mirror and sat on Mum's plush-upholstered piano stool. The time had come for Mum's mannequin to prove herself: to strut her stuff in the real world, she who had been for so long trapped between mirrors.

The big central looking glass was the only part of the table Mum ever kept clean. The table's mirrored top was dusty and greasy, hidden under empty jewellery boxes, old Mother's Day cards, tissues, a big plastic tub of all-purpose moisturiser. I piled this junk to the sides, clearing a space to work. I pulled open mirrored drawers, discovering foundations, eyeliners, shadows, gels. Not just Mum's home-mades – real products. I laid them out. I knew what I was looking for. I knew what I was doing. Mum had taught me well. She had awoken these dark and liquid eyes. She had put this slim and swaying figure into motion. Now her creature sought her own life, through me.

I dipped a small, semicircular sponge in a bowl of water and squeezed it out, and again, until the water ran clear through my fingers. I picked up a compact and ran the sponge in circles through the foundation. The stuff was cold and clinging, tightening as it dried. I leant forward as I worked, dipping, wringing, dabbing, smoothing. My reflection entered the yellow cloud cast by the bulbs around the mirror. My face was as smooth as a doll's. I ran a little purplish powder along my cheekbones, sculpting them. With brush and pencil I refashioned the sockets of my eyes, adding and subtracting shadows. I closed my eyes and ran blues in layers over my eyelids. When I was done my eyes were set like jewels. I drew a little kohl along the inside of my eyelids, behind the lashes, and leant forward, staring into my mother's eyes.

I looked exactly like her. You could not have told us apart.

An hour by car. Two hours by train and bus. Around 4.30 on Saturday afternoon the bus dropped me off on a stretch of main road, woods to my left, fields on my right. There was a lane here the bus couldn't negotiate, through woods and up a shallow hill to a hamlet that had fallen out of the usual channels of communication. I met no traffic on my way up the hill, no people. The air was still, the trees silent. My own movements sent cold fingers down the insides of my thighs, where mum's nylon hose rubbed my shaved skin. Mum's batik dress was long and tatty, tight and fitted round my belly and under my ribs.

At the top of the hill the trees gave way, the green tunnel parted and the village spread out before the eye, even and neat and simple as the setting for a model railway. There were no streets as such, just a horseshoe of houses around a rough-mown green. The houses shared no common style. It was as though a collector had gathered them here – someone with an eclectic eye for the rural vernacular. That this idyll came with a price tag was evident from the cars parked on the green. Aside from a couple of distressed 4by4s, they were all business saloons, showroom-clean.

The hamlet lay about a quarter of a mile away from the base, and far from the main gates. (There, young protestors had set up much livelier, more newsworthy camps than any Mum came near, though the woods they infested were hardly more than a large hedge, barely concealing the chainlink from the road. By night, tents and tarpaulins made looming, organic shapes in the headlights of passing cars.)

The camp Mum went to lay past the hamlet, and well out of sight of the base, where the ground fell away into a secret valley. It was an afternoon's walk through woods to find the wire with its concrete fence posts turned to totems, painted with eyes, with snakes, with spiders dropping on wet silver ropes.

There was no centre to the camp, nothing to really 'find'. Glimpses. A sheet of tarpaulin. A curl of pale smoke. Furtive things, hidden in plain sight. By then, of course, it was too late – the place had you surrounded.

There were women all around me, hidden, hissing at me. They were squatting in benders made from old tent canvas. They were crouching in teepees and yurts and behind screens of dead branches. They were hiding in nettle patches, hunkered down there like animals. Mum had told me they had their own religion here. Arachne was their goddess – web-weaver, binder of souls, symbol of the connected earth. Only now did I see that their trees were webbed with wool.

I ran my hand over a skein of black wool, knotted between the low branches. The hissing all around me died away. The oak was mostly dead. New growth burst where it could through the bark, so that the shape of the thing was hardly tree-like – more of a hedge.

I palmed the screen aside.

What had I expected? A room. A hollow tree that was at the same time a cabin. A home. A simple pallet bed. A rug. A pile of books. Not *this*. Between the roots of the great oak there was a kind of fox scratching. It was shallow. Filthy. It wasn't even dry.

The tree wasn't hollow. Lightning had split and scarred it, torn half its growth away, and over the years the trunk had swollen in a great horseshoe around the blighted part, making a crouch-hole only a dog could have sheltered in.

Ragged plastic sheets hung from low branches. Squatting among a heap of green nylon refuse sacks, Mum looked up from her work. Black wool. Busy fingers. Filthy hands. A web wove itself over the earth towards me. Mum stood up. She was wearing a striped jersey and sailor's pants. Her feet were bare. Her toes clutched at the woollen web, tugging the clews.

I wanted to speak, to greet her, but words were dangerous here. My voice had begun to crack – it would have betrayed me. Mum cocked her head. She dropped her wool. Her fingers folded themselves into fists. Her busy toes. She followed the skeins towards me on shuffling feet. The blow was so fast, I didn't even see it coming.

Now there were women everywhere. Running toward me. Kneeling by me. Wide-eyed. Hands upon me. 'Who are you?' 'Who are you?' 'What do you want?'

My feet were tangled up in the woollen web. Women dragged me from Mum's lair and the web followed me, tugging the branches towards me, shredding leaves into a green rain. Hands grabbed for me, but I was too heavy for them. Down I went.

'What did you do?' Hands tilted my head back. Blood ran into the back of my mouth. Through a pink mist, figures flitted back and forth. My feet were entangled. I couldn't get them free.

'Now calm down,' someone snapped, as to a child.

Dad brought home the remains of Mum's camping kit. The tent he'd bought her had vanished. Her sleeping bag was damp and smelly and there were green stains on it that would not lift. I laid the bag across the lawn to dry. Her aluminium cooker was more or less complete. I set the pieces out in a row along the conservatory steps and cleaned each in turn with soapy water and a wire brush. Just above me, behind glass doors, a serviceman wandered to and fro, eyes hidden behind black glasses. He put me in mind of an animal kept too long in a cage. Dad watched him from his desk, a dispassionate lion tamer.

That evening Dad and I drove to the hospital where Mum lay recuperating from a lung infection. The hospital was built on a chalk hill overlooking the port. Old barracks and defensive structures had been torn down and ground under to make room for the hospital which, from the sea, had all the appearance of a bigger, better fortification.

Dad went inside, leaving me to wander round the weedy paths, the flights of cracked concrete steps, the pot-holed roads. You needed first gear to reach the car park here, so there was this constant whine in the air – a common mechanical labour renewed again and again and again. In the dusty banks and verges that bordered every metal-railed stairway, I found nubs and flecks of red-pink brick – remains of the old fortress – and in between were thready weeds with bright blue, pink and yellow flowers.

From this high vantage, I could see how the port city had been constructed over a network of mudflats and channels. In between there were islands, but they were bridged over in too many places to really count as islands any more. In fact the whole estuary was so heavily built upon that roads and waterways blended in the eye, and it took an effort to pick them apart. I looked at my watch. Dad was taking a long time. I went inside to look for him.

I hadn't seen Mum since I'd tried to visit her *incognito* in the camp. Dad had warned me that the sight of me would upset her, but my nose was already healed, more or less. If Dad had let me, it would have been the work of a moment for me to hide the bruising with make-up.

The hospital floor was a mottled red vinyl that looked as though it had been poured and left to set. Every few yards, at a stairwell or junction, there was a vending machine. I tried to get a carton of drink. I put in my money, typed the code. The metal coil shuddered, turned, stuck. There was a notice, red capitals on white self-stick plastic, telling me not to rock the machine, which anyway didn't help and set off an alarm that everybody ignored.

Mum's ward had this easy to miss open-plan arrangement – impossible to say where the corridor left off and the ward began. Mum was alone, lying with her back to me. I watched her a while, not saying anything, then I went away and looked for some magazines to flick through. My emotions were so mixed up, my attention so fractured, the articles might as well have been written in a foreign language.

Dad turned up eventually, approaching from the wrong direction.

'Where've you been?'

Dad told me Mum was 'on the mend'.

'When's she coming home?'

'Have you been in to see her?'

'She was sleeping.' Of course, she might not have been sleeping at all. She could have been just lying there.

I wanted to go see her again but Dad was keen to get

going. 'School tomorrow.' As though my bedtime were any different from his.

It was nearly dark by the time we got going and still Dad was hunting for words, the right spell to lock down whatever he'd seen, or learnt, or been told. No lid he tried seemed to fit. 'The camp's got your Mum pretty messed up.' The form of words he picked – 'your mum' in place of 'Sara' – was a measure of the trouble we were in. He was trying to establish something. He was trying to set this down. To be clear. 'She's upset.'

They'd wanted his signature.

'Signature for what?'

He hadn't signed.

'For what? Dad?'

'She's upset.'

'Dad.'

He pulled the car to the kerb. We were nearly home; halfway through the housing estate. It was Dad's usual short-cut, he knew the way. There was no need for us to stop. He rubbed his hand across his eyes, faking a headache, thinking that I could not see his tears.

'Please Dad.'

Dad undid his seatbelt and put his arms around me and held me. It was horrible. Unbearable. I was pinned by my belt. I couldn't reach to undo it. I couldn't hug him back. I was stuck there – his object. And here he was, holding me, shaking like an injured dog, faking everything, telling me everything was going to be all right, pretending (this was worst of all) that it was him who was comforting me.

*

The town I grew up in was a friendly place. At least, it was friendly to us. Because of the hotel, we were known to people – a local business, a source of summer jobs. Women fussed over my father. Febrile with a late and hopeless heat, they imagined they could save him from his 'impossible' wife. While Mum remained in hospital under psychiatric observation, they steeped us in sympathy and relationship teas. We whiled away hours like that, separately and together, in strange sitting rooms, breathing stale desire.

Some of those women tried to get to Dad through me. One in particular, distracted from her main purpose by what she called my 'charm', decided to pull up her top and get her tits out. They were very large but her nipples were tiny. Sucking one was like rolling a sugar cake decoration around in my mouth.

She helped me with her hands and tongue. She was quite rough. She took my hands and placed them on the back of her head. I wound my fingers in her hair and dared to pull her onto me. She made a little moan and slid me right down her throat. I rocked against her. After a minute of this she gagged and pulled away. 'There are condoms in that drawer when you're ready.'

I had never handled a condom before. I couldn't make it unravel. Maybe it was inside out. I turned it round. That wasn't right either.

'Give it to me.' The moment she leant over me I began to wilt. She wiggled me about and took me into her mouth again but it didn't do any good.

'Do you mind if I wank for a bit?' she said, trying to turn me on.

'No, I don't mind.'

She laughed. 'You're such a gentleman.'

This is the sort of thing you say to a child.

I moved around the bed, curious to see her put her fingers inside herself, but all she did was fiddle. It reminded me of Dad worrying at a grease mark on our immaculate bar top. I ran my feet along the insides of her thighs, and she seemed to like that. She took hold of my foot and rested it against her sex. She rubbed my toes against her, making them wet.

At last she took pity on me. 'Well,' she said, gathering her clothes, 'that was naughty.'

I used her bathroom. Her medicine cabinet was full of products she had brought back from overseas trade fairs; pharmaceuticals with names unsuited to the domestic market. Polysilane Upsa, Neo-Angin. Smecta. Spassirex. The shower looked fancy, but it wasn't up to much. I remember the whine of the pump, and a sound in the pipes like a child draining juice from a carton.

The way home from her house led me beside the river, along the track I took to school. Its bark-chip surface had worn away, and the ground was soft after days of rain. I should have known better than to attempt the track in trainers. The wet soaked through my socks.

A serviceman picked his way towards me. I recognised him by his hair – albino white and wild. He was in trouble. His vest *tick-tocked*, *tick-tocked*, useless in this maze, and he wove from one side of the track to the other, unable to plan his line. How easily he might have stumbled off between the trees. The river ran behind them, sluggish and slow-moving; it made no sound.

Dad's blinded servicemen didn't often come this way into town. Their goggled, low-resolution blindsight handled the box-like architectures of the housing estate much more easily. The ambiguous and busy undergrowth of the track tended to confuse them. Here, they'd have been better served by a stick, a dog, a sense of hearing.

The white-haired man walked with a defensive, mechanical stiffness. I recognised it. I recognised *him*. We approached each other. In army boots he overcame the uneven ground. My presence confused him. When I veered left, he veered right, straight towards me. I skipped to one side to avoid him. He stopped and turned to me. The sun glittered off his goggles and winked in the lens of the camera mounted on his left earpiece. His chest chattered monotonously as he stood, perfectly still, the machine at his hip repeating, in regular pulses, the scene before him. Boy against foliage.

I said, 'Good afternoon.'

His face showed no recognition. His hand worked at his fly and his erection slid into the light, hard and white and as long as a dagger.

EIGHT

'What do you do, Conrad?'

We are sitting, Hanna and I, against the up-turned hulk of a fishing boat, staring at the waves.

'I work for an AR company.'

The contrast between Hanna's life of muscular simplicity and my day job could hardly be greater. Hanna planes and scrapes, drills and sands. I spend my days stroking glass panels, bringing images to life against their printed target. This is what AR stands for: Augmented Reality. 'We turn newspapers and magazines into rich media. Every newspaper photograph becomes its own TV channel ...'

The ocean has piled the shingle steeply, and even on a day as calm as this, the waves churn and plunge with a terrible violence. No way could you ever swim in this. The pebble bank is very high, and where we're sat, half way down its stepped incline, we have no view of the desert expanse at our back. Even the tops of the lighthouses are hidden. We are trapped between the pebble wall and the roaring sea.

'Basically,' I tell her, 'it's advertising. It's about laying an advertising layer over the physical world.'

'Is it difficult?'

'Not especially. Mathematically it can mess with your head but intellectually it's on a par with casting a ghost onto a sheet of glass. An old stage trick.' The core of our AR business is a billboard system. Image recognition software running on a smartphone or a pair of web-enabled spectacles sews moving pictures over a static target. Someone walking past an ad for the latest movie will see the hoarding spring to life, screening its trailer.

'And everyone can see your ghosts?'

'Anyone stood behind some web-enabled glass. It's all a bit art-student at the moment, but there's a lot of commercial interest.'

Hanna thinks about this. She says, 'But it's all the wrong way round. People are having to go out of their way to see your advertising.'

'What do you mean?'

'They're having to put on funny glasses, or raise a phone to their faces. Who goes to that much trouble just to see an advert?'

'At the moment, yes, you're right.' I pick up a pebble and throw it into the sea. 'But web-enabled glasses look like they'll be flying off the shelves next year. It's only a matter of time before the web becomes wearable, just another form of clothing between you and the world.' Biting the bullet, I describe the future as my employers

64

see it: a giant mall overlaid with proprietary information. 'Sale, Last Three Days!' 'Next Bus 5 mins.' 'NOW – Happy Hour.' Image overlaid with image, veiling the Real with arrows and exclamation points.

'Bloody hell,' she says.

I put what gloss on it I can, 'With AR, you can thread private and public spaces through each other. You can turn public spaces into private screening rooms. Augmented Reality will change how space is used.'

'You mean you're privatizing it.'

'What?'

'You're privatizing civic space.'

'No—'

'Yes. That's what you're doing. You're doing away with personal perception. You're directing people to see things a certain way. You're telling people what to pay attention to.'

People who know nothing about advertising always assume people are defenceless against it. 'That's not going to happen.'

'Really? Why not?'

I do my best to explain why AR is worthwhile. Virtual Reality was crack cocaine, spiriting its wraiths away to NeverNeverLand, and that is why it never really took off. Augmented Reality is different. 'AR exists to heighten the present moment ...'

'Conrad.' She waits for me to look at her. 'It *stifles* the present moment. It replaces reality with a – a recording.'

How easy for Hanna to take the moral high ground, free of the burdens of ambition or responsibility or any interest beyond her own self-fantasy! 'For fuck's sake, you're surely not going to tell me that your bloody boat trip is *authentic*, are you?'

Hanna smiles and shrugs and backs off and pretends not to understand. Of course she understands; she's not stupid.

Hanna spends the rest of the day indoors with her maps and guides, her lists of foreign vocabulary and her text books. (Her language teaching is supposed to feed and equip the couple as they circumnavigate the earth.)

On board the boat, meanwhile, Michel plugs a loft-lamp into the extension lead and fits a sheet of ply across the width of the cabin to make a desk. The cabin doubles as his study.

He helps me on board. 'You'll like this,' he says. Shoved deep in the bows is a grey plastic attaché case. Inside are maps. He spreads them over the plywood table.

A lot of the hills round here are called islands. Isle of This, Isle of That. 'It's in the place names, see? The land round here has been dry land, farmland, for only a couple of hundred years.'

It has been easy, an enjoyable thing for Michel to re-imagine this place, to make islands of these gentle hills and to trace and shade with a blue pencil the line of imaginary coastlines of the future. When we were children, school friends, Michel and I would play this same game, poring over my Dad's old maps of the town, seeing which streets we could inundate, transforming familiar ground with a meshwork of inlets and peninsu-las. There is something magnificent in the continuity of Michel's obsessions. He hasn't changed at all.

At the same time, how can he be so childish? 'So how

far into your book are you?' I say, to prick his fantasy.

'About three hundred thousand words.'

Which shuts me up.

He folds the maps away. 'This stuff's just the scene-setting, the research. In the end, so long as you've done it, so long as important bits of it are parked in the back of your head, none of this world-building nonsense matters. But I thought you'd like to see it.' He knows I do not take his literary ambitions seriously.

'So what's next?' I ask him.

'I'll have to find myself an agent.'

'Good luck.' But he has read my reaction, and gauged my disapproval, so there is no point in my keeping silent. 'And this book of yours is going to help fund the voyage?'

'That's the idea.' Then he casts his hand around the cabin and says something so off-point, so unexpected, it is night before I think to measure its implications. He says, 'If, that is, we ever sail.'

Come nightfall, it is raining – a proper ocean squall, sudden, short, the wind a knot trying violently to solve itself, the rain like spray from a fire hose.

We can none of us get to sleep. Around midnight Michel and Hanna stumble out of their bedroom fully dressed and make tea. Mugs in hand, we brave the weather. Laughing and cursing, we clamber aboard the boat.

We stand, the three of us, in the cabin, looking through its rain-beaded Perspex at the silhouettes of the inland hills. These are the same hills Michel pointed out to me this afternoon. They mark the old coastline, before the land was claimed and drained for pasture. The villages perched on these hills (Isle of This, Isle of That) were ports, once upon a time. Big, successful towns – their skylines are dominated by churches so big they could be cathedrals. These days, of course, it's all overpriced coaching inns, antiques, second-hand bookshops, cloth mice.

The sky is clearing, but the hills are smudged, as though a thumb has smeared charcoal into the orange haze cast by port cities to the west. Standing here, it is easy to imagine the flood to come.

Lift the boat from its trestles.

Watch the trestles twist away on the dark water, disappearing behind the house.

Then, lift the house.

There is Hanna, working indoors, surrounded by her books. Turn the house slowly round so she can face the sea. She raises her head. She sees a flash, a storm, and she smiles to think of all she has to learn.

On board the boat, meanwhile, Michel (eyes down, pen poised, a head crammed full of fantasy) does not feel the subtle current bearing him inland, over flooded levels, past the comically bloated corpses of drowned cattle, towards the hills the maps have down, even now, as islands. Isle of This. Isle of That. On the shore, axes ring out as the townsfolk, troubled by a revenant folk-memory, chop wood for boats of shallow draught and, salivating, eye the skies for teal, widgeon, wintering geese.

Rushes grow up to tickle the branches of dying trees and nowhere is there a defined boundary between land and estuary.

Here and there, banks of shingle rise incrementally above the shallow sea like a new medium, neither sea nor land – an unreliable medium where men and livestock founder and blue lights flicker mysteriously in the hours before morning.

Of the towns the miniature railway once served, only roofs remain. A bell sounds under the waves at every turning of the tide, from a church built beside an old military canal. The waterway's route is marked now by the makeshift floats – old soda bottles, plastic canteens that once held washing powder, all treasured now and irreplaceable – that mark the dropping points of lobster pots.

Fishermen appear, steering strange coracles. Oyster divers, boys with bags around their hips and wooden nose plugs, dive for a catch that breeds within the rotten brickwork of the canal. Lobsters and crabs have scratched themselves crafty tunnels here, switchbacks, false entrances, so that the boys come up with their fingers bloody, nipped by claws.

North then, crossing over the drowned canal, careful to avoid the tower where the bell rings out each turning of the tide, to the mirrored waters that once were marsh, and will be marsh again, to where Hanna spins, safe in her chalet, anchored to the shingle by the strangest material: filaments of copper wire, optic fibre, plastic pipe, their uses uncertain now, forgotten, as the future pins the past under the water, drowning it.

'If, that is, we ever sail.'

Already afloat on a sea of words, already embarked upon his private voyage, Michel stands at the porthole, pointing out clusters of light on the hills. Old port towns, landlocked by centuries. They were islands once and now they're islands in his head, and he is happy to have found a way, half-way respectable, maybe even remunerative (his book might be good, for all I know) to live inside his ideas of the Fall.

As he talks, I feel for Hanna's hand. I take it in my own. Gently I squeeze.

She runs her thumb across the back of my hand.

A few nights later, there is a party.

Michel chivvies us into the truck. It's a two-seater, I'm riding in the flatbed. A motorcycle tyre makes a seat for me. It feels as though I'm sitting on a toilet. Hanna tucks me round with the fleecy throw she's fetched from the sofa.

'I'll be warm enough.'

She tucks the blanket round me as though I were her dolly.

Michel hands me a can of beer then climbs behind the wheel. He takes the shingle road gently, then speeds off like a dog out of the gate as soon as he hits hardtop. The reclaimed land – old marsh, made into weedy fields – is flat and monotonous. It won't admit its closeness to the sea at all – you have to search for clues. I glimpse the top of a red sail behind a hedge, and we shoot by the entrance with a sign, crudely done, for a water sports school. Hard as I look, I get no glimpse of water. We drive past an army artillery range – a long run of chainlink and nothing else to see. A grassy blank. I would like to drive this road some time. It weaves and rocks: an hypnotic rhythm, like something from a driving game. I remember my beer. I pull the ring and the can explodes. I lean forward, keeping the stuff off myself. The wind whips the foam welling out of the top of the can and trails it into the dark.

Michel drops a gear, and then another, and the truck

tilts sharply. I brace myself. Brambles choke the narrow lane that leads, steep as a funicular, up through a tilted zone to the mainland proper, and the west.

The road bends back and forth, following the old shoreline. Solid land on one side of the road slides and slips away from the other in muddy, fertile gobs. This soft slippage suggests less the action of ancient tides than the recent melting of a candle.

We pass through old, landlocked harbour towns, one after another. Through the windows of old coaching inns I catch glimpses of red linoleum. The forecourts of the timber merchants are piled with shipping pallets. Teenage girls with bare legs are smoking together under the grey-orange lights of station car parks.

We pick up speed on a dual carriageway between hillsides cut up into cereal fields: enclosures as vast and arbitrary as strip-mines. Ragged hedges. Crows. By now I'm frozen to a popsicle, I've got my hands stuffed in my jacket and still I can barely feel my fingers. My head is a block of ice; even blinking is a struggle. Most of this is wind-chill. But something is happening to the weather, too. Gusts beat about the truck like starlings scrapping over a piece of bread. There's a band of cloud moving in from the sea. It's so low it looks more like a wall, and above it, catching the last of the light, are towers of brighter cloud, as smooth as porcelain – the prows of strange ships riding a dark tide into harbour.

Off the main road, Michel slows sharply for blind bends in the dusk, then brakes and turns. The truck rumbles and sways, finding its balance on an exhausted gravel driveway, all mud and hardcore and potholes. I lever myself up and round to lean on the roof of the cab. The drive is lined with trees. It curves steadily. On the left are fields, to the right a bank of rhododendrons – the truck's headlights rummage through their gloss, leathery green.

The house comes into view. It's a big, no-nonsense place, its white stucco luminous in the dusk. It's a couple of hundred years old, from the look of it. It has not been long abandoned. There must be two, three hundred people gathered on the lawn, in vans parked up on the gravel turning circle, and in the house itself. The windows have no curtains, and you can see inside every room – they're all lit up. The electricity is still connected, or it's been jemmied on.

The garden is ornate and disorganised. Many shrubs are hidden under wet clothes and sheets of muddy canvas. Teepees make angular shadows under the trees. Cigarette ends tattoo the darkness. Fifty feet away, a pampas grass has been set on fire. It burns with a roiling, liquid flame. The air stinks of petrol. There's a dip in the land behind the house. Behind it, trees make a dense black screen – a false horizon. There's a sound system in the dip; its noise seems to be emanating from within the earth. Its industrial beats melt to form something ponderous and wet – a faltering heart.

In the middle of the lawn, a boy with a shaved head is pouring petrol onto a pile of furniture and floorboards scavenged from the house. There are upholstered chairs there. Leather trunks. Clothes. A child's bed. The boy takes a swig of petrol from the can, flicks a lighter in front of his face and blows fire. A cheer goes up and the heap explodes. The boy falls back, rubbing his face. The bonfire catches in stages, a staggered spectacle, the turning on of civic illuminations. Somewhere deep in the pile, batteries pop. A pair of silk knickers rises on the expanding air and catches fire.

Hanna takes my arm and squeezes. I turn to her, thinking she must be enjoying this, but her expression is carefully blank. Coming here was Michel's idea, not hers. Michel, grinning, waves his phone in the air, saluting us, and wanders off, snapping pictures as he goes. Then Hanna moves away and I am left alone, wondering why the hell they brought me here. What's here for me? A bunch of kids on heat, demonstrating their lack of materialism by destroying someone else's stuff. It is an unpleasant reminder that the human world falls apart, not through catastrophe, but from mounting internal failure. I wonder where the house's owners are.

Partygoers gather round the flames, shouting. They seem determined to incite my paranoia. I step away from the noise, but my gaze is held by the shapes in the flames – turned wood and latticework – and metal-salt colours spilling from the curtains jumbled on top of the pyre. I'd lay money not one kid here has a clue how to turn wood, or make a chair, or knit a blanket for a child. They still live in a world of affordable plenty. Stuff, for them, is a utility, on tap. They rate this evening a misdemeanour, like flooding a public bathroom. Everything can be replaced. They believe this. Soon they will wake to discover that, blinded by fictitious capital, they have been torching what few riches were left.

The world ends, not with flood or plague or famine, but with a man torching his own house.

A boy tries to sell me a can of lager from a barrow parked under a tree. Rebellion against the market system can only be taken so far.

The kitchen has been left more or less intact. There has even been some attempt at catering. There are plates piled on every surface. By the sink there are plastic washbowls full of punch, black under the weak fluorescent light. It's crowded, as kitchens always are. Near the door, surrounded by girls who crowd her round like acolytes, I see a woman in late middle age. She's standing with her back to me. Her hair is grey and shaved so short I can see her skull.

'Mind,' comes a voice beside me.

I cannot move – neither do I want to.

'Fucking *mind*.' Someone opens a fridge door into my foot. I move aside, lose sight of the woman a second, and push through the crush only to find that she is gone.

I look around for something, anything, to drink. There's a half-full bottle of vodka on the windowsill. I need something to steady myself. I need room to think. She looked like Mum. She looked *exactly* like Mum, the last time I saw her alive. It cannot be her – but what if it is? Her being here would solve all mysteries – all, barring the mystery of how she could possibly still be living.

In the hall the stairs are jammed with girls waiting miserably for their turn on the one working toilet. 'I'm off to shit in the garden,' says one, the fattest of them, barrelling me into the wall as she goes. 'Mind,' she says.

'Mind yourself, you fat fuck.'

She hesitates and turns, squeezing her fists, the flesh squishing like dough, but the urgency in her bowels overcomes her annoyance with me. Someone on the stairs calls me a cunt. This, from people like this, I can live with. I take the stairs at speed. Hands and feet whip out of the way of my feet like fish darting for the shelter of rocks. 'What's your problem?'

74

My problem is I've lost my mum.

The upstairs rooms are empty. Not unoccupied. Empty. Everything has been dragged out of them, even the carpets.

'Mum?'

I move from room to room.

'Sara?'

It cannot possibly be her. The world cannot possibly knit itself over so well. There are no miracles. 'Mum!'

I take a breath, or try to. I feel as though I have been kicked. Air rattles in, as eventually it must, clearing my head. The fit – what else would you call it? – it passes.

On the stairs, Hanna has joined the queue for the toilet. It's much shorter now. 'Everyone's gone to piss in the garden.'

'I'm surprised they don't just use the rooms.'

'Christ.'

'What?'

'I'm sorry, Conrad.'

'What?'

'This.' She glances round her, wincing, as if afraid of what new thing she might see. 'It's horrible.'

The front door glass is bashed in. A hand reaches through and fiddles with the lock. The door opens and a boy enters, trailing a guitar. He wanders into a room and strikes up a folk song. Come the end times, we shall have no chairs, no beds, no blankets for our children. We shall have folk-singers, and we shall kill them with rocks and cook thin strips of their flesh over fires conjured from their smashed guitars.

Hanna and I stand shivering in the gust from the open door. (The weather is definitely turning.) Horrible, the paint-spattered carpet. Horrible, the inept graffiti on the walls, and the shattered light-shade over the door, and the fragments of coloured glass from the panel the boy has idly smashed. Yes, horrible. Yet these judgements don't just spring up from nowhere. 'The thing you have to bear in mind, Hanna, is that everything's still more or less in favour of being sensitive and civilised. And this stuff can turn on a penny.'

Hanna's not interested in my cleverness. Probably she gets enough of this sort of thing from Michel. 'They've ruined it,' she says, a brave bourgeois, standing up for value.

I go and swing the front door shut. Squares of coloured glass crunch beneath my feet. I pull a blue square free of its twisted leading. 'Close your eyes.'

'What?'

'Close them.' I stand beside her, and raise the jagged colour to her face. 'Okay.'

Hanna stares through the glass at the blue-tinted hall, wide-eyed, a child. 'Oh,' she says. She smiles. Nothing is horrible any more. Everything is new.

This is a trick I have learned how to pull. This is my work. With tricks of mathematics and optics, we augment reality, smothering surfaces in warm, spicy notes of brand belonging.

I turn, distracted by a voice.

'I lived free among free women.'

That woman even sounds like my mother. She's back in the kitchen again. How the hell did she do that?

'There were no inhibitions,' says a boy, egging her on.

'None, sonny, none.' She is not my mother. She does suggest, with uncanny physical precision, what my

76

mother might have become. She says, 'We lived a life of perfect freedom together.'

The kitchen is less busy now. I go over to the sink, but the vodka has disappeared. I rinse out a cup and dip it into a washbowl. The punch is as thick as blood. There are slices of orange floating in it.

The boy says, 'What was it like? How did it feel? Describe your freedom.'

'Licky.'

'You were licked?'

'I lived among tongues. Among women's unfettered tongues, singing, crying, tasting, supping. Tongues loosed in the mouth, free to probe and explore the soft mouthy interiors of the self, to sense and express.'

Hanna comes and stands beside me. She snaps open a can of lager. The woman like my mother says, 'There developed among us an unexpected appetite for the anus. For the wrestle of probing muscle and sphinctered round, for the negotiation between these intimate forces.'

'At all times of day and night.' The boy has her rhythm now.

Hanna peers into my cup. 'What the fuck is that? God.' She takes a mouthful of beer and swills it round her mouth before swallowing. 'Let's get out of this shithole.'

She leads me back to the lawn. Someone is throwing books into the fire. I feel the need to comfort her. I put my arm through hers. 'He probably thinks he's being ironic.'

'I can see why Michel wanted to come here,' she says.

So can I. If he's any sort of writer, he'll be sat up in a tree somewhere with a view of it all, taking snaps, scribbling furious notes.

Hanna surveys the house, the grounds, the fires. She says, 'You sink and you sink and you sink and one day you look in the mirror and there are creases around your eyes that weren't there last year and you've done nothing, absolutely fuck-all that adds up to anything.'

'Yes?'

Hanna makes a face. She is presenting herself to me, delivering the elevator pitch for 'Hanna'. It's not rehearsed, exactly – it's not cynical – but she wants me to know she is more than just another counter-culture youth. She wants me to think well of her.

But it is painful, to have to listen to all her hackneyed dreams of secession – her plans to flee her self in other lands, on other shores, and in among the poorest of the Earth: sea gypsies and shrimp farmers, fishermen and cockle pickers. These are communities Hanna has read about and with whom she declares a powerful if abstract affinity. 'I want to be among people who work with nature,' she says, 'who work with their hands.'

I remember the time Dad blew up about Mum joining the protest camp – how she'd be used, abused and very likely raped. A funny thing to say in front of your son. Now I understand his frustration. Listening to Hanna is like watching a car accident from the vantage of a hill. The distance giving you the view takes away any chance to intervene.

Dry land is portioned and parcelled and privatised beyond all saving – this is Hanna's argument. And if this is the way she thinks, I can understand Michel's deep appeal for her. She has fallen for his millennial poetic.

There's no denying the intensity of Michel's myth-making. A glint of morning silver in the dusk. A spark of spring renewal in the dying king's eye. Where it all goes wrong – wrong enough to matter – is his insistence that escape is a real possibility. Hanna dreams that come the Fall she will literally sail off into the sunset with Michel. She genuinely imagines they can live off the sea.

She's not ignorant. She's spent time on the ocean. She knows what she's doing. 'Most sailing clubs are friendly, they can usually tell you which skippers are planning long trips. It's not so hard to find a berth, if you're willing to work.' But this is the problem. All Hanna's practicality, her experience, her determination, even her intelligence, are only making her more stupid. Stupidity isn't a lack of knowledge, or a lack of intelligence. Stupidity isn't a *lack* at all. Stupidity is a force. It's an energy. It has hold of her now and it is not going to let her go.

Michel is by the bonfire, stomping up and down in his heavy boots. I have never seen him dance before. He isn't very good. He smiles at us, creasing his eyes against the smoke from his roll-up. Hanna leans in to speak to him. He shrugs, smiles, carries on stomping. He's still clutching his phone. Is he still taking photographs? It would be like him. I'm surprised at people's easiness with it. Even with things as they are, the police still turn over in their sleep now and again to seize some online prey.

Hanna takes my hand and leads me back up the slope, past the house. We are leaving him here. Hanna is driving me home.

The weather front I saw building earlier this evening hits land. Hanna's faster than Michel behind the wheel and she punches us into the open mouth of the storm. The rain is so heavy it takes all the power out of our headlights. Hanna finds the switch for the fogs but the rain simply reflects the light, make visibility even worse. I wish to God she would slow down.

Lightless, winding, the road leads through uncertain country into the shelter of tall hedges. Rain shivers off the sides of barns and silos. A magnesium yard light throws the shadow of a tractor across the lane. On a sharp bend, our own headlights are repeated in tiny shards off the eyes of cattle pressed together in a barn.

Suddenly there are leaves hanging motionless in the air before us, glittering in the headlights, fluttering in space as though suspended on thin wires. It's not a big tree. As trees go. We skid, swerve, the truck slipping into place, nose to tail across the narrow road, as neatly as a wedge fits a crevice. In the split-second before impact I catch a glimpse of Hanna, hands still at the wheel. My heart swells to see her sitting there, so calm. I wish there was time for me to hold her.

We hit the tree side-on. The noise is immense, complex, horrible. Something punches a hole through my side window, passes behind my head, and stabs the cabin ceiling. In the time it takes me to inhale – I'm still half-convinced that my brains must be spattered across the roof of the cabin – the cabin light comes on. The branch that nearly killed me is knotted and grey and lichenous. A spider, a tiny red body cushioned on long hair-like limbs, climbs from the branch onto the light housing, as the light fades and dies. Everything turns silver suddenly. I imagine another car, swooping towards us, and glance in panic at the side mirror. It's still intact, and hanging there like a picture expertly framed, the moon shines through a rent in the clouds.

Hanna's airbag, deflating, leaves her with her head cushioned in the laminated shards of her side window.

'Hanna?'

Her eyes come open.

'Hanna?'

She takes a breath. She blinks. She looks at me. She says nothing. Glass falls like rain from her lap as she opens her door and climbs down from the truck.

'Hanna.' Slowly, testing for damage, I clamber across the cab to the open door and let myself down to the ground. The ground isn't solid at all – I'm balancing on branches, on crushed twigs and leaves. I put my hand out to steady myself and the wing-mirror gives under my hand and I barely keep my feet.

The rain has stopped but the gale is at its fiercest now. It tore the tree out by the root, and the tree brought down a low wall as it fell. Clumps of brickwork are scattered in puzzle pieces all over the road. I step from the shelter of the cab. You would think these high verges would shelter us from the wind; instead they channel it. Tree and truck together make a complex voicebox through which the wind passes, moaning and whistling, struggling to speak. The wind is so strong I can barely stand up in it. It's stripping the tree. Something, a nut, a fir cone, damn near takes out my eye. I open my mouth to shout, and the next second I'm spitting out leaves. 'Hanna!'

She's leaning against the tailgate, braced against the wind. As I watch, her energy fails her; she slips down off the panel and lands in the road.

I offer her my hand.

She looks up at me and dares a smile. She yells, 'Does this happen to you a lot?'

The road's on a sharp incline, which makes moving the tree much easier. It is quite small. You would think it would take more mass to shove a branch practically through the roof of our cabin. Hanna, still shaken, accepts my offer to drive the truck for a while. There's some comical business, trying to work out how to reset the engine after its bag-deploying stall. I ease the truck past the tree, and foliage crackles beneath our tyres. The truck's sides sing as they scrape against its branches.

'Gun it,' says Hanna. 'We have to get home.'

I'm more worried about the rubble from the wall than I am about the tree, but we get past without a blow-out. It's cold in the cab now, the glass in both side windows put out, but the rain has stopped for now and our windscreen, cracked through and crazed in its lower left quarter, is still somehow holding together. No way am I letting us go over twenty with the windscreen like this.

The coast road is awash with refuse spilt in the gale. The wind's first violence is past, but it's still strong enough to be sending cereal cartons bounding along the gutters. A tea bag catches in our wipers, and is snatched away. Through town after town, our passage is lit by the flashing indicator lights of parked cars. Their alarms, triggered by the gale, howl and hoot as we go by.

'How does it feel to drive?' Hanna's worried about the truck. She can't understand why we are going so slowly. She does not know, as I know, intimately, what flying glass can do to a person's face.

'It's fine.' I keep the needle stuck at twenty, the engine whining away in second gear. In places, even the litter is overtaking us. A signboard for a local paper goes skidding under our wheels. Plastic bags flock in the branches of overhanging trees. We have only one headlight now.

Half-way down the vertiginous lane to the levels I brake to a halt and together we wrestle with a buckled wheel arch to stop it rubbing against the nearside front tyre. Now, of course, it starts to rain again.

I am gripped by a sudden desperation to be behind a door and contained within walls. I let the needle go to thirty, trying all the while not to think what will happen if the windscreen gives way.

The levels offer no obstacle to the wind; it gathers walls of rain about itself, becoming visible, and dances circles round us as we drive. Sudden gusts break up the rocking rhythm of the road, and Hanna flinches every time rain comes into the cabin. My hands are frozen and wet on the wheel.

The gale is at its fiercest when we reach the shingle, but here there is almost nothing for the wind to toy with. No litter, no foliage to toss about. Not even sand. I can hear the sea over the sound of the engine but I cannot see it; it lies beyond the shingle bank, where the automatic lighthouse blinks but does not turn. The snap of its easy illumination nags at the eye in a way the wheeling light of the old lighthouse never would.

Outside the house, the boat is rocking on its trestles. A tarpaulin has come loose. It snaps and writhes, a fantastic pennant, over the roof of the bungalow.

'Christ.'

Hanna leads me to the door, undoes it, shoves and shoves. Behind us, the boat creaks and strains, eager to fall. 'Hanna?' I'm offering help, but what comes out of

my mouth is a lamb's bleat against this roaring wind.
'Hanna!'

'There.'

The electricity is out. Holding hands like bashful school-children, we stand in the dark of Hanna and Michel's bedroom looking out at the storm. Beyond rain beading the window pane, there is nothing to see. There are no street lights. The house itself might be sunk in a deep hole, or sealed inside a gigantic tin, were it not that it bends and flexes with every shift of the wind. The house is adapted to storms. In the changing pressure it contracts and swells like a lung, popping and squeaking.

We are in the bedroom because the boat may at any moment come crashing into the living room. Outside, pebbles grind together under the beating of irregular waves. I wonder how high the water is now. I wonder how high the tide comes, relative to the land. Were the currents to shift, the prevailing winds to change, how quickly would the sea eat through this place?

Lightning flashes, bringing the answer to life with a dreadful clarity. I can see the sea! This has to be a trick of the light. The sea is swelling into view, out beyond the shingle. It vanishes for a second. Then lightning strikes a second time – a tree, thinly rooted in the surreal greener-than-green ocean.

Another flash. (The world is reduced to a series of stills.) A grey container ship shows up starkly against the radium green ocean, the ceramic-white sky. Its prow, as straight as a piece of creased paper, cuts the black water, raising a wound webbed with foam. At the back of the ship, the helm and living quarters rise as a stack of grey boxes. A red painted line runs round them like a strip of packing tape. What's a ship this big doing so close to the shore? Is it being steered towards the shelter of land, or are the waves dashing her helplessly towards these banks? Another flash, and the ship is poised halfway down the sickening descent of a coast-facing swell. Its right propeller is lifted into the air and a line of water, thick as shaving foam, clings like a hand to the grey circle made by its spinning blades. In the electric flash, the ship appears reduced, tiny, as simple and smooth as a plastic construction model.

It vanishes. I turn to Hanna. I cannot see her, but I wait, and she is looking at me, straight at me, in the next lightning flash, her lips slightly parted, as though she would speak, but in the darkness no sound comes, and there is no more lightning. We stand there in the dark waiting for light, and there is no light at all anymore. I have to do something about those parted lips, I have to, and she meets me, her lips meet mine, while all around us the house breathes its heavy sigh.

It happens easily, the way water spills and finds its level. A steady and fluid descent. Clothes. Bodies. Her flesh is tight and hard and efficient. She pulls me onto her and into her as though clambering into a piece of gym apparatus. I pin her arms to the bed, less from passion than from the simple desire to catch my breath. Her hips arc against me, gently now, pulling me against her pubic bone. Her desire is heartbreakingly pure. She will not let my tongue inside her mouth. 'Little kisses,' she whispers. 'Little kisses,' all the while stretching her legs, lifting them, stretching herself wide for me. The smell of Michel on the sheets only steepens the rate of my fall into her. The thought of him where I am now, his wet in with hers, makes me climax so fast I have no time to withdraw. I come deep inside her. She gasps.

'Hanna—'

'It's okay. Doesn't matter.'

I don't even go soft.

After a time, she fetches me out with her hand. 'Do me like a boy.'

'Hanna.'

'Go on,' she says, pulling herself wider, hands under her knees. 'I want to be filled.'

We are sitting at opposite ends of the sofa, eating breakfast. Anyway, toast.

Half way through the night I panicked and left the bed Hanna shares with Michel and came to sleep out here. There wasn't any need, as it turns out. Michel isn't back yet. I wish to God I'd stayed in bed, pressed up to Hanna. Her small brown hands. Her breath. Perhaps we would have done it again. *Again*, that magic word. Imagine it happening all over *again*.

It's not going to happen now. Everything has acquired a predictable awkwardness. Words are setting over our intimacy like a scab over a wound.

Hanna asks, 'Where will you go? When you get back.'

'I'll see if I can find a flat near where I used to live.' I tell Hanna about the old factory, its interlinked brick courtyards, its dogs and its motor scooters, its life, its noise.

'It sounds fun,' Hanna says, as unconvinced as I am.

When I go back I will go straight to work. I will pick up where I left off, if the company will let me. I will earn money and pay rent, and life will acquire whatever new shape it will.

I think right now I would actually feel easier with Michel here. 'When's Mick back?'

'Oh—' Hanna's dismissive gesture is somehow more undermining of her relationship with Michel than anything we did together. What we did probably doesn't count for much, after all. People do things. If they only get the chance. *Again*. God, I would give my right arm for *again*. She is the most beautiful thing I have taken to bed in my life.

'Tell me about Mandy.'

Another unavoidable topic. She knows Mandy was my girlfriend; that I lived with her, and I have left her now, and feel guilty for it. She does not know the full circumstances. I have so far spared her – spared myself – the details.

'The thing is, falling in love is about falling in love with a world.'

New to the city, and ever more out of touch with my father as he pursued his own strange course, I fell hook, line and sinker for Mandy's world. And though my love for Mandy has long since evaporated, I still love Mandy's kitchen. I'm still deeply infatuated with her pillows, and her shoes. I love her scarves and her seven different kinds of toothpaste. 'There was a flavour for each day of the week. And she had these little porcelain bottles of essential oils gathering dust on her bathroom shelf.'

'I don't know why you came here,' Hanna says. There is a chill in her voice. I have revealed too much of myself. The inner shallows.

She is thinking about last night, and wondering how

much of what I did with her was directed at her; how much at the boat, the shack, the shingle, the lighthouses. 'We fall in love with a world.' How stupid.

Too late now to tell her it was all for her. Too late to convince her that she is something new, unlooked for and extraordinary. Too late to tell her that she has changed my game.

'You asked me here.' Words build their own defences around me, unasked. 'Mick asked me.'

'That's not what I meant. Don't be angry.'

I take a breath. 'Michel wanted to show you off to me – is my guess.'

'You think he's that egotistic?'

'You. The boat. The book. The life. Not in a bad way. He wants me to know that he's happy.'

'He does?'

'He knows that his happiness matters to me.'

'Right.'

'We've known each other forever. Did he not tell you that?' Indeed, the amount of damage I could do right now, with a few salient memories, is dizzying. 'Do me like a boy,' indeed. Not that I will say anything. If history teaches us one lesson, it is that all breakages must be paid for.

'Yet you fucked me.'

'I did.'

'I'm glad you did.'

'Not as glad as I am.'

This, at least, raises a smile. 'And Michel?'

'It's all right. You think I'm going to say something? I'm not going to say anything.'

She says nothing to that.

Christ.

'Will you? Tell him?'

Hanna waves her hand, of course not. 'Things happen.'

This is such an accurate echo of my own internal dialogue, I can't help wincing at its vacuity. No. Things do not just 'happen'. This is more than chance – this is choice, this *was* choice. 'I wanted you.'

She looks at me.

'I still want you. I know we can't, but there you are. Because you're gorgeous, Hanna. You're gorgeous. Among your other qualities.'

Your tiny breasts. Your small brown hands. Your wit and your stupidity wound round each other like a mechanism set to shake itself to pieces. Little kisses and spread thighs. The drama in you. The impatience. The bloody *life*.

Bone-thin boats carve the cold green water under Mandy's window as she dictates ideas into her laptop. I imagine her discussing her injuries on public radio, in sprung rhythm, wedged between a folk singer and the COO of a hospice charity.

Hanna, luckily, is much more interested in what I think about Michel. Whatever else you say about infidelity, it does bring problems into focus. And here they come, a whole parade of them. Has Michel always written? Will his writing find a market? What will a writer do aboard a boat all day? Will it be good or bad for his writing, this voyage they have planned? The more Hanna talks, the more anxious she becomes. She is as doubtful as I am about Michel's commitment to their voyage. 'The thing is,' she says, 'I can't handle that boat on my own.' She's couching all this in practical terms, but the image I'm getting of her is of a woman already abandoned, as her man sails away on an ocean of his own invention.

Oh, let go, fool. Let go and float. Pay attention to the things of the present. Hanna's small feet. Hanna's small breasts. Hanna's small mouth. Make it smile. Make it gasp. *Again.* Seize the day. Seize her. This moment will not come a second time. I reach over and stroke her neck, hit the button of her shirt, hold it between my thumb and finger, daring her to let me, daring her to say 'Again.' 'When will Mick be home?'

She moves towards me. 'How will he *get* home?'

She has a point. I undo a button. Michel's among friends, and he will be able to cadge a lift eventually, but this place is hardly on anyone's way anywhere. Most likely some roads are completely closed. A button comes free. He might not get here for hours. For days. The entire beach is cut off. A button. A button. The mainland has sunk. Here's all that's left. She shucks her shirt for me. I hold her hands. 'What do you want to do?'

'He'll turn up eventually,' Hanna says, without worry, without enthusiasm. I lie her down on the floor. She barely moves, and then, feeling me draw near to my climax, she paddles against me, wriggling clear. I won't have it. I won't. I come down on her, hard, her bone a hot bar across my erection as I fill her again. Her eyes are glassy with an emotion stuck uselessly between anger and hunger. I grip her, fixing her, and kiss her lips.

At last her mouth comes open.

And, after a minute or two of this, here they come, the bloody words. Too soon, too soon – I am still just about inside her, for heaven's sake – yet I cannot help but vomit them up. 'I know you want me to apologise.'

'No,' she whispers, hushing me. 'No.'

'It's all right. I'm not bloody going to.'

I roll off her and she staggers to her feet – I have been very rough with her – and she goes to the window to study the sky, her figure outlined against the boat, the half-finished ketch that will, finally and forever, take her away from me.

And him. If she takes Michel away, I may never see him again, either.

'Come see.'

I stand beside her, resting my hand on her hip. 'Around here,' she says, 'the sea comes up higher than the land. You can see it sometimes. Some tides.'

So it is true. Last night – the swollen green dome of the ocean, rising above the shingle like the top of a monstrous head – it was not just a trick of the light. The sea impends here, and the land is a bowl, waiting to be tipped, to be dipped, to be filled with the sea. It doesn't make sense, how the land bends here. Not falling away. Falling *up*.

The first line of Michel's novel reads:

Why run off to sea when the sea will come for you?

NINE

Occasionally Michel came home with me for tea after school. Dad wouldn't be home until six-thirty, and Mum was busy upstairs, so we pretty much had the run of things. The kitchen staff were old hands, they knew what they were doing, so at this time of day the hotel looked after itself.

Out the front, the hotel made a big display of its picket fencing and ornamental dry-stone wall, but round the back the grounds abandoned all pretension and blended with the surrounding farmland. The fence separating the hotel garden from the river track was rickety and loose. I held a strand of barbed wire for Michel to duck under. 'Mind the ditch.'

The lawn needed cutting.

'Now I see why you come to school looking such a mess.'

'No I don't.'

'You look like you've been pulled through a hedge backwards.'

I didn't argue. Knowing Michel he probably had photographic evidence. Michel's love of photography caused him a lot of trouble at school. One of his community service clients had phoned up to complain.

In an effort to stem his voyeurism, the school had told his mother. Now Michel was without a camera and lived with the constant threat of having his photographs discovered. 'I've got them hidden.'

'Yes?'

'I'll show you sometime. They're wrapped in plastic. They should be all right.'

'I mean, it's not as if you were taking photographs of them in the bath or anything.' I wanted to show willing, to be outraged on his behalf.

'I did, once or twice.'

'For fuck's sake, Michel.'

'I'm joking,' he said.

Now Michel spent his Thursday afternoons helping out the school caretaker. Of course it was impossible for the school to impound every photograph he had taken. He still had his collection, buried away: ancient faces caught unawares, flesh rilled against the bone, and how the weight of life and time bore down on every dusty room.

I led him round by a crumbling brick path to the conservatory. Sunlight bleared over panels of dusty glass, framed in dark green wood. When the hotel had regular guests, this had been our breakfast room. Now it was Dad's workshop. The heating was turned off. The pipe that ran around the circumference of the room was no longer the scalding-hot hazard it had been. (We'd lived in terror of a guest's child one day getting a hand stuck behind it.) Now Dad was getting by with a bottled gas heater that made an obscene lapping sound whenever the bottle started to empty. Three cement stairs led to the house proper. Dad's vests were hung up on pegs beside the door. A black padded chair sat in the middle of the room. A medical examination lamp leant over the chair, perching on shiny tripod feet. A workbench ran along the long wall.

The floor was strewn with explicit magazines. Dad had been cutting pictures out with scissors and sticking them on pieces of A4 card. A plastic bulb of paper glue had been left to harden in the sunlight.

'I should explain.'

'This'll be interesting.'

'They're for our guests to stick up over their beds.'

'Uh-huh.'

Erotics were a part of the visual world Dad worked to restore. The trouble is, below a certain resolution, the most explicit image loses its erotic charge. Dad's vests offered his soldier-patients, at best, a twenty-by-twenty pixel field of view. 'Then there's the edge detection problem.'

'Keep going. You're funny.'

'One serviceman complained that Dad kept showing him pricks.'

'You really think you can talk your way out of this?'

'Oh, what's the use?' I threw up my hands. 'We're a family of pornographers. Dad straps schoolgirls to his desk and I violate them with this.' I waved an ophthalmoscope around.

Dad's researches into prosthetic vision – a spin-off from his constant tinkering – had brought him into contact with a loose, international network of hobbyists and junior researchers – men and women he met only as stuttering ghosts on his computer screen. For them, or for the brand they represented, he stitched fabric and webbing and copper lugs into visual vests for blinded servicemen.

Michel and I tooled around with Dad's kit. Michel took off his shirt and put a vest on, and a pair of black goggles to hide the world from his eyes. The camera mounted on the side of his goggles plugged into the vest. 'It needs turning on ... There.' I reached to touch the switch. It was hidden by a curl of hair over his ear. 'Okay?' I drew away, fingers tracing his temple. I went to the switch by the door and turned off the conservatory light. It was just about dark enough, a summer evening. The setting sun had fallen behind a line of trees. There was a torch in Dad's desk drawer. I swung it around a few times in front of Michel's goggles.

'I can't make any sense of this,' he complained, his vest chattering, his eyes hidden behind the big, blacked out lenses of his goggles.

'You're getting there.'

'How?'

'You're turning your head to follow the torch.'

'I am?'

'Yes.'

Like everybody else, Michel imagined that once you invented something like this – something worth an article or two, a local headline – then a grateful world would see to it that you were properly recompensed. Michel thought

Dad's work explained how we'd ended up running this sprawling hotel.

But the hotel – this great, absurd shell, vanishing year by year behind walls of tangled and untended green – had been Mum's waste of money, not Dad's. The guests didn't have too bad a time of it, but the rooms we lived in were cold, draughty and uncomfortable and there were too many of them. There were rooms no-one went into from one year to the next – rooms Dad warned me to stay out of because of some newly discovered dereliction: faulty electrics, or spreading damp.

We put Dad's gear away and I led Michel upstairs to my room. Michel paused on the landing, looking up the stairwell at the light escaping from Mum's apartment at the top of the house. The light was strange up there: pools of taupe and rose spilling from desk lamps draped with hand-dyed silk. Mum was flirting with arson again. We heard furniture being shifted around.

'Who's up there?'

'That's Mum. She's sorting out her stock.' Bags of cosmetic-grade glitter. Clear plastic boxes full of sequins. Rolls of cloth. Reams of hand-made paper. Boxes of ribbon. An easel. Bags of unopened paints. She was saying she was going to sell it all. I couldn't imagine how.

She was going off to the protest camp again – the third summer in a row. Her ambitions for it were more realistic this year. At any rate, more muted. She no longer expected the camp to transform her life. She no longer imagined that it would ever save the world. She just wanted to see her friends.

The militants, on the camp's other side, had been edged off their narrow purchase, their tents and shelters grubbed up, and boulders dumped between the trees to stop them reoccupying the space. They had adopted other causes, other interests. Squats and demonstrations. Agitprop. The women Mum camped among were too remote to matter much, and the authorities had left them alone. They were not as doctrinaire as they had been. 'You can come and see me,' Mum had said to me – as if I could ever be persuaded to go there again.

'Jesus,' said Michel, entering my room. 'Is this all yours?'

'Well, it's my room,' I said. 'The furniture belongs to the hotel, really. Apart from *that*.' I pointed at the dressing table – the mirrored table Dad had bought Mum as a wedding present. This was the table which was supposed to make Mum feel like Gloria Swanson whenever she sat at it to make herself up for evenings of parties and premières. Life takes its own path, of course, and now the table was mine. Mum didn't want it any more. Since her hospital spell she had lost her liking for mirrors.

The dressing table drawers opened stiffly, crammed to jamming with photographs in yellow paper wallets.

While I rifled through them, Michel waited on the white-painted bench that ran round the bay window. It was massively uncomfortable to sit on. The cushions slid about on the paint so that you were always slipping off. Still, visitors here invariably headed straight for it, suckered, I suppose, by the novelty of the thing. Squirming for purchase, determined to enjoy his window-seat moment, Michel studied the photographs as I handed them to him.

'Here they are.'

The water meadows captured in our family snaps were buried now, beneath the asphalt and paving of the

housing estate. There, in their perfectly square bungalow, under its red-tile pyramidal roof, Michel lived with
his mother.

Michel wanted to know how ground water had moved
about the meadows, before the builders canalised it,
piped it, buried it under chicanes and driveways and
mini-roundabouts. He wanted to know what the land
would look like once the estate fell apart, as it surely
would one day. The End Times were on their way. He was
convinced of this. He was trying to work out what life
would be like here, after the Fall. He liked to imagine
himself preparing for disaster, steadily, calmly, over
years. He imagined himself holed away in some brake in
the woods, his life made rich and strange by its privations
and narrow compass.

Still, after Michel's recent run-in with the school, I
couldn't altogether shake off the suspicion that, as he
worked through our photographs, he was actually studying me. My bobble hat. My pantaloons and pushchair.
Mum's hand in mine, pulling me to attention. 'I'd better
start cooking. Dad will be home in half an hour.'

We went downstairs and Michel sat at the kitchen
table, watching me chop vegetables. He had this intense
look – you'd think I was performing surgery. 'You can
cook,' he said.

Dad had one of those Japanese knives; the weight of
the blade did all the work. You just had to mind your
fingers. It was the easiest thing in the world to cut up
a few vegetables, throw them in a tray and bung them
in the oven. The fish went on top about fifteen minutes
before we sat down to eat.

'You cook fish,' he said.

'Do you like fish?'

'Sure.'

It felt good to have found something I could do and that Michel couldn't.

Dad walked into the kitchen and dropped his briefcase by the piano. 'Hello,' he said, in the voice he used with our guests, and gave a reserved-judgement smile. The photographs were spread out on the dinner table. 'Goodness. Conrad. You're showing off your baby pictures?'

Mum came down to eat with us more or less when I called her. She wasn't usually so accommodating.

Dad asked her, 'What time is your train tomorrow?'

'After eleven.'

'After eleven?'

'Quarter past eleven. Eleven twenty. Eleven twenty-one at the third beep.'

'I can run you down in the car, but you'll be waiting there a while.'

'You can run me down in the car?'

'I can run you over.'

'You can run me over?'

'Do you want me to give you a lift or not?'

'No, Ben, it's okay.'

'You'll have to make your own way to the station then. I need the car. I'll be leaving around eight.'

I said to Michel, by way of explanation, 'Mum's off on a protest.'

'Sara,' Dad said, 'is going to get herself cold, wet, scared, arrested and very probably beaten.'

'Jesus Christ, Dad.'

'Certainly kettled. Hosed. Maybe gassed.'

Mum joined in, mimicking him. 'Blinded. Blown up.'

There was an awkward silence as Mum and Dad re-membered, far too late, what I'd told them about Michel's family.

Michel looked from me to Dad and back again. 'What? You want me to say "beheaded"?'

'Let's all calm down,' Dad said.

'Let's not,' said Mum.

I said, 'Let's just eat the fucking fish I caught.'

'*Caught?*'

'Cooked. Let's eat the fucking fish I cooked.'

'Does this sort of thing run in the family?' Michel asked Mum, trying to jolly things along, to give as good as he was getting, to join in.

Mum said, 'You wouldn't believe the things that run in this fucking family.'

'Enjoy your tent that I paid for,' Dad said.

'I bloody will, Ben. Thanks.'

When he left (by the front entrance, off to the housing estate and his widowed mum's bungalow) Michel said to me, with admiration, 'She's quite a character, your mum.'

The following morning I traipsed after Mum to the station, 'helping her with her bags', breathing in her second-hand smoke. She had no time for my preferred, round-about way into town. 'I need to get going.' She had us cut straight across the estate.

Our hotel used to have a view. I remember clover. Watercress. (Peppery – it made me sneeze.) Now even the water was gone: canalised, buried deep, a maze. I remem-ber them lowering big concrete pipes into the ground. Diggers and pile-drivers and drills. Lakes of mud.

The housing estate was made of all the same shape of

bungalow: small, square, with roofs of red tile. The roads were curved, generating fractional differences in the sizes of neighbouring gardens. Because the bungalows were all exactly alike, the people who lived in them had each tried to make their own bungalow stand out from all the others. The walls were clad in a smooth render, and each house was painted a different colour. Eggshell blue. Sand yellow. Moss green. The driveways were different. One had tarmac newly laid. There were marble chips in it. It looked like a cake. Others had laid various grades and kinds of gravel. Someone had laid bark chips. Each bungalow had a garage, and each garage had a different kind of door. Some were metal. Others were wood, with little windows. On and on like this, your head ended up full of this junk: how some verges were well-tended, as though for a game of miniature bowls, while others were overgrown, a mass of weeds, dandelions and clover, and still others were so bare and dusty they looked new-sown. On and on and on. Mum had told me that places like this matured; that new trees would grow. But here she was, going away again. For all her efforts the world had yet to be saved; and the estate looked as raw and as ugly as it always had.

On the railway platform, Mum stared down at her great, clod-hopping black boots. She was trying to find words. Something right for the moment. 'I thought you were going to walk with me.'

'I did walk with you.'

She ground out the butt of her cigarette. 'You lagged behind.'

'I wasn't lagging behind, I was trying to catch up with you.'

'We didn't talk at all.'

'You didn't want to talk to me.'

'I did.'

'Well.' I told myself I was not going to cry. I was bloody well not going to.

Mum stared at her feet, casting glances that never quite reached me. For one horrible moment I was sure she was going to try to apologise. 'Christ, it's cold,' she said.

'It's going to be colder in the tent.'

'Will you visit me?'

'No.'

'Give me a hug.'

Her head rolled against mine. Her newly shorn hair bristled against my cheek.

'What?'

'You feel like a man.'

'I do?'

'I'd better go,' I said.

By the time I saw him, standing at the far end of the westbound platform in army drab and big black glasses, I was on the footbridge, crossing lines. Committed to departure. His hair, too long for regulation, made a white halo against the shredded sky. At his feet, a duffle bag almost as big as he was.

A grey mitten of cloud folded itself over the sun and the man's hair went out, went grey, became unremarkable.

What could I have done? What could I have said? I couldn't even be sure that this was the same man who had exposed himself to me. Mum waved, dismissing me, and I returned her wave automatically, a puppet strung on wire. Impossible, on such weak evidence, to break the conventions of farewell. So I left her there with him.

Normally I would have walked back along the river; instead I found myself heading for the estate, the way I had come with Mum. It didn't matter anymore. The water meadows were gone and nothing would bring them back. Michel was wrong. If the world fell apart tomorrow and humanity vanished in a puff of smoke, the waters here, cracking free of their concrete prison, would never run as they used to run. They would find new courses. The old stream beds – ribbons of silt and sand that webbed this place, mystifying gardeners – would blear and vanish over time, a network of collapsed veins. Michel's bleak, muscular view of collapse was no more than a boy's romance. No one can say what will succeed our present dispensation but one thing is for certain: it will not resemble the past.

TEN

I am glad that I live within walking distance of the Middle. I need the air, after a day spent in an office chair, rolling from desk to desk in an open-plan office lit only by a narrow lightwell.

This city picks and scratches at itself like an animal kept in too small a cage, pining for its lost reflection. It obsesses over its own archaeology. In the shade of parking garages and electricity substations, stubs of classical brickwork, lacquered with a weatherproof resin, poke up through gravel beds and well-tended lawns. New buildings clad apologetically in glass contort themselves around the city's ancient leavings. They hollow themselves out where they can; they arc above, they grope beneath. At its centre the city has begun to resemble the root system of a neglected houseplant. The Middle has packed itself around itself to the point where its surface has eroded away entirely. Inside its tangle of windowless malls and pedestrian bridges, its banks of stairs and escalators, its short-haul lifts and cantilevered walkways, no-one thinks about 'ground level', or even expects the numbers on the lifts to match up. There is something exhilarating about this – some atavistic hint of forest canopy.

I keep my glasses on for the walk home. I want to keep tabs on illusory light. It's easy enough to find if you know where to look – spilling from this atelier or that; welling up through the stairwells of the more on-trend basement clubs. Augmented reality is still the preserve of the very few, the initiated, the early adopters. Geeks, frankly. More rarely you sometimes see its early, clumsy forays into the real world. A shop-front spills its frocks onto the sidewalk. They pick themselves up and spin away down the road. A traffic experiment – ghost barriers descend across a road held up anyway by red lights. Cutting through a mall, I see movie actors wandering through crowds who are queuing to see their latest releases. These avatars go largely unseen, though they're swollen to more than life-size – seven-foot giants of the half-silvered screen. A few spectacled punters have spotted them, but they are already too sophisticated, too jaded, to want to interact with them. This is one of the difficulties with Augmented Reality. The bald idea has already worn thin. My half-silvered, AR-enabled spectacles are new (and expensive – the firm bought them for me). But Augmented Reality – the pasting of images over the real – is *old*: old as the ghost train and the distorting mirror.

*

I have moved back to the old locomotive factory where I used to live, before I met Mandy. Developers have taken down one whole corner of the building; of course they have left the facade. It's supported on iron braces, a gigantic theatre flat. They are planning to put something glass in place of its stacked-matchbox apartments and its flights of heavy, narrow stone stairs.

This redevelopment has reduced the number of apartments and puts pressure on the rest of the building, because nobody living here wants to move. There are even families here, their children living three to a room on stacked bunk beds. The rooms are so small, the ceilings so high, people have subdivided their own living spaces vertically. Every few years the freehold company turns over in its sleep and orders the removal of these treehouse mezzanines, thrown up in contravention of the building code. The ban never sticks. The courtyards are stacked with lumber.

The loss of one whole corner of the building has set the landlords subdividing again. Someone else was already living in my old apartment, but I have found another, higher up in a neighbouring wing, with a view of an identical courtyard. This apartment has been cut up into two: a cursory division of space that gives my neighbour and me half the enjoyment of the living room window. The party wall has been roughly cut around the profile of the frame. We have a pane each. There's gap between the wall and the window, wide enough to pass notes through. Not that we do.

There are inconveniences, living here – chiefly the noise and the moths.

The man I live next door to has been stamping and

shouting in an effort to get the family below us to shut up. They have an autistic child. It's hard to tell sometimes if she's crying in distress or simply hooting. Unconsciously, her parents have been placating her – or at any rate, drowning her out – with a wall of sound. Music, variety shows, film-clips, game loops. Noise-suppressing head-phones worked for a while. Then construction work started behind the factory facade. At work, tying illusory sound to illusory vision, we use cranial gloves to stimu-late the acoustic nerves. This is kit even the brashest early adopter would hesitate to sport in public, though the pundits say its day will come. Moving about my flat with its meshwork on my head makes me feel like a cyborg in a movie, but I value the near-silence it generates, and I can play music through it without disturbing anyone else.

The moths are a bloody nuisance, to be honest. They are small and white and they fetch up everywhere, a little pile of wings and dust in the corner of every windowsill, the back of every drawer.

It's nearly a year since I returned from visiting Michel and Hanna, and ironically enough it's me who lives the kind of cramped and straitened life they spent so much time and energy preparing for. Living here requires a kind of sea discipline. You let things slip just a little in this box, and all of a sudden you're ankle-deep in chaos and kipple. Even when the place is tidy and half-way clean, I can't bring anyone back here.

There are a couple of women at work who are fond of me. It's all very casual. A night out and a room in one of the boutique hotels round the back of the Ministries. I don't really have the money for this kind of thing, but

I'd sooner spend my money like this than on a bigger apartment, further from the centre.

Right now, and like everyone else in the company, I am pretty much living to work.

The company's been going for about six years and it needs to become more than just a handful of graduates and freelancers with a common idea. Money would make a real difference, but there's precious little of that, so we pull monstrous hours instead, bonding over our mutual pain and exhaustion.

What do we do? We play three-dimensional animations over printed targets, turning a headline, say, or a picture, a logo or a photograph, into a multimedia portal. The work is simple to explain, and it's relatively easy to generate business. The problem is in making any real money. Because the technology is new, we have to spend a lot of time educating our clients about what is possible (a constantly evolving brief); at the same time, we're constantly being blindsided by competitors who stumble across technology and outsourcing arrangements that undercut us – sometimes by tens of per cent.

Work here is a potent cocktail of commercial promise, too much encouragement, and the imminence of collapse. People new to the company quickly become addicted to the adrenaline. We rely far too much on interns, burning them out and replacing them like cheap batteries. They're all would-be entrepreneurs, creatives, video artists, writers. They've put their personal ambitions on hold to be a part of this bigger thing, this young company that could so easily swallow the world, if only it were given the right breaks. They are young, and their arrogance is neatly balanced by their insecurity. They want to be part of something bigger than they are.

I've been here a little over three years, and by many I'm counted an old hand. I no longer get off on the company's narrative. I'm not cynical about its prospects, but I'm prepared to be realistic. This company, so small, so undercapitalised, could well remain small and under-capitalised forever. It doesn't have to die, but nothing says it will ever actually come to life. Things can stay half-realised forever. Companies. People.

These days, I prefer the company of the coders. I haven't much in common with them. There's not a mathematical bone in my body. I don't share their love of trivia, their taste for science fiction, their distrust of the body. What I do enjoy – what I admire – is their love of the work for its own sake. These are the people who wander round the office abstracted all day, shifting several dozen variables around in their heads, trying to make them fit, trying – in their own arcane manner – to assemble them into something beautiful. Beauty counts for a lot with them, though some of them have a funny way of showing it.

I thought at first that Ralf's persistent star rating of everything from a cup of coffee to a gallery visit was a tiresome conversational gambit. I've come to understand that it is actually a kind of fetish – without it he would be lost in a world robbed of meaning.

'How did the presentation go, Ralf?'

'Three stars.'

'Weren't you at your sister's wedding last weekend?'

Ralf strokes his goatee beard. He's a couple of years older than I am, due for his thirtieth birthday next month, but he has to grow his bristles out a lot to make them show. 'I would struggle to give it more than two.' Ralf shaves his head. He is heavy-set, with sloping shoulders. He wears baggy jeans, and stands always with his legs splayed. He looks like a three-stage rocket.

Ralf likes putting people right. You come up with a theory about something, and Ralf says, 'I think we ought to label that an *hypothesis*.' It's the easiest thing in the world not to take him seriously and I should know because for the first couple of years, I really didn't. I knew he was talented. I knew he knew far more than me about subjects I considered 'my own', including some corners of the fashion business. But even while we worked together, brandspacing the show factory of a major automobile manufacturer, still I considered him one of the backroom crew – one of life's more capable functionaries.

Since coming back to work, however, I have been struck by the sheer adultness of what we cheerfully call 'the dev team'. They have quietly acquired an independent existence. After work they gather in their own preferred members' club. Past the listed frontage its interiors are retro plastic and bespoke plywood. There is a noisy dining room on the third floor. In each cubbyhole there is a jet-lagged sprawl of men and tablets, laptops, clever phones and empty cocktail glasses. This is where the true if unacknowledged movers of our industry come to relax.

Ralf has brought me here tonight to talk through some work. He has not told me what. 'What will you drink?' he asks me and before I can answer he has snapped his fingers at a passing waiter. I have never seen anyone do that – let alone get away with it – outside of an old movie. I sense some shift, some change in him. I was expecting to meet the rest of the dev team here tonight, but Ralf and I are on our own.

'I want to ask you something.' Ralf's show of self-possession would be unremarkable in any other man. Coming from Ralf it's frightening.

'Go ahead.'

'How wedded are you to your work?'

What kind of question is that?

'I don't mean the company,' says Ralf. 'I mean the work.'

I shrug. 'The work's the work.' This will hardly do. I try again. 'The work's the important part. The company—' I'm not sure where I'm going with this. 'The company can get in the way of the work. If you know what I mean? It's a frustrating time. What about—'

'Drink up.'

'We've only just got here.'

'Put your spectacles on,' Ralf says. 'I want to show you something.'

Ralf must be on better relations with the club than I realised, because he has mounted this surprise of his in their basement – a cramped, windowless null-space that must once have been furnished, going by the patches of glue still adhering to the poured concrete floor.

The room is quite empty. I stand, waiting for the system to kick in and for something to appear in this neutral and depressing grey interior. After a while I reach up to reboot my spectacles.

'There's no need. Leave it. It's working.'

'It is?'

'It's working.' Ralf's eyes glitter in the half-light. It occurs to me that he's not wearing spectacles. Whatever

111

it is he wants me to see, *he* will not see it. He says, 'Why don't you explore?'

I walk round the room, trying to prepare myself for God knows what surprise.

'Stop. Now. Take half a step to your left. Yes. Now, turn a little to your right. There. Now. Gently. Sit down.'

'Sit down?'

'Yes.'

I make to sit on the floor and the back of my knee catches the edge of something. I jolt, turn, and straighten in a single movement, staring at empty space. I reach out and touch—

'There you go.'

I explore it with my hands. It's a chair. I step back and take off my spectacles. A regular chair. Chrome, wood, a padded vinyl seat. 'Oh. That's neat.' I look around the room. 'You hid the cameras, too.' There they are; I can see them now. There is one in each corner of the room.

'Of course. If you'd seen the cameras, you'd have guessed the trick straight away.'

I put my spectacles back on. 'What happens if I move the chair?'

'Let me show you.' Ralf picks up the chair and carries it across the room. The lines of the chair stutter in the air, wheel, turn to grey-blue wireframe, and disappear again in an instant. He sets the chair down and steps away. The chair folds itself out of the air, folds itself back in again and disappears.

'It's brilliant.'

It is. The effect is seamless. I step towards the place where I know the chair to be. It takes me a moment to spot the four spots, grey on grey, where the chair's feet

112

connect with the floor – a junction no camera trickery can mask. 'What's all this for?'

Ralf barks one of his trademark humourless laughs. 'You tell me. Seriously. Tell me. I need to know.'

As if I'm not pulling fourteen-hour days as it is. 'Well, Ralf, I think it's a great demo, but—'

'I'm leaving the company.'

'You are?' Does the dev team know? Does the company know? What will they do without him? 'What will you do?'

He casts his hand about the empty – the *seemingly* empty – space. 'This. Ideas like this. Ideas without an immediate return. I want to play with this stuff, and I want you to monetise what I come up with. If you can. If you can't, then probably they weren't good ideas in the first place. That's the thing, you see. I have lots of ideas. I just don't know how to rate them.'

I don't understand this. 'And for this you need to quit your job?'

'I'm setting up on my own.'

'Oh.'

'Will you join me?'

'Oh.' Christ. 'How?' This whole conversation is becoming more and more strange. 'Who's going to pay for all this?'

'I will.' He sees my confusion. He smiles. 'Whose club do you think this is?'

This certainly goes some way towards explaining how Ralf – Ralf, of all people – gets away with clicking his fingers at the staff.

Strictly speaking, Ralf does not own the club. His sister manages it. Strictly speaking, he doesn't own the building. The family do – at least, they run a property company that operates, not just these premises, but the entire block and several beyond it.

I've acquired ideas about what money looks like from our interns. They all come from money – how else could they afford to work for us? I thought money came well-dressed, labouring under brittle, cutesy names like Flick and Roddy. I always assumed the dev team were safely proletarian – grafters on a credible wage. Strange that money could throw up a sport like Ralf. Ralf the work-aholic, Ralf the star.

It doesn't take me long to decide to accept his offer. The company we've been working for has had six years to break through and in that time the technology we pioneered has matured. It's become cheap. It's become easy to use. We're a ponderous service company trying frantically to reinvent ourselves as a portal for user-generated content, all on a shoestring and a series of half-baked promises from various government-sponsored industry foundations. We won't be the first outfit in this sector that's been encouraged to death. It's not anyone's fault. It's just the way of things. The first person through the door almost always gets shot.

Ralf wants me to handle business for what amounts to an inventor's atelier. He wants to stay on the dirty, techni-cal side of the IT divide, establishing patents for software engines which I'll go on to sell to bigger, public-facing companies. But if we establish just one good idea, and get bought out for our trouble, I will count this venture a success. We are not living in the nineteenth century. The pace of change far exceeds any individual talent – even one as focused, as monomaniacal as Ralf's.

For a while, Loophole (the name was my idea) is a sofa in an out-of-the-way corner of the club's sheltered and heated tea-garden. We lounge about under canvas in oversoft armchairs, overheated laptops scorching our knees as we hammer out, like struggling poets, a form of words that will get Ralf's work noticed. Ralf's family have money, and this cushions us, covering our own needs. It will not drive the company – for that we need investment.

This is my job. For eighteen frustrating, toe-stubbing months, the only work I find for us is old work, throwing together image recognition systems to paste virtual movies over billboard posters. Ralf is patient with me, but I can't help thinking that I'm scoring three stars at best. This is my fault. I'm the one charged with dreaming up new applications for imaginary light, but I have to bring in money as well, and here I am reaching for easy solutions, again and again.

By the time of my thirtieth birthday, Loophole is two. A weedy toddler, it employs six people to crunch code in the club's refurbished basement – a start-up company indistinguishable from dozens of others all crammed in the same three-block radius, all of us more or less dormant as we wait for our long-talked-about spring: the moment everyone is wearing spectacles and drinking in imaginary light as unthinkingly as they run water from a tap. 'Because that's what it will take.'

Michel accepts another cocktail from the tray and sits back in his chair. It's autumn but hot, and the roof-garden stinks, quite frankly, of damp vegetation and rot.

Michel came to celebrate my birthday, not sit through my litany of professional disappointment, but I cannot stop. 'When people go out of their way to adopt a new technology, they want something useful for their effort, not gimmicks, not games, not even stories. And the fact is, AR is *all* gimmick. That's its point. It gimmicks and games the world. You know, Hanna had this pinned years ago, when you first introduced me to her. She knew straight away it was arse-about-face.'

Michel nods and smiles, patient with me. He is surely weary by now of my mordant view of my work.

Outwardly the party is a success: an exclusive club; friends and workmates; even a girl who's sweet on me, off snorting cocaine with her girlfriends in the upstairs loo. The fact is, though, the club is the club – our workplace, a budget option. The colleagues outnumber the friends. Plus, I discovered today that Mandy has been given her own programme on national radio. For some while she's been reading her poetry at comedy clubs and bars across the city. She has become a minor urban celebrity. Now, with her 3.30pm slot, there will be no getting away from her. She has new hands now. Slimmer. Stranger. Too many fingers. She shows them off in the mugshot the newsfeeds have run. Becoming writer in residence at a service hospital south of the city, she lucked into some neurological experiment or other. They give her a cachet, those wild arachnid hands. They've pushed her up the rankings faster than any improvement in her poetry. I don't know why I feel angry. A defence mechanism, I suppose, knowing what I did, or rather, failed to do for her. Perhaps somewhere, in her ever-expanding opus of radio-friendly doggerel, there is a chilly piece about me. Maybe there isn't even that.

Michel, meanwhile, has sold the film rights to his first novel. *The Shaman*, it's called, and though the book advance was tiny, times being what they are, the film option was so big Michel's agent thought it was a printing error. Even parcelled out the way it is, in dribs and drabs over a dozen years, and hedged around with all manner of new writing commitments which Michel must religiously fulfil, the deal is a life-changer.

'Bryon Vaux wants an original treatment for the next one.'

The name means nothing to me.

'You know. Vaux. *Friendly Fire*.'

Friendly Fire came out a couple of years ago. It was the culmination of a long line of modish, cynical war films that compensated for acts of unlikely heroism 'in the field' with liberal conspiracy theories back home.

'I've not seen it.'

'Be happy for me, Connie.'

Jesus. 'Of course I'm happy for you, Mick. What am I saying? Why do you need me to be happy for you? Fuck you.'

Michael grins, at which point it occurs to me that he is working and writing for one of the most powerful media producers on the planet. He is more than a friend now. He is a contact.

'How's the family?' (You can almost hear the crunch of gears.)

Michel nods – a successful sommelier contemplating his cellar. 'Not bad at all, thanks.'

Michel and Hanna's daughter is exactly the same age

as Loophole, and a deal chubbier and healthier. They've had to abandon their sailing plans because of her, though the runaway success of Mick's writing would probably have scotched them on its own. This is the first time I've seen Mick since that visit, and I haven't seen Hanna at all. She never comes into the city; perhaps, even if she did, she would avoid me. I think of her sometimes. Who am I kidding? I think of her all the time. Her hands. The taste of her mouth. Christ, and since then she has had a child. Impossible not to wonder about that. 'Do you still have the boat?'

Michel nods. Without enthusiasm, he says, 'We'll have it finished, then decide what to do with it.' The boat was their project, the thing that bound them together, the myth they shared. Now that they have some, they're throwing money at it. But they have a child now. They don't need a dream.

'He wants to shoot something on those new cameras.' So much for a proud father's tiresome anecdotes about his family. Michel wants to talk business. We're back with Vaux again. 'He wants the next one to spill out of the screen, out of the cinema, I mean. To be distributed. I told him some of my ideas. He's keen.'

'That's great. Great.'

It's not until the following morning, waking in an unfamiliar bed, that it occurs to me – Michel is trying to put some work my way.

Eight months on, Michel brings Hanna and their daughter Agnes into town to see what Loophole has made for them.

We're meeting just outside the north-eastern suburbs,

where the railway, after passing through several deep cuttings, embraces the earth at last and disappears into a mile long tunnel. The tunnel's brick ventilation chimneys crop up in the portfolios of virtually every film and photography student in the city. Not that you can see the chimneys now the bracken is out. The hills' trademark gold and brown is vanished for the summer under this shaggy, silly green.

Where the tunnel begins, so does the granite, and the suburbs leave off entirely here, lending the city a sharp edge you would otherwise find only in storybooks. The houses rise in tiers against ferny rock-faces. They are always wet, even at the height of summer, because this is where the peat beds drain. At night, the culverts echo round the town, filling the streets with a sound that is part magical river, part overworked toilet mechanism.

The station is built into the foot of the gorge, and the road bridge runs over the rail line at an unlikely height. I lean against the parapet, a favourite of suicides and graffiti artists, waiting for the train. I recognise Michel by his thinning hair, Hanna I do not clock at all at first, and little Agnes is hidden from me by the natty pink parasol attached to her buggy. There is a lift to street level, a new all-glass contraption, already tagged. Mick and Hanna are practised pack-horses now; ignoring the lift, they carry the buggy out of sight, up flights of covered stairs. They're flushed when they emerge from out the entrance. Michel sees me and makes some comic business, staggering towards me. Hanna's got the buggy. Agnes is asleep.

'Don't worry about her,' says Hanna, loudly, in reply to my murmured hello. 'At this time of day she'd sleep through the Last Trump.'

119

Michel says, 'Nights are a different story.'

'Here.' I rummage about in my bag and pull out two pairs of goggles. 'Gifts.'

They are similar to the goggles Dad's blind soldiers wore years ago. The cameras in their earpieces are smaller and neater now. The lenses are half-silvered, rather than black.

The top half of her face hidden behind balloon lenses, Hanna takes my hand and lets me lead her over to the parapet and a view over the city, rising behind industrial parks and new housing estates. Michel stands a little behind her, resting his hands on her shoulders.

'Ready? Blink twice.'

I dig out a pair of goggles for myself and, as I turn to face the city, the lenses blink, shiver, and seem to fill with blue paint. The paint drains away until the lenses are half full. 'Try not to move your head.' The paint spills and spreads over the city. The land turns blue, then freezes and fractures. Planks, spikes and planes of blue fall from the buildings and bed down between them. The blocks turn and shuffle.

The city is buried under a torrent of blue geometric shapes, a child's building blocks, dropped and scattered, none of them smaller than a house. There are glitches. One high tower stubbornly clings to its blue coat. Elsewhere, landmark buildings have evaporated entirely, deleted by the program as it struggles to integrate reality and artifice.

(Ralf grew up playing console games whose squirrely physics engines sometimes allowed cars to ride along the undersides of overpasses, or avatars to sneak through the netherspace between two imperfectly adjoining walls.

120

At low moments he jokes that, if nothing else, at least Loophole has managed to revive these mistakes at a grand, city-spanning scale.)

The core illusion is starting to take shape. It appears that a blue lid has descended over the capital – a lid pierced to let through the spires, towers and chimneys of its tallest buildings. It is not yet fluid, not yet a flood. There are too many gaps, too many rectilinear holes. But as we watch, so Ralf's program renders its effects at finer and finer grain, until at last it really seems as though the city is flooded with blue paint.

The graphics engines kick in then, turning the flat blue to a living, moving sea. Technically speaking, Ralf's *coup de grace* is trivial, but even over the sound of the traffic I hear Hanna's gasp.

Imagine the city's rivers rising unstoppably, and breaking their banks. (The mainland has sunk. Here's all that's left …) The waters spread and slow, pooling here, threading there, exploring and rejoining. New islands form. The rail terminus upon its little rise becomes an island, while to the north the city's royal parks and theatres, its pleasure grounds and colleges, are made an island chain. The southern half of the city is almost entirely inundated. The towers of the large estates rise dramatically above the little waves, their lower storeys drowned. I take Hanna's hand in mine. 'Why run off to sea when the sea will come for you?'

I say it softly; too softly for Michel to hear.

Hanna shoots me a nervous half-smile, her fingers nerveless, waiting for me to let go of her hand. When I don't, she moves away.

I lift the goggles from my face. 'So there we are.' Michel

is still staring out to sea across the city, caught between realities. We have captivated him. Good. This being, after all, what we set out to do. 'You like it?'

Of the gloomy vision encapsulated in Michel's bestselling book, and rendered positively apocalyptic in Vaux's forthcoming film, Ralf and I have so far generated only the sunniest, smoothest caricature. Michel's narrative demands much more. It calls for foam and breakers, smashing tides and rips. But we have to begin somewhere.

'It's amazing,' Michel says.

Hanna says nothing. She cradles her goggles in one hand and rocks the buggy against her hip with the other. The child is awake now. Hanna takes down the parasol and chucks her under the chin. Agnes turns her heavy head and blinks at me, her eyes wide, her mouth pursed in outrage.

She looks exactly like me.

There's a cafe nearby I know is good, its interior a thick froth of old attic tat and second-hand furniture. Setting this pair down to eat anything in it is much more of a problem than I anticipated. They don't eat meat any more. They want to know the source of everything. They are concerned about their sugar intake, about the tolerability of wheat, about the sufferings of the rural poor. The coffee has to be absolved of crimes against humanity. Hanna subjects even the muesli to interrogation. 'Do you think these Brazil nuts are sustainable?'

'I should think so,' says the waitress, playing along because she knows me, because I come here for breakfast every day, because she expects we'll have a laugh about this later.

Michel's woodland redoubt, Hanna's waterborne odyssey – it saddened me when they abandoned these innocent, impractical escape plans, and chose a more ordinary life for themselves. But here they are embracing something even more childish. Do these two seriously imagine that global collapse might still be averted – averted simply by everyone clubbing together for the common good? They are becoming the sort of tweedy vegetarians who take used carrier bags with them when they drive to the supermarket in search of organic salad. Seeing them sip their microbrewed coffees, it's not hard to imagine what the End Times will actually look like: a planet of corpses clad in 'I Told You So' unbleached cotton Tees.

I don't feel like laughing, seeing what I have seen – Agnes's scowling, furious, vengeful baby face. I wore that very expression in a photograph I still own. I can picture it exactly – me in my pushchair, my mum behind me, and all around us the water meadows seeming to go on forever (though even then there must have been plans afoot, in some grey municipal office somewhere, to grub them up).

Is Agnes mine?

Hanna and Michel have both put on weight. New motherhood is alibi enough for Hanna's slight and pleasant filling-out. Michel has no excuse. He has been passing his good fortune straight to his stomach, snacking inappropriately on the gooier, oilier brands of fairly traded flapjack.

What if little Agnes is mine? If she is, then these two make no sense at all.

I'm not at all surprised that, once they no longer had to worry about money, Hanna and Michel decided to have a child – or changed their plans around a child they hadn't expected. Why look the gift horse in the mouth? In these happy circumstances, I can imagine Hanna letting her dreams of escape fall away, replacing them with something more normal, more adult and – yes, why not? – more comfortable. (The boat is gone. Sold. The beach house, too. They live in the suburbs now, though I don't suppose they call them suburbs. They live in a puddle of satellite green, twenty minutes' drive from the nearest railway station. The train into town takes an hour.)

But if Hanna had the slightest suspicion about the child's paternity (and how could she not?) why on earth did she go through with the pregnancy? Why would she give her life up to a lie, and for the sake of a future quite different from the one she was planning for herself, and was working so hard towards?

If it's my child – and of course it's my child! just look at its *face*! – then Hanna is using her to freeboot on Mick's fortune, binding him to her in a way he wasn't bound before, when she couldn't even say for sure whether he'd help her crew her boat.

'You know,' says Michel, 'there is another reason we wanted to come see you today.' He takes Hanna's hand. Hanna stiffens. Smiles. Tries to.

Christ. He knows.

He says, 'We wondered if you would be prepared to be Agnes's godfather.'

'What?'

Michel says it all again, word for word, laughing – dippy old Conrad, tuning out of the world, as usual. 'Well?' He talks about this as though it was another piece of work he is pushing my way. He wants to help out. He wants to get me involved. I wish Hanna would say something. Or do I? Christ, I don't know. What would she say?

Agnes. Just look at her. Sleeping again. When she sleeps she looks just like her mother.

When she's awake—

Vaux's film company approves our work on *The Shaman*. The executives there are so delighted with our AR visualisations, they try to steal the underlying code. I keep Michel out of the loop while we sort this one out, because Michel and Bryon are working hard on the screenplay and I don't want to throw grit in the works. Chances are Vaux, from his lofty perspective, probably doesn't consider this theft at all; just a piece of business as usual.

But we have patents pending on the realtime mapping algorithms that drive our flood simulator, and we need to establish priority.

It's a struggle to remain patient and civil with these people, but it eventually pays off: Vaux's production company offers to buy us out. I'm resistant at first but Ralf is passionlessly pragmatic – the money they are offering us will pay for another year's R&D. 'We either have faith in our ability to come up with the Next Thing, next year, or we don't,' Ralf tells me. 'If we don't, then why are we in this business?'

He's right, of course – and on the back of the cash, plus the goodwill we generate by being 'businesslike', we begin to expand, a semi-autonomous skunkworks, exploring the possibilities of immersive 3D.

We move piecemeal into proper premises. This, again, is through Ralf's family's property contacts. There is a heritage cable TV company rapidly haemorrhaging in a building not half a block from our basement den. So we hire rooms, one by one, in their offices, and like insects, we begin to eat our host from the inside. Over the course of a year we pick up their outgoing CFO, their personnel manager and their PA/receptionist. To our neighbours it must seem that the building is being steadily and stealthily infiltrated by the mentally disturbed. Abstracted young men and women in fashionable glasses are constantly wandering in and out of the building. They walk a little way, a few metres, and maybe they get as far as the corner of the street, when some internal battery fails them, and they begin to slow. They come at last to a complete stop, heads raised to the middle distance, oblivious to the business around them. There they stand, in the middle of the pavement, peering up and through delicatessens, hairdressing salons, bars and production offices, as though lost in a jungle. They stare and stare. Eventually, they wander back to the office again. What do they see? What do they hear?

Indoors, insulated from real-world distractions, we dream up proofs-of-concept. We calculate the physics needed to sail a boat through London's flooded streets, and brainstorm a gondoliering game, where you have to navigate through the shallower waterways and you fall into the water if you punt your boat out of its depth. Over a single, frantic weekend, we write the bible for a speedboat racing platform. Our games are games you can play outside, on foot or on a bicycle or from the passenger seat of a car. We web them through the real – skeins of narrative and incident and dayglo animation. They're not subtle, and they're not meant to be. They're not very easy to play, and they do not have to be. They stutter and tilt, not quite welded to the world they are trying to inhabit; their glitches will be ironed out in time. Meanwhile our office walls vanish under flowcharts and storyboards, sketches and wireframes and quickly rendered avatars with bulging pecs and massive breasts.

Six months into our work, Ralf is invited to dinner by the chief operations officer of a major telecommunications company.

I've had a bone-shakingly bad day; everyone has been shouting at me, so it's hardly surprising I take the news the way I do. *I've lost Ralf.* The company is done for. I spend until about half past two in the morning drinking at my desk, trying to work out my exit strategy.

In the morning Ralf comes into work as normal and asks me how you're meant to tackle a crème brulée. 'I mean, are you supposed to eat the topping or what?' I know then that our business relationship is safe. Cast iron.

In the year that follows, and as our reputation spreads, Ralf gets invited to dinner after dinner. They're a lot longer and more expensive than any dinners I'm ever invited to. At least once a month, some headhunter or high-echelon executive sits Ralf down in front of the incomprehensible tasting menu at a prestigious hotel ('What's ceviche?'). It's my turn now to play the backroom boy, arguing contractual points over a working lunch of finger food and soup. I'm in my thirties, old enough not to mind the chop and change of status, but Ralf's dominance – I'm tempted to say his celebrity – does surprise me sometimes. You should see the girls he goes out with now. The terror on his face.

Ralf is Loophole's golden goose, there's no hiding the

fact, and everybody wants a piece of him. Eventually the temptation gets too much and I ask him, straight out, why he stays. 'Because, you know, you could write your own ticket.'

His face falls. You would think I was jilting him. 'We're having fun, aren't we?'

He is, after all, the same old Ralf.

By the time we've all reached our mid-thirties, what Hanna and Michel most resemble – this adventurous yachtswoman and her bestselling husband – are a couple who work in financial services. They have that kind of house, garden, summerhouse and car. They have that kind of life, their talk less conversation now than camouflage, as they adopt the political coloration of their highland home.

I see them regularly because of this godparent business. The pressure of his success is taking Michel away from home at weekends, to conventions, launches, premieres, private screenings. When the event is something Hanna wants to go along to, I come over and take care of Agnes for them. We go to zoos and parks, visit festivals and wave our flags in civic parades, we watch movies and tap our feet in folk concerts. It's exhausting. One afternoon while I'm clearing up their kitchen I go to put bread in the bread bin and I find a tortoise in there. A wind-up plastic tortoise. For one horrible second it looked like some sort of super-cockroach. I take it out, stare at it, run it under the cold tap, shake water out of the mechanism and put it on the draining rack. Outside, a sudden gust sends rain rattling against the rigid plastic tunnel that covers their swimming pool. The wind sweeps off the mountains here without warning. The evening sky glitters uneasily. Far off, too far off to be heard, there is lightning.

Loudly, over the sound of her platform game, I ask, 'Agnes? Do you want an umbrella?'

Agnes glances round. She's five now, and insists on wearing scaled-up versions of the clothes her dolls wear. The controls of her games system come with safety straps to stop her accidentally hurling them at the TV. She looks like the prisoner of a dystopic police state. Her look is blank, uncomprehending. She hasn't eaten anything in hours.

'I think you should have an umbrella.'

'No,' she says.

'Agnes, you need an umbrella. A banana. I mean a banana. Oh, God.'

One warm weekend in October I take Agnes to the coast for a last-chance spot of beachcombing. It's so hot when we get there, Agnes is shedding her clothes all over the rocks. She's still scared of the sea. When I suggest that we follow a line of wooden markers across the sand to a low wooded island, its all-year conifer green flecked pink and turquoise with rental bikes and ice-cream, she balks, as though the tide were pouring in already on great coasters.

'I'm sure it's fine.'

Children and dogs are scampering through the bright standing shallows. It looks from here as though they are stamping a vast mirror to pieces. Agnes shakes her head, wide eyed and solemn. Instead, she wants me to splash with her across a tidal puddle that has formed at the foot of the boat ramp, far away from the sea.

'Again.'

'Let's go again.'

'Come on, I'll take your hand.'

We're playing this game for at least half an hour, and I have this vision of myself, in clear view of the ocean, striding back and forth across this puddle like a trained dolphin swirling round its pool, not quite bright enough to understand the nature of its imprisonment.

Come early evening I'm driving Agnes back home, crawling up the motorway with an operetta hammering the speakers, when she says, 'Will you come to ours for Christmas?'

'I don't know, love.'

'Mummy and Daddy are going to ask you.'

'Are they?'

'They say you shouldn't be alone at Christmas time.'

Hanna and Michel are back home by the time we arrive. Michel's already in his summerhouse, working. Hanna makes a pot of coffee for me, to set me up for the drive back to the capital. 'Thanks for today.'

'It was no problem at all.' I take a seat at their kitchen table and leaf through Agnes's storybooks. She's tucked up in bed now, but she's not asleep. I can hear her, faintly, cheerfully chuntering to herself. She has a torch in there. She stays up all hours, playing, telling stories. I wonder why they've not had a second child.

While the coffee is heating up on the hob (for all their creature comforts they have never succumbed to a complicated coffee machine) Hanna moves around the kitchen, stacking, sorting, putting away. She has help – cleaners, an au pair off and on. I think she is making all this work for herself now just to avoid me. It doesn't often happen that we're alone, without Michel or Agnes somewhere around. I'm surprised Hanna's put Agnes to bed, to be honest. The girl's sharp as razors – an effective chaperone. Which reminds me. I repeat to Hanna what Agnes said to me in the car.

'Jesus,' Hanna laughs, 'we're going to have to watch our mouths around that one.' She rescues the jug from the stove and pours. 'So, will you come? Seeing as you're aged and infirm and in need of help.'

'Lonely, too.' The coffee's too hot to drink. I blow on it. 'Bloody lonely, don't forget.'

She throws a biscuit at me. '"It was weeks before the neighbours noticed the smell."'

'If you put it like that, I can hardly see how I can refuse.'

'Michel's Mum is coming, too.'

'Poppy? Really?'

'Just for a day.'

'I should hope so.'

Hanna doesn't seem to want to hurry me out of the house particularly, yet what can we say to each other while the matter of Agnes, and Agnes's paternity, remains unbroached? The older Agnes gets, the more convinced I am that she's mine. The facial similarity isn't definitive, but it's still there. Her long, slightly mournful upper lip, and her nose, a little snubbed. (It lets her down, a little heavy for her face.) More, it's her manner. Well, her mannerisms. The prim way she tells her stories, her eyes sparkling. Her easy and comical outrage. A dozen tiny gestures. They remind me of my mother. When that happens, something cold and clinging fastens itself around my guts and I know that, sooner or later, for the girl's sake, I am going to have to say something. I will have to.

131

It would be unfair not to. It would be wrong.

If they hadn't made me the girl's godfather, and weren't as a family so comfortable to be around, I think I would have said something by now, and hang the consequences. Given my mum, and what she did to herself, it is essential that they know. But I am Agnes's godfather, I play with her almost every other weekend, and she has come to matter to me in ways I could not have predicted. Once I tell Hanna and Mick that I think Agnes is mine, then I will lose her, if not forever, if not entirely, then for a long time, and there will always be this cloud over us. This is a sacrifice I know I must make, but frankly I haven't the guts.

At the door, as I'm saying goodbye, girding myself for the drive back to the city, Hanna says, 'I've never understood why you and Mick are so hostile towards Poppy.'

Poppy? Poppy. How old must she be now? Well into her seventies, I would have thought. I haven't thought about Poppy in years, and when I have, it's always been with affection, or at any rate, with amusement. 'I think "hostile" is a bit strong.'

'No,' Hanna says, 'it isn't.'

'Well. You probably had to be there. Good night.'

'Good night, Connie.'

I lean in for a kiss but she has already turned away; she is closing the door on me.

ELEVEN

'Come on, Connie,' Dad called, swinging my bedroom door open. Since about half-past six he had been trying to rouse me. He was leaving early. He had a conference to attend, a presentation to give. Something very last-minute and, by the sound of it, important. He was stressed. 'Are you at cricket practice this evening?'

Groaning, I pulled the duvet over my head.

He stepped into my room. 'There isn't time for me to give you a lift into school.'

I flung the duvet off and sat up. '*Shit.*'

'Conrad.'

'Sorry.'

'You're just going to have to lug everything in yourself.'

Usually, when there was an evening practice, Dad gave me a lift to school in the car. Getting there on foot was not easy, given the sheer amount of kit I had to carry. I had my own bat, my own pads, my own gloves – last year's unlooked-for birthday present.

'No problem,' I said.

'I'm sorry, Conrad.'

'S'okay.'

'I'm sorry.' For one horrible moment it looked as though he was going to hug me.

'Dad, it's okay. Just let me get dressed, yes?'

He remembered himself. He forced a smile. 'What do you want for breakfast?'

'Eggs?'

'Sure.'

Dad clattered around in the kitchen while, piece by piece, I assembled myself. Textbooks, uniform, kit. Bits of sleep-deprived brain.

Dad called up the stairs, 'Have you got everything?'

'Everything but the kitchen bloody sink.' It was embarrassing, striding onto the school cricket pitch in such brand-new gear. It must have cost my parents a small fortune.

'Jumper?'

'In this weather?'

'Jumper.'

'Okay, Dad.'

I threw the whole lot into a leather-handled green canvas bag that, by disregarding a hundred years of innovation in man-made textiles, was an embarrassment in itself.

I lugged the bag downstairs. The key was hung up as usual by the side door. Dad kept our car parked among all the others out the front of the hotel. I went out with my bag. I was still dozy, running on habit, and it wasn't until I turned the key to open the boot that I remembered I wasn't getting a lift. Before I could catch the boot lid it swung up on its spring.

Mum lay curled up inside, barefoot, in denim shorts and one of Dad's cast-off jumpers. The chalk-white shapelessness of her legs made it clear to me, straight away, that she was dead.

My eyes drank in strange details – hairs on her calves; her rough, blotched knees – as though death were an extreme form of bodily neglect. Her face, blue and swollen and bovine, was only partly visible through the fog that had collected on the inside of the bag. She'd taped it around her throat with brown tape. It was one of our big freezer bags from the kitchen. Near where her eyeball had stuck to the plastic there was a white patch, a writable surface, 'BEST BEFORE' in clear cut-away type. Her bottom teeth were visible. They were very small.

'Conrad!'

I dropped my bag and turned.

Dad stood at the entrance to the hotel. He had an apron tied around his middle, protecting his suit. A spatula in his hand.

Things slowed down around me, or seemed to, driven out of mind by the clatter inside my own head. It felt, for a moment, as if I hung outside myself, watching myself thinking.

Mum in the boot – whose doing was this? Mum's own. The bag around her head was sign enough of that. The stench of whisky and bleach. For years, and wordlessly, Dad and I had been living in anticipation of this moment.

Batting it away. Facing it down. All for nothing. Here it was at last.

But this was not what was supposed to happen. It was supposed to be Dad who had found her like this. Dad, called away at short notice on a last-minute trip!

I had opened the boot instead. *I* had discovered her. 'Dad?'

He just stood there in the shade of the portico, shoulders raised in a half-shrug. Nonplussed.

Who had invited Dad to this last-minute conference? Was the conference even real? Mum had planned this. She had expected Dad to find her here as he got ready to go, filling the boot with vests and goggles and all the rest of his visual paraphernalia. It hadn't been enough that she had decided to destroy herself at last. She had wanted to destroy Dad, too. She still could.

All right.

I turned.

Dad had gone back inside.

It was clear enough what I had to do. I had to go back inside and find him. Warn him. Tell him. At least if I told him what she had done, then he would be prepared. Seeing her there, dumped like a deer in the back of a poacher's car, would no longer be the killer shock that Mum had meant it to be.

The trouble was, I didn't know if I *could* tell him. I didn't know if I had the strength to go back into the hotel and catch him as he came out through the lobby, asking for his car keys.

And what if I did tell him? What then? Dad runs pell-mell to the car, to see the thing his wife has made of herself, and he sinks to his knees in the car park; or he hugs me, hugs me like he hugged me when we drove back from hospital, hugs me and trembles and fails and falls apart in my hands the way he did before, and across the road the estate just goes on and on and on, its roofs a burial ground of red pyramids—

Dad was back in the kitchen, cooking bacon and eggs. He had his back to me, shoulders hunched as he nudged food around the pan. The pressure was back on him again. When Mum left for the protest camp, there were always a couple of days of decompression, and Dad brightened. Soon enough, though, he was fretting over her absence just as much as he had been fretting in her presence. How was she? What was she up to? Was she well? Was she safe?

Now I would have to rob him of that and lay upon him something new – a burden unimaginably heavier than the one he was used to. 'Dad.'

'I told you I couldn't give you a lift to school.'

'I know, Dad.'

'I told you.'

'Yes, Dad. I'm sorry.'

He clattered a couple of dishes out of the Welsh dresser. 'What are we going to do?'

'I'll go get my kit.' I stood up.

'No!' He stared at me. 'I'll drive you in.'

'You don't have time.'

'I'll drive you in.'

'Yes?'

'What time does your practice end this evening?'

'Six. Quarter to six,' I said, 'I think. Dad.'

'Okay, I can pick you up on my way home. Now, have you got everything?'

'Yes.'

'Here you are.' He shuffled from the counter to the table, put down my plate, and moved away.

'Dad.'

'Uh-huh?' He was stacking the dishwasher now. He was pottering about the room, still with his back to me.

'Dad, aren't you going to eat anything?'

'I'll eat when I've dropped you off. Come on, Connie, hurry up with that. We have to get going.'

I couldn't tell him. I didn't have the courage. After I had gone to school, unprepared and all alone, he would find Mum in the boot of his car.

The boot.

The boot was open.

I had left the boot open, and the key in the lid still, and my kit bag on the ground in front of it. Anyone could walk by. Anyone could see.

The world fogged over. I wrestled out of my chair, took the plate to the bin, emptied it there. Dad didn't see. He was clearing up. 'All done?'

'Sure.'

I staggered out the room, along the hall, through the side door, and round the side of the hotel to the forecourt.

The violence of what Mum had done to herself, the hurt she had meant to inflict, made it impossible for me to picture her properly. It wasn't Mum in there. I kept telling myself this. No telling what it was, what filthy horror, but it wasn't Mum. Who had it been who'd taken me for walks through the water meadows? Not her. In its madness and monomania, this *thing* had stolen Mum from me. I would have to get rid of it. I would have to get rid of the body.

There was the car. The boot was still open. The key was still in the boot lock. My green canvas bag was still on the ground where I had dropped it.

I closed my eyes and shuffled forward. I reached out, paddling my hands blindly in front of my face, because if I could find the lid without having to open my eyes I could shut the boot and I wouldn't have to look at her again. I was afraid to breathe because worse than seeing her, far worse, was that smell, that bleach and whisky smell that I couldn't be sure was even her, but which surrounded her, defining her.

My hands made contact with the lid. I grabbed hold for balance. I had to breathe. I had to. And it came – the smell was stronger now, scraping the back of my throat, forcing tears from my eyes.

'There you are.' Dad was standing on the porch, shrugging on his jacket. 'Have you got everything?'

I picked up my sports bag. Pads and bat and gloves. Jumper. I hefted the sports bag in both hands and dropped it between Mum's legs. I swung the boot down.

It didn't latch. The lid didn't close properly. I stared at the lid of the boot, at the angle of it, a mouth slightly parted. I heard Dad's footsteps approaching.

I couldn't bear to open the boot again. I got all my weight on top of the lid, and the latch clicked shut.

It was as I was climbing into the passenger seat that it occurred to me what a calamitously stupid thing I had done.

I had to tell Dad what had happened. I had to tell him what he could expect to find when he opened the boot.

But when I did – when at last I mustered the courage to tell him, then he was going to ask, Why did you shut the boot? Why did you drop your sports bag on top of her? What on earth did you think you were doing?

And it was all going to be worse, ten times worse than before – even more grotesque than it had been at the beginning.

Still, I had to tell him.

'Penny for your thoughts?'

'Oh, Christ, Dad. Nothing.'

'Well, strap in, don't just sit there like a lemon.'

When was he most likely to find her? When was he going to need to look in the boot? When we got to school he would park up and I would get out and open the boot and there she would be. Of course Dad wouldn't see her then, because he'd still be at the wheel, waiting for me to slam the boot shut. He would drive off with no idea of what he was carrying with him, no idea at all that he was driving it around, and when he did find out, the very fact that he'd been driving it around would be enough to destroy us.

'You knew.'

'Dad, I—'

'You saw. You knew.'

I had to get her out of the boot. There was no way I could do it before the end of the day. If Dad opened the boot before I got back home from cricket practice – well, there was nothing I could do about that. But if the boot stayed closed till I came back, then there was still a chance.

I was going to have to take the car. There was no other way. Now and again Dad had taken me to a nearby disused airfield, an old wartime place, just a strip of concrete that was too expensive and too much trouble for the farmer to grub up. He'd put me behind the wheel of the car a few times and taught me the basics. He reckoned that the sooner I started to learn to drive, the safer I'd be. That was what he told me. I think the real reason was that he enjoyed it – just him and me in the car, doing stuff, away from home and all its pain and fret.

I figured that in the middle of the night, with no traffic to get in my way, I should be able to wrestle the car away from the hotel. Once I was out in the country I could just – what? Leave her somewhere.

Leave her anywhere. It wasn't as though I was trying to hide her. What would be the point of that? I wanted her to be found. I just didn't want Dad to find her, not like this.

The hotel driveway was steep, but if Dad parked where he usually did, I'd be able to get the car out and onto the road without having to start the engine. The trouble would come on the return journey. Suppose I managed to drive all the way back home – how was I going to manage the drive? How was I going to get the car up the steep drive and back where Dad had parked it?

This couldn't possibly work. This had the logic of a nightmare. Something was going to go wrong.

'Conrad?'

We had stopped. The engine was idling. We were outside the school gates already.

I climbed out. 'Well, have a good one,' Dad said, putting the car into gear.

'Wait!'

He looked at me.

'The boot.'

He didn't say anything. He didn't know anything.

'In the boot—'

Dad put the handbrake on.

My courage failed me. 'My kit,' I said.

'Oh,' he said. 'Go on, then.'

I got out of the car. I rarely came into school by the main entrance and the place – the clock tower and the low, slate roofs of the quad – seemed utterly strange to me, grandiloquent and Gothic, not any part of my real life.

Dad wound down his window and called to me, 'I'll pick you up tonight.'

I went round to the back of the car. I pushed the catch, the black rubber diamond. The catch was stiff, the mechanism was under tension, because the boot was overstuffed. I tried again, pushing harder, hard enough to hurt my thumb, and the lid popped up. The smell was a stench now. Dad was bound to smell it the moment he got back to the hotel and got out of the car. He was going to be driving and the heat from the engine was going to warm up the whole car, never mind the heat from the sun as the day went by, and he was going to smell it, how could he not? Him, or a guest at the hotel, passing by. Smelling it, he was bound to investigate it. He was going to open the boot. He was going to see her there. And he would know that I had seen her, too, and said nothing. Twice.

I was going to have to tell him now, after all. It was too late for me not to. I had to explain. I pulled out the sports bag from between my mother's legs and I slammed the boot shut. 'Dad.' First, I would tell him what had happened. I would get him out of the car and I would tell him what happened, what she'd done, and while I explained, I would keep myself between him and the boot, until he was ready. I would at least manage the moment as best I could.

Dad tapped the horn and drove away.

'Dad.'

I watched him go, out through the gate, onto the road. Dad.

I picked up the bag. The bag smelled. I carried the bag into school.

Because the term was nearly over, the teachers were operating on autopilot. There were no tests, no questions, no discussions. In their place came interminable periods of private study. We were left to read whatever we wanted. During morning break I went and checked something out of the library, a big thing, something to hide behind, and that's what I did – I hid. At lunch I walked round the sports fields, avoiding everyone. Especially Michel. I didn't want him caught up in this.

The smell had spread to my clothes now. It was everywhere. On my fingers, from the handles of the bag. Around the lockers, where I'd left it. The corridor. Everywhere. Was there anywhere now that did not smell of what I had done?

What I had done. What *had* I done? Why was I taking on the burden of what she'd done to herself, that mad and vicious bitch who stole my mum from me? Dimly, in as much as I could feel anything in this buzzing confusion, I was beginning to understand that anger was my friend. I needed it. It was the glue that was holding me together. Without it, what was to keep me from spinning apart?

The day was a ragged, half-glimpsed thing, uncon-
vincing in every way. In the final period before the end
of school, marooned together in 'private study', Michel
tried to get me into conversation about some book he'd
been reading. Yet another apocalyptic science fiction
'masterwork'.

'I'm not interested.'

'No?'

'I'm not interested in any of that shit.'

And that was that.

I took the usual track home, on the look-out for servicemen. Their blindsight, useless as it was in many ways,
unnerved me. Blind to so much, they would sniff my
secret out, their remaining senses tuned to an exquisite
pitch, lapping horror from the air. I met no-one. A flash
of white between the trees turned out to be the rusted
corner of an abandoned refrigerator, one of that sarsen
circle that marked Michel's redoubt. So much for his
hideaway – even summer undergrowth could not conceal
it.

The wire fence. The ditch. The lawn. Coming home
this way, I could not see who was parked out front.
Ambulances? Police cars? How easy it would have been
for me if Dad had already opened the boot. How easy, and
how terrible.

But Dad, none the wiser, was in the conservatory with
one of his clients, a serviceman stripped to the waist,
the visual vest bound round him like a piece of antique
underwear. A truss. I tapped the glass.

Dad started and turned. I had surprised him. The
light must have been at my back because for the longest
moment, Dad did not recognise me at all. He stared at

me through the glass as if I had been a ghost. At last he assembled a smile. He waved me in.

The serviceman was wearing the vest back to front. Some found they saw better that way – through the skin of their backs, rather than across their chests. Just as a blind person reading Braille truly reads (their visual cortex lighting up like a Christmas tree under the fMRI scanner), the serviceman, hooked up to Dad's vest, truly saw. When Dad swung his torch from side to side, the serviceman moved his head, tracking the light with the camera mounted to his heavy black eyeglasses. Though he was seeing through sensations on his back, he didn't attempt to turn his back to the light. A nubbin on dad's remote control operated the camera's zoom ring. Dad pressed it and the soldier, convinced that things were hurtling towards him, staggered, throwing out his arms to protect his face. Dad nudged the nubbin again – again the soldier stumbled.

'Thank you, sergeant.'

The soldier's face was a zipped bag. What emotion was he not showing? He put his clothes back on – clothes issued to all service personnel on their discharge from hospital. Baby clothing remade to an adult physique, with pockets and belt-loops to cushion their infantilisation.

Dad turned to me. 'You're home early.'

'So are you. I thought you had a conference.'

'I had a conference.'

'You did?'

'It was very nearby.'

'Oh.'

'Just the morning session.'

'Right.'

'Where's your cricket kit?'

'My—?'

'Your bag?'

'Oh.' The pads, the bat, the gloves. 'Oh.'

'Aren't you supposed to be at cricket practice?'

'Oh. Yes. God.' I felt my face burning. Burning and blushing, all because of a missed sports practice. Tears. I felt them welling. All the stored grief of the day, released at last, by such a trivial thing. 'Well, don't worry,' Dad said, taken aback by my reaction. 'It's all right. Just run back.'

'I don't want to.'

'Conrad?'

'Please.'

The serviceman rocked from foot to booted foot, waiting to be dismissed. He'd forgotten he was not under orders any more.

'Well, I'll see you tomorrow,' Dad said, taking and shaking the man's hand.

'Yes.' Still no expression on that tanned but too-smooth face. No embarrassment, and no relief. 'Tomorrow.' His vest click-clacked as he navigated his way to the three concrete stairs, climbed them, found the door-handle, and opened the door.

When he was gone inside the hotel, Dad turned to me, questions in his eyes, but the few seconds' grace the interruption had made had been enough for me. I was sealed again. Bottled. In control. 'Okay.'

'Okay?'

'I'll be off.'

'I'm sure you'll be fine.'

'I'll see you around six.'

'I'll come pick you up,' he agreed.

It was nearly four in the afternoon. Now I had somehow to get through two more hours – two hours in which, left to his own devices, Dad might, for reasons obscure to me, find a reason to look in the boot of the car.

And then what? Why should it ever come to a stop? What was there to prevent things going on like this, hour after hour, day after day?

We lived so near the school, I wasn't even particularly late for practice. Hill said something routinely sarcastic. 'Nice of you to turn up.' Soon enough I was brought in to bowl.

At that time I was about the fastest bowler the school had, which isn't saying much, but at least we kept a steady length. I found myself facing a boy called Martin. Nothing I came up with fazed him. I threw him a leg cutter and instead of blocking it as he was supposed to, he leant his bat a foot wide of his wicket and clipped the ball as it passed for an easy four. And I was done.

'Next up.'

I glanced at my watch as I took up position on the field. It was only twenty past four. Time was crawling by. The next bowler, Merriman, managed to knock Martin out of his complacency; he scooped the ball like a beginner and suddenly everyone was yelling at me. I flubbed the catch: the ball slipped through my fingers and, falling almost vertically, hammered the toes of my left foot. I staggered around like a wounded deer while everyone groaned at me.

'Thank you all. If you can, get some catching in before Saturday.'

Puzzled, I looked at my watch again – it was ten to

six. First, time had practically stopped. Now. it was racing out of my grip. Nothing added up. Nothing made sense.

In the shower room, people left me alone. The shame of my missed catch steered them away from me. This far into the tournament they feared a jinx.

Dad was waiting for me out the front of the school. He was standing, leaning against the car. When he saw me, he said, 'Where's your kit?'

I had left it behind. I couldn't bear the idea of opening the boot again. I couldn't bear it. 'It's in my locker. There's another practice at lunchtime tomorrow.'

Dad shrugged and went round to the driver's side and started the engine.

I climbed in beside him

'Come on,' he sighed. 'Let's go for a drink.'

And so it went on, and on, and on – it was never going to stop – there was never going to be an end to it, never. Now we were off to the Margrave, with its lead-roofed veranda smothered in lilac. Beer straight out of the barrel, because the barrels were kept directly behind the bar. I was old enough to drink if Dad bought. This had become our summer treat – a half, maybe a pint, in the pub around the corner, away from the smell of Mum's patchouli, clary sage, dyes, inks and paints.

The Margrave had no car park as such – just this verge, badly churned, along the lane that turned from tarmac outside the pub, to gravel and dirt where it became no more than the driveway to the mill house at the bottom of the hill.

Dad, an old hand at this, reversed us down the lane about as far as you could park without blocking the drive. From here the lane descended, unlit, through a tunnel of trees to the mill house, the millrace, the river. It was part of our cross-country course.

He ran the nearside tyres up on the bank a little, so that we both had to climb out the passenger's side. I stood by the car, fearing to breathe. The odd thing was, I couldn't smell a thing. Nothing bad, anyway. The earth churned by our tyres, and a cut-grass smell, and something dusty and ticklish from the field behind the hedge.

'Come on, then,' Dad said, pocketing his car keys.

There was a slatted bench in front of the house, under the soft leaden roof. It wasn't a whole lot more comfortable than the window seat in my room at home, but Dad wanted us to sit outside. He took off his jacket – in summer he wore this ice-cream linen jacket – and dumped it on the bench beside me. 'Mild?'

The local mild was frothy and liquorice-sweet. 'A meal in itself.'

We drank. We talked cricket. At least, I set Dad talking about cricket, knowing how reliably he would spin off if I gave him his cue. The daylight was going. A lamp blinked on above our heads and within a minute the air was a blizzard of moths.

'I might walk home,' I said at last.

'Okay.' The hotel was only round the corner – closer, if you cut the corner and followed the river. 'Can you manage in the dark?' If he'd known how treacherous the ground was along the river bank, how precarious the brick edging of the millrace, he would have tried to stop me. Instead, he accepted what I told him: my shortcut home was simply a stretch of our cross-country run – not difficult at all. 'I'll be back after this,' he said, lifting the remains of his pint. I was fairly sure he would stay for another. There were men here he knew, and he would stay to talk with them tonight, making the most of his little moment of freedom.

'Sure, Dad. Thanks.'

I headed down the lane, down the hill, into the dark.

Half-way down I stopped and turned. I watched the top of Dad's head as he entered the pub. Even if he came out again he wouldn't see me. The glare from the porch lights would blind him to movement this far down the lane. The stars were out. No street lamps. No house glow.

I took out the keys I had filched from the pocket of his jacket and unlocked the car. The rubber button gave against my thumb. The boot was on a spring, it pulled away from me and swung all the way up before I could catch it. I stared into the boot. There was nothing to see. It was too dark to see anything. Was she even there? Imagine her awake, her head wrapped in that plastic bag. Jesus. I put my hand out, imagining her there, willing on the original, familiar horror of her presence to bat away the terror that she might have climbed undead from here, be standing at my back …

The touch of her hand, so dry, so cold, so stiff, was an electric shock, knocking me back and away. I paused, trying to gather my breath again, trying to force it down, trying to cram it into my lungs. My eyes began to accommodate the deeper darkness of the boot. There were cryptic shapes there, hard to separate and decipher.

I had no choice. I had to reach inside. I had to touch her. I leant in and found her arms and got my hands under her armpits. The cold there was a shock. It dizzied me. I pulled at her, shifting her about in the boot. Lifting her into my arms was impossible. Though thin, she was too heavy for me.

Low laughter came from drinkers on the veranda.

I reached for her feet. They felt small and familiar. I gripped them roughly, as you would clasp a nettle. I figured the harder I squeezed, the less I would feel. I had them now in my hands. I pulled.

Her knee joints bent stiffly, smoothly, as though steeped in cold oil. Was this the onset of rigor mortis, or the end of it? I pulled her round so her legs dangled over the lip of the boot. I had to reach in further now to lift her hips up and out. I bent down and wrapped my arms under her legs. My head pulsed as I pulled at her. It was no use. I had somehow to get my weight behind her. I would have to prise her out of the boot. If I climbed in there with her, maybe I could push her out.

I was practically on top of her now, fumbling for the right hold, and suddenly I could not bear it any more. I rolled out of the boot and sat down in the road, clenching my teeth against the sound rising in my throat.

Her feet dangled in front of me.

I had an idea.

I shuffled around and leant my back against the boot, my head between her legs. I clamped her legs to my shoulders and clambered onto my knees. The tarmac bit into my knees as I hefted her up. With the backs of her knees round my shoulders, I tried to stand, slowly, straining. I paused half-way, getting my balance, poised like a weight-lifter, one leg locked behind me, the other bent forward. At least this way I was facing away from the boot. I took a deep breath, held it, and stood up straight, trembling against her weight. I tottered forward and she came with me, out of the boot. Fresh from its baking confines, she came out cool, inert as earth. There was a double jolt as first her shoulders and then her head bumped against the sill and slid away. Her weight was too much for me. I dropped her and her head smacked the tarmac.

I staggered forward into the dark and froze, listening. I couldn't hear a thing. No murmurs, no laughter.

Mum lay sprawled on the tarmac – an indeterminate shape. I could not be sure what I was actually seeing. She lay every which way. She made no sense. I reached for her in the dark. I found her feet again.

But I couldn't just drag her. Not over the tarmac, Christ. (My knees stung where I had broken the skin trying to lift her from the boot. They were wet, bleeding.)

There was a blanket in the boot, laid there to stop luggage sliding around. I found it bunched up in a corner. I pulled it out and tucked it under her feet. I tried to tie it around her ankles but the blanket was too small, the material too thick. I tucked the corners around each other so the blanket protected her feet as I dragged her down the road.

I reached under her arms and her head flopped against my belly. There was a little starlight now. The plastic bag around her head had stuck against her face. That eye was still open, a black pebble pressed against the plastic.

I started to drag her along the lane and the blanket gave way immediately. I laid her down again, took up the blanket, shook it out and spread it beside her. I rolled her onto it. Sitting down in the road, I took hold of the edges of the blanket and pulled. The weight of her pinned the blanket against the road. It didn't move.

Now I straddled her and gathered the corners of the

blanket together, bunching them in my hands. I tried to lift her. Her arms trailed on the ground. Her head dangled and swung as though her neck was broken. My back sang. I couldn't possibly manage her weight, lifting her at such an unnatural angle. I couldn't lift her. I couldn't drag her. It was impossible. Panic strummed my bladder.

Then it came to me. I sat down in the road and I took off my trainers and slipped them onto her feet. With my shoes protecting her heels, I could safely drag her along the tarmac. The only problem was the amount of noise we would make. I took off my socks. I tugged the socks over my trainers to dampen the sound they'd make against the surface of the lane. I knew what I was doing now. I was no longer afraid. A thumping numbness had overcome me. I reached under her arms and I lifted her against my waist; her head lolled against my stomach. The tarmac felt smooth and cool against my feet as I pulled her further into the dark of the lane. Even with socks over them to dampen the sound, the heels of my trainers rattled and chocked, but at the top of the lane, around the pub, nothing moved: the drinkers on the veranda had all gone inside.

The trees parted above me and the tarmac gave out. The ground was warmer here and gritty, smothered with dirt and twigs. I was nearing the mill-race. The sound of rushing water overlaid every other sound. Where crumbling brick embankments canalised the river, turning it past what was now the front door, a wooden railing guarded the drop. I laid my mother's body down in the dark and pulled the socks and shoes from her feet. The flagstones were slippery under me as I tugged the body alongside the balustrade, to where water spilt over the weir.

A light beside the porch snapped on. I wheeled round, dazzled, and stared at the glossy black door of the mill house. The lion's head knocker. The little glass eye of its spy-hole. Had my movements triggered the light – or had someone turned it on from inside the house?

I pulled my mother by the arm. The arm gave slowly, turning and articulating like machinery. I let go and it stayed in the air, pointing back at me at an unnatural angle. I crawled around her and sat down and got my feet against her and pushed her underneath the balustrade. The uprights of the balustrade were close together and she was too tall to simply slip between them. I pressed my foot into her stomach. The air remaining in her lungs escaped and the bag around her head inflated like a balloon. The plastic sticking to her eyeball peeled away. The black pebble disappeared. The bag misted, saving me from the sight of her face as she fell through the balustrade. The rushing waters masked all other sounds. I barely heard her hit the water.

The porch-light went off. After all, it was only a security light. I stood up and the light came on again. I put my shoes and socks back on, gritting my teeth in concentration.

A new plan was forming in my head. Up till now I had only been concerned with getting the body out of the boot. Mum's eventual discovery was something I had been prepared to leave to chance. Now I realised that this too could be managed. There was a way I could tie everything up tonight, and I would not even have to tell a lie, or not much of a lie. What could be more natural than for me to run back now to the pub, breathless, staring, haunted, close to tears? I would tell my dad I had seen

Mum – spotted her on my shortcut home. That Mum was floating in the river. Dad would follow me down the track, over the bridge, along the bank of the river – and there she would be. Together we would find her, and terrible as this would be, it would be better, unimaginably better, than what would have happened if I had not intervened.

I leaned over the parapet. I could just about make her out – a pale shape, rotating slowly in the middle dark.

I'd forgotten to take the plastic bag off her head.

I closed my eyes, trying to work this out. I wanted her body found, of course. The sooner the better. *But with the bag over her head?* Who puts a bag over their head before jumping in a river?

I was going to have to find her and take off the bag.

The bridge was fenced off to stop sheep wandering off the common. I was half-way over the stile when I heard:

Click-clack.

I froze.

Click-clack.

I knew this sound.

The porch-light went out. (*Click-clack.*) I waited, my eyes adjusting little by little to the dark. I heard nothing more beyond the race of the water. I saw nothing at all. Even my mother had disappeared. No white shape blurred the millpond's soot-black surface. She had been carried downstream.

I climbed off the stile.

Click-clack.

I was being watched.

I waved my arms. I was out of the range of the porch-light, but even in the dark:

Click-clack.

There was a soldier out there, watching me. My movement was enough to trigger his visual vest! I tried to find my voice, but no sound came. I hunted the darkness for a halo of white hair, but all I saw were the ghost limbs of distant trees.

I moved forward.

This time there was nothing. Perhaps it was too dark here for the soldier's vest to respond to my movements.

I climbed off the footbridge. I strained my ears. If he were moving, then I would surely hear him, vest or no vest. I could see the pattern of bushes and trees now, the river bank, the fence line – enough to know I was alone here. Unless, of course, he was hiding from me.

I clambered along the edge of the race, clinging to the stiff woody stems of the rhododendron bushes, and hurried bent-backed along the river bank, hiding from shadows. Away from the sound of the millrace there was nothing to hear, unless you counted, just at the threshold of hearing, the low arterial thrum of the bypass on the other side of the valley.

I ran along the river bank, all the way to Michel's circle of fridges. Try as I might, I saw no pale shape – no white-haired soldier; and no pale body either, spinning in the river's dark. I had in the end to abandon my search for her. All the way home, along the track the soldiers used sometimes, I slouched, defending myself against a blow, an assault, a confrontation. It never came.

I had not imagined the sound. In the end, though, I had to concede that the sound was not proof of anyone's presence, let alone the presence of a blindsighted soldier. Heard over the sound of the millrace, well, that 'click-clack' sound could have been anything. The catch of a gate rattling in the wind.

More strange – though I had no room to deal with it at the time – was the disappearance of Mum's body.

THE SHAMAN

The opening passages to *The Shaman*, Michel's first novel, go something like this.

A subtle current bears Cole inland, over flooded levels, past the comically bloated corpses of drowned cattle. Rushes grow up to tickle the branches of dying trees. The new coastline rises incrementally above this shallow sea: an unreliable medium, a waterland where men and livestock founder and blue lights flicker mysteriously in the hours before morning. Inland, axes ring out as the locals, obeying a long-suppressed folk-memory, chop wood for boats of shallow draught and, salivating, eye the skies for teal, widgeon and wintering geese.

Cole is an old man now, perhaps the oldest in the

village, his long life earned through guile and a fertile imagination, but he has grown weary of the land, weary of the tales he tells and all the claims which he exerts there. Discontented, he makes for the open ocean, seeking renewal, perhaps – or extinction. But he is, after all, just a dotty old man, the genius of his own place but a fool beyond it, and the sea wall, long since submerged by the rise of the world's oceans, presents an absolute barrier to his ambitions. No way can his keel-less and homemade raft negotiate the surf that wall kicks up.

So the urge to flee dies in him, as it has died so many times before, and Cole contents himself with a wet and exhilarating attempt to explore the ruins there. The waves will not allow him to get close, and every so often the foamy break threatens to overturn his craft, but Cole persists (it is his chief quality), filling in with his imagination what will not reveal itself to his eye.

Of the houses that were ranged along the sea wall, only stumps of masonry remain to cut the surface at ebb tide. Under the sea's merciless action, these stumps are falling away very fast – faster than the seaweed and the limpets can colonise them. There is something proud about their ruin, as though they would sooner be extinguished than be subsumed into an age to which they do not belong.

Time is getting on. Cole steers away from the wall, toward lagoon-smooth inner waters and his first acts of daily ritual. Adaptability is his great strength; his only virtue. The old world dies. The old man lives.

Away from the churn thrown up by the submerged

wall, Cole throws out his primitive sea anchor – a wicker dog basket, attached by its handle to a length of plastic clothes line – and waits patiently for the bell to sound. Cole understands, better than most, the flow of waters round these parts, and comes to this spot once, sometimes twice a day to hear the church bell in its squat and flooded tower not far beneath the waves. The changing tide sets it ringing, three times, sometimes four. Once, at full moon he heard it sound a dozen times, and trembled, expecting a marvel. A big wave. A flood. A great bubble of marsh-gas. Nothing very surprising happened. The tide was higher than usual, flooding his nephew's pig pen. In the next village, a two-headed calf was born. But that's foreigners for you.

The church beneath his rough-hewn craft stands beside an old canal. The route of the canal is marked by makeshift floats, soda bottles and plastic canteens, treasured, irreplaceable.

And here, as he predicted, come the lobstermen – if you can call them men. No men of Cole's age round here could do what these boys do. Diving from a coracle into that muddy murk, armed only with a nose plug and a scrap of sack-cloth, is work for strap-ping youths, whose lungs have not yet succumbed, as their elders' lungs have succumbed, to the region's vapours. Here they come, not one of them over fif-teen, their heavy shoulders rippling as they ply their ash paddles, naked but for their loincloths, and these they strip away before they dive.

Lobster pots are useless here, where the rotten brickwork of the canal offers the local crustacea unmatched shelter and plentiful grazing. No, they cannot be tempted out – they must be manhandled, dragged from their crevices. The boys, saluting Cole with upraised oars, prepare to dive. Each manoeuvres his unstable reed craft about his float, then stands and strips, squeezes the wooden peg over his nose, and wraps his hand in sacking as a glove, protecting his fingers from his quarry's pincers and its fierce fight for life.

Cole dresses. He shrugs on his leather coat, winds strings of beads around both wrists, and slips the knuckle-bone necklace around his neck. A folded cloth protects his head from the sharp edge of the broken porpoise skull he now proceeds to tie around his head.

Cole sings.

He sings for the fertility of the canal, to this great, dark, weed-furred slot that brings increase and plenty to the people of his village.

He sings words of comfort to the mother lobsters, heavy with eggs, honouring the sons they'll lose today. Cooked and eaten, their children will be trans-mogrified into the sons of the village above the water, and Cole sings of this alchemical pact between sea and land, between heaven and earth.

Much of his song is lost on the boys, who spend a minute, even two minutes at a time deep under the waves, hunting their vicious and spiny catch. This old man's not some mere entertainer. He's not singing to them. He's singing to the lobsters. He's singing to the spirits of the sea, propitiating them, so that the harvest might go smoothly, and no diver lose a thumb. He's singing – *for* – them. When the boys are done they gather round him, pull the biggest and best lobster from their scuttling catch, and two young, smooth-loined boys board his craft. One pins the creature to the boards. Its tentacles quiver, its claws creak open and snap shut convulsively, it legs scrabble like an old man's fingers upon the deck. The other raises a knife and stabs it expertly, and with a show of great violence, through the caudal nerve at the back of its head.

The shout goes up – 'Ai-eh!'

Now that supper's sorted, it is time for Cole to steer for dry land. There is much he must arrange for tonight's ceremony.

Cole's hold over the village depends in part upon his independence from it. Shamans do not live among the people. They inhabit and embody the wilderness, weaving nets of meaning that bind the human to the other. They are, at best, half-beast. To keep the villagers balanced on the edge between fear and yearning has been his life's project, and, to his dismay, this balancing act is only going to get harder as he ages. As a young man, he always fancied himself some hermit of the hills – a man wise in council, modest in his demands, yet living well enough off the gifts of a grateful people.

But hermits die by the dozen round here – men and women who have been too proud or too stupid or too stubborn to learn the skills of a fast-degenerating world. The countryside is amok with toothless old skeletons who, for a crust of bread or a sliver of widgeon, will bore you into the ground with fairytales of the great past: of hollow metal birds that crossed whole oceans, and tablets of great worldly wisdom that you could slip into your pocket, of pills to cure fatigue and blight, and heroic feats of observational comedy, and images of copulation everywhere. But these has-beens are no advertisement for the lost age. They sleep under the boles of trees, set traps for mice and hedgehogs, shit on footpaths, spread disease. The young go killing them for sport sometimes, hating these revenants, these senile, sniggering idiots who, in their distant youth, enjoyed a world these boys will never know.

Cole punts as far up the river as he can (a little less each year, he acknowledges; this world's built for the strong, not the 'spry') and ties up the raft to the stump of a streetlight. He walks the rest of the way, feeling more than seeing how the road bed curves and bends..

The cemetery is reached by a narrow track across ground so soft the trees here cannot reach their full height before they succumb to their own weight. They do not die, but, falling, sprout from their topmost side, forming natural hedges, barricades and nooks. Here wild dogs made their nests, till Cole flushed them out with fire and made his home here, fellow with the dead.

Which is to say, Cole lives within the dry-stone bounds of the village cemetery. Villagers are not permitted to explore the hallowed ground itself, on pain of instant execution. Exactly what form this formalised murder would take, how public the event would be, and even how Cole, an old man now, would

163

accomplish it against a young man fighting for his life, are questions Cole has never needed to resolve. The taboo has never been tested, nor is it likely to be. What, aside from an overwhelming urge to desecrate, would convince a marked, already mutilated felon to risk capital punishment, just so that he can say he's wandered around a few abandoned white goods dumped in a swamp?

For this, to the bemusement of outsiders (whose scepticism, if they are fools enough to express it, is quickly and permanently silenced) is the site Cole has chosen for the town to bury its dead. A flytip full of fridges.

He ties a kilt of stoat-fur round his withers with a cord woven of virgins' hair (on and on and on, over half a million words of this shit and counting, the literary equivalent of diarrhoea – once begun, why stop?) and brushes fallen leaves from his white-goods' lids with a mop made of strips of rabbit fur and on and on and on.

TWELVE

Poppy is afraid to leave her home unattended over the holidays, so Michel and Hanna have arranged to celebrate Christmas early.

I arrive just a couple of hours before Poppy is due. Michel's mood darkens as we wait for his mother to arrive. 'The thing about Mum is she's never here on any proper day. Flag Day, Christmas, birthdays, she's always a couple of days early or a couple of days late and it's always by special bloody appointment. Everything becomes about *her*.'

Michel turns over his resentments like a child sorting through a box of toy cars. Meanwhile Hanna runs after Agnes, trying to contain the whirlwind of the girl's 'tidying'. 'Agnes! Agnes, for God's sake, I just put that *away*.' At the door of the kitchen she turns. 'Please, Mick, not in front of her. *Agnes*!' She swings the door shut, but her voice is hardly muffled. 'Agnes, what did I just *say*?'

Michel casts around as though he has mislaid something. Losing one half of his audience has thrown him out of his stride. 'Fancy an espresso?'

Succumbing to convenience at last, they have bought themselves one of those machines that make thimblefuls of rocket fuel out of pre-packaged coffee cartridges.

Since he embarked on an original film script with Bryon Vaux – they must be on their twentieth rewrite by now – Michel has developed a cast-iron ritual. It's the only way he can meet his obligations to both Bryon and his publishers, who are still expecting a book a year from him. He writes, long-hand, in the garden or the summerhouse every day. Poppy's Christmas visit is breaking the habit of many months and he's as jittery as a chain-smoker attempting a cold-turkey withdrawal.

I'd like to say something to distract him, to take his mind off work, but the first thing that comes out of my mouth is, 'How's the film?'

'Christ.'

'That good?'

'We're gearing up for production.'

(I hide a smile at Michel's use of the royal 'we'. Once the cameras start humming, Michel's involvement will surely be at an end.)

'You must be excited.'

'I'm up and down into town, with Bryon Vaux yelling in my ear, typing on-the-fly revisions on the train. It's a bloody hopeless way of working.'

'But you must be nearly done if you're shooting in January.'

'Are you kidding? Do you know we actually had an executive production meeting the other day about how immersive entertainments should be set out on the page? We're going to be rewriting this bastard all the way into April's edit suite.'

The doorbell rings, saving me from any more of Michel's unbrookable enthusiasm. 'I'll get it.'

Poppy is about a foot shorter than I remember, and her skull has retreated from the surface of her skin, her face a mass of lines. I give her a hug. She doesn't know what to do with it. She pats my back, a bird beating its broken wing, spastic and frightened.

I sit her down in the living room. Michel's vanished. Hanna tries to usher little Agnes in to say hello. Having chattered non-stop about Grandma's visit for days, Agnes hesitates, half-hidden behind the living-room door, her smile a *moue* of shyness. It doesn't take her long to thaw. A few minutes later she is badgering Hanna to assemble her puppet theatre so she can give Grandma a show.

'I'll do it,' I offer. How hard can it be?

'No!' Agnes scolds me. 'Not that there. That doesn't go— Not like that! That's the wrong way round! *No!*'

Hanna brings in cups of tea and Poppy and I snatch a little conversation between the adventures of Little Red Riding Hood and Mr Punch. Michel has still to reappear.

I try to get Poppy into conversation, but she's tired and a little bit grumpy and everything seems to be a trial. 'Oh, the garden! I've got no-one to help me, you know.'

Poppy is happiest just listening to her granddaughter, so I leave them to it and find Hanna in the kitchen, still preparing dinner. 'Dinners,' she corrects me. 'I want to get ahead.'

'I'll help you.'

Out in the hall, Michel finally greets his mother, with a not-very-convincing show of surprise. 'I was off in the summerhouse! I didn't know you were here!'

'Daddy, come and sit down!'

'Hang on, love.'

'Daddy! You're interrupting the show!'

'She's doing a show.'

'Yes. I can see—'

The door clicks shut, cutting off their conversation.

'Here.' Hanna hands me a bag of sprouts. 'Peel these fuckers.'

'Is Michel all right?'

Hanna makes a face. She runs water in the sink and drops potatoes into a bowl. 'We've had a bit of a barney with Poppy this week.'

'What about?'

'Agnes has a school project for the holidays. They're supposed to find out what they can about their grandparents. Mick asked Poppy to bring over some stuff about his dad. She said no, that she couldn't get up in the loft to get it. It was all packed away. And when Mick offered to drive down and help she said she wasn't interested in a five-year-old's school project.'

'That sounds a bit direct.'

'The thing is, Mick doesn't have anything of his father's to show his daughter. Not even a photograph.'

It occurs to me that the video clip of his father's head being kicked around a dusty parking lot in the middle of a desert must still be floating around in the aether somewhere. Nothing really gets deleted any more. Nothing really gets forgotten.

After dinner, once Agnes is in bed, Poppy digs about in her handbag and hands Michel a cheap plastic wallet. 'Look,' she says, 'I've brought you the photographs you wanted.'

'Well.' Michel flicks through the plastic leaves. 'What is this?'

'I just brought what I had. There aren't many. I had a sort-out.'

'That's great.' In silence, Michel turns over the pictures. 'I'll scan them and you can take them home with you.'

'Oh no, dear. They're yours now.'

'But you'll want to put them back in the albums. Won't you.'

'I've given you the album.'

'What album?'

'That album.'

'This is an album?'

I know what Mick's getting at. I remember from my time in the bungalow on Sand Lane, Michel's family photographs were fastened with adhesive paper corners onto the thick black pages of old-fashioned albums. Every photograph had a description written underneath in white ink: Michel's father's meticulous signature.

'Where are the albums?'

'Oh, they were taking up too much space.'

'You've thrown them away.'

'They're not your albums anyway, Michel. They're the family's.' Poppy has a way of talking about the family that makes you forget there's only her and Michel in it.

'No,' says Michel, warming up, 'they're not the family's, because you've thrown them away.'

'They were taking up space!'

Michel flicks back and forth through the wallet – there are barely a dozen snaps in it. 'How am I supposed to know what these are? Or where they were taken? Who is this here? Christ.'

'I've written what they are on the back,' Poppy tells him, her voice tight and high in the back of her throat, defending her corner. And so she has. In biro. She has been very careful not to press too hard, so the writing on the back of each photograph has come out faint and spidery and barely legible. How typical of Poppy, to cook up a pointless task for herself and then make a difficulty out of it.

After Poppy has gone to bed, Hanna, Michel and I stay up drinking. We need to decompress. Even setting aside Michel's spat with her, Poppy is a heavy presence. She is incapable of saying what she wants, while being utterly ruthless at getting it. Hanna has spent the entire afternoon trying to establish whether she takes milk in her tea any more.

'Oh, don't worry, dear.'

'Yes, but do you want some?'

'I often have it without.'

'But do you want any?'

'I'd be very happy with a cup of hot water.'

'But I've just made you *tea* …'

'If it wasn't for Agnes,' says Michel, 'I'd never have invited the old sow.'

'Don't say that.'

'It's true.'

'Well, I'm glad *I've* seen her. It's been years.'

No-one is interested in my sentimental reunion.

'God.' Michel shakes his head. 'Agnes is besotted with her. She spent all last week asking when is Grandma going to get here? How long is Grandma staying? Is she staying for Christmas? You'd think Poppy would have made an effort.'

'But Agnes knows Grandma isn't staying for Christmas Day.'

'I'm not talking about her staying, Hanna, I'm talking about the photographs.'

'Oh. Well. That's not about Agnes, is it? That's about you and her.'

'What did I do?'

'That's not what I meant.' Hanna corks the whisky and gathers up our glasses, policing us. 'Agnes will be all right.'

Michel says to me, 'Mum thinks I want to trash her house. She thinks I can't wait till she's dead, so I can get my hands on all her *things*. It's why she's thrown so much away. The albums. Dad's medals and letters.'

'I'm sure she doesn't think like that.'

'This is exactly the way she thinks. How else do you explain this shit?' He waves the plastic photo wallet at me. 'She's afraid of me. No way is she letting me get my grubby paws on the precious *things*. Not by the hairs on her chinny-chin-chin. Grandma's built her house of bricks and lit a fucking big fire in the grate.'

Hanna comes back in to announce, 'I'm going to bed.'

But Michel has the bit between his teeth. He continues, 'If you had any idea how often I've sat on Agnes's bed of an evening, tucking her in, explaining to her why we never go to see Grandma.'

'Well,' I say, 'why can't you go see Grandma?'

171

'Because we're not invited,' says Hanna, drawn back into the conversation in spite of herself.

'Come on, you could just turn up if you wanted—'

Michel's eyes go wide. '*Turn up?*'

Hanna says, 'Agnes has only ever been to Sand Lane once, when she was a baby, and then only because we invited ourselves.'

Michel says, 'We're never fucking doing that again.'

The next morning I come downstairs to find Agnes playing by herself, singing and laughing at the top of her voice, the way children do when they are trying to block out something bad. In the kitchen, Michel and his mother are already at each other.

Michel says to Poppy, 'Look, I don't want to take it. I don't want to take anything off you. Jesus. I just want to copy stuff.'

'You'll get it all when I'm dead anyway, I wouldn't care.'

'Why wait?'

'I'm not having you clambering about the loft. I'm not having you up there stamping about in my things!'

'Morning.'

Poppy runs to me, as best she can. 'You speak to him!' There is something magnificent about Poppy – the way she assumes I will take her side.

'Speak to him about what?'

'He's going on about his father's *things* again!'

'Michel. I have told you before. These heirlooms traditionally belong in the family home. Now stop badgering your mother.'

Poppy's self-satisfaction is priceless. 'You see?'

172

Hanna comes in and sends Poppy and me packing. 'There's croissants and coffee in the sun lounge.'

'Oh, I couldn't manage a whole croissant.'

'Whatever. Agnes! You see that Grandma has a good breakfast.'

Agnes, an eager gaoler, leads Poppy from the room.

'That,' I say, 'was brilliant.'

'Fuck off, Connie.'

'And a merry Christmas to you.'

In the sun lounge, Poppy is staring at her croissant with revulsion, as if it were a dead rat or a large turd.

'You know how this all started, don't you?' Poppy says, picking up her knife with a shaking hand.

Agnes is here to help. She tears her grandmother's croissant in two and, with a sidelong look, shovels the larger half all the way into her mouth.

Poppy, oblivious, ineptly butters the shred that's left. 'It's because—' It suddenly occurs to her that Agnes is in the room. But Agnes, aware that another wave of boring grown-up gibberish is about to break over her lovely Christmas morning, is already on her way out.

'I'm going to rehearse a show!'

Sotto voce from Poppy: 'Agnes had a *school project*.'

'Well.' I go over and close the door. 'I think it's normal, when you're a child, to want to know about your grandparents. It's normal to be interested in that stuff.'

Poppy flaps her hands in irritated dismissal. 'It's not *her*. It's the *school*. It's ridiculous.'

'Perhaps you should write a letter to the school explaining how ridiculous it's being, and Agnes can take that in as her holiday project.'

You can say these things to Poppy because her

173

self-defence is seamless. She only ever hears what she wants to hear. This has nothing to do with her age. She was always like this. In fact I would go so far as to say that, after a gap of almost twenty years, she hasn't changed.

'Michel's never shown the slightest bit of interest in Louis until now.'

Louis? It occurs to me I've never heard the man's name before. It's always been 'Dad' from Michel or, from Poppy, 'Michel's father'.

'This isn't about Michel,' I point out.

'He's never asked for anything of Louis's before. He's just got it into his head.' She makes it sound as though he's contracted an infection.

'Is that a problem? Why is that a problem?'

Poppy's trouble is that she has never really believed in communication. Information goes in but it never comes out, and if you force it out, it emerges so tortured, twisted, hedged around with all sorts of mysteries and qualifications, that it's worse than useless and obscurely upsetting. 'I had nothing from my family. I didn't have anything of my mother's or my father's. Anyway, I don't want to have to explain myself to you.' Poppy is in tears now.

'You don't have to explain anything to me. Come on, Poppy.'

'My home was sold from under me. Why should I have to explain myself to you?'

The next evening, once he has seen Poppy off at the station, Michel comes home and we try scanning and printing out Poppy's photographs so that Agnes can have at least a couple of pictures of her grandfather for her Christmas project.

I suppose I had a very romantic notion of what a writer's study should look like. Waxed floorboards. Kilims draped thickly over a daybed under the window. African masks on the walls. A desk piled with manuscripts and obscure books.

Michel's den isn't remotely like that. It is tiny, carpeted, and brutally functional. The walls are bare. The window is too high to see out of. On the far wall there is a small MDF bookshelf, stacked with copies of his own books. The desk is a sandblasted glass sheet on unvarnished wooden trestles. There's a laptop, connected to a larger screen. A landline telephone. A desk lamp.

Michel sits at his screen. 'Can you go round and sort the scanner out?'

The scanner/printer sits on top of a small drawer unit behind the desk, out of his reach. There's nowhere for me to sit so I sit on the carpet, slipping the photographs out of their plastic wallet while the scanner clunks and whines. It is warming itself up, checking itself over with a painful attention to detail, like a geriatric man recovering from a fall. 'It says it has low ink.'

'It always says that.'

There are only three pictures that are any good, and even these are misframed. Either the top of Louis's head is missing, or an ear, or his feet, as though some malign supernatural force had sought to presage the ugly manner of his death. He doesn't look like a soldier, any more than Poppy ever came across as an army wife.

He looks worried in these photos – the very picture of introversion. As for Poppy, you would expect her to exhibit, if not a certain stiffness, at least a sense of make-do-and-mend, a resourcefulness that, even if it had not been there to begin with, would have been forced on her by years of relocation, loneliness, and the narrow social confines of the army life. Many years have gone by. It could all have been worn away by now, but the thing is, I have no memory of her being any tougher than she is now, or any more straightforward. 'How long was Louis in the army?'

'All his life.'

Which shows how much I know. 'What did he do?'

'He handled drones. Haven't I told you all this?'

Disposable drones for mine clearance – lumbering, sand-ballasted, pressed-paper robots on all-weather tracks. Cardboard kamikazes. Not a front-line man at all. Just another code monkey who strayed too far, too confidently or carelessly down the wrong alley, not five hundred yards from the edge of the diplomatic zone.

'Do you think about him much?'

'What? No,' he says. 'No, not much.'

'Do you remember him?'

'Of course I remember him.'

'It's just— How old were you when—?'

'Can you move it up? The photograph.'

I open the lid and nudge the photograph back into alignment on the glass.

'No. Up. *Up*.'

I open the lid and turn the photograph around on the glass.

'Now what are you doing?'

'Up was down.'

'What?'

'Look, it's no good just going "Up, up" – my up is not your up.'

'For God's sake.'

'I'm sorting it out. Look, is that better?'

Michel grunts.

What captured Poppy's gaze to make her frame her shots so badly? I imagine her always over-thinking things, turning every task into a problem. I must get his feet in. I must get that tree in. I mustn't let the sun in. Let's not have that stranger in the frame. And – oops.

'Mum asked me if you were seeing anyone.'

I have to think about this. 'That was nice of her.'

'Okay, let's have the next one.'

Strange that Louis should ever have sported a uniform, or even joined the service at all, with a job like that. You'd expect that kind of role to be outsourced, given to some tiger-economy whizz-kid earning two dollars an hour off some privatised military consultancy.

'Did your Dad—?'

'She spotted it straight away,' says Michel, cutting across me.

'Spotted what?'

'The likeness. What do you think?'

'I don't know what you're talking about,' I tell him, fussing the originals back into their wallet.

Michel's machine is not up to copying subtle gradations of gray. The pictures aren't coming out well. All you can see of Louis's face is his glasses.

'Yes, you do.'

'No. I don't.'

'You don't have to play games, Conrad. Agnes is all water under the bridge as far as I'm concerned.'

I keep my head down. 'Well, that's good to know. Any time you want to tell me what you're on about …'

'Come on, Conrad.'

'You're as bad as your mother.'

The printer churns and churns.

It's well into the next day before I get the chance to speak to Hanna. After the midday meal we drag a complaining Agnes out of the house for a walk, past the riding school and down and up a wooded dip to a churchyard with a view of the mountains. The landscape is spectacular, but my attention is drawn more to the gravestones. The stones are white with frost, but the china photographs pinned to them have absorbed the heat of the day. The photographs are clear of snow, and gelid water clings to them like tears. The faces of the dead peer from their pockets with a certain truculence, as though to say that they cannot be so easily effaced.

We stand around while Mick takes photographs with this bulky antique camera Hanna bought him for Christmas. Films for the thing are made by this tiny, specialist company you have to hunt for on the internet. Hanna is cold and wants to go home, but Michel wants to stay and try again to engage Agnes's enthusiasm for snow. The girl shows no interest in the stuff. She just sits there, crouched in her fun-fur on her plastic toboggan while Michel, bent-backed and drip-nosed like something out of a Hogarth painting, weaves round the gravestones, rolling up a snowball for a snowman's head.

Hanna takes a picture of them with her phone. 'Bless.'

'Poppy said something to Michel yesterday.'

'Yes?'

It is my chance. It may not come again. 'Something about us.'

178

Hanna's face locks down. 'Us?'

'You and me and Agnes. Michel's pissed at me today.'

'Really? I wonder what that's about,' she says, already moving away from me.

I follow her, wracking my head for something to say. Stupid, to have begun so obtusely. Stupid, to have begun with Poppy, and her random, gnomic pronouncements. What could Poppy possibly know? What could she have picked up? Whatever else she is, Poppy is not and never has been stupid, and she has mistrusted me from the first, ever since I went to stay with her and her son in Sand Lane. It doesn't in the least surprise me that she's been keeping an eye on me. But what can she have seen? That I am in love, always in love, and hopelessly, resignedly, above all, pointlessly, with Hanna? Perhaps.

A couple of weeks go by.

I've an afternoon of investment meetings today, so I'm on a train bound for the Forum, the city's business centre, where all young entrepreneurs go to die. The rail line rises on brick arches above football fields and allotments, creeks and disused embankments. This was the old Middle, its leavings torn down after the last war. The gap was left as a memorial. Today it has its own value: an extra lung for the ever-expanding city. Over sheds and shacks, prefabs and mobile homes, half a dozen angels hover in the clean and cloudless air. They're motion-capture figments – real-time feeds that Ralf has pasted on the sky for me. If I took my spectacles off, they would vanish.

Imagine them: jobbing actors, they have turned up to work in hastily constructed motion capture studios.

They have pulled on black Lycra bodysuits stitched over with ping-pong balls, and they are spending the day performing simple, iconic actions in front of a green screen – walking, running, sitting, falling. Their movements, abstracted into three-dimensional vectors, will be used in our first big field demonstration, where we will animate whole avatar armies.

Creatures made purely of light and movement, our strange angels hover above the weedy lots, limbering up for some apocalyptic event. Over the earpiece, Ralf asks, 'Well? How are they coming through?'

I crane and twist my neck, fretting under unfamiliar gear. They are made of points of light; only in motion do they make sense as bodies. They walk, run, sit, fall and dance in mid-air. 'Are you trying to skin them? I'm getting only data-points here.'

'Hang on,' he says, 'I'll come see you.'

A minute later, here he is, inside the carriage, grinning, in his usual T-shirt-and-baggy-jeans combo. He looks out the window, following my line of sight. He frowns. 'They're skinned for me.'

Were I not so conscious of the amount of gear I'm lugging around, it would be easy for me to forget that Ralf – the Ralf sat here, opposite me – is an illusion. Ralf is leaning towards me, eager, earnest, his foot an inch away from mine in the packed and airless carriage. And if I kicked him, my foot would go straight through.

As it is, I'm feeling hot and self-conscious and eager to be done. Even by the chromed, futuristic standards of the financial district, this equipment of mine is absurdly conspicuous. Item: wraparound shades. Item: an electrode stickered not so subtly to my throat, to pick up speech I no longer need to utter. (In a year or two, everyone will subvocalise their calls by choice. This, anyway, is what the pundits are saying.) Item: a headset cradles my head with transparent silicone fingers. (Phoned sounds are crude intrusions – we bypass the ear entirely, and excite the auditory nerve, creating synthetic soundscapes that merge seamlessly with context and environment.)

Ralf tilts his head at me. 'You don't seem happy with this.' His voice comes alive in my head, subtly smoothed and delocalised by the software. The link is not very good – Ralf's lips move but his voice seems to be coming at me from the back of my head.

'The thing is,' (I say, speaking in perfect silence – electrodes parse the throat's intention tremors into speech) 'we create phantoms.' I nod out the window. 'That's all they are. That's all they can ever be. They're completely ephemeral.'

'You can interact—'

'Only according to the narrow rules of a game. You have an object made of light. You manipulate it, scroll through it, open and close it, shrink and expand it. God help you should you ever try to lean on it, or sit on it, or make your home in it, or, well,' and I nod out the window at our angels, 'take it out on a date.'

We are leaving them behind now. Illusory Ralf has to turn in his seat to see a processed point-of-view of them as they flex in the sky, invisible to the gardeners, dog-walkers and six-a-side football teams toiling on the ground below. The view vanishes behind the blue glass wall of an office-block.

'So you interact. Okay. What does that mean?'

Ralf turns back and makes a face. For him, this is an

irrelevance. Everything is a game to him. He lives inside the game, and when he is outside the game, he pretends himself inside, for fear of what he might find Out There. The unmediated real. The world. Chaos.

'Don't you see? The stuff we make is doomed to a life in inverted commas. We're not even building in light. We're building in *irony*. Everything we make is steeped in the stuff.'

The train makes bathetic, burst-bladder sounds as it slides over the river towards the north shore.

'You know,' Ralf says, 'you worry too much.' Around him, bleeding away from his stolid outline and mispro-portioned goatee, I begin to catch glimpses of the wiry, physical man who actually occupies the seat opposite me. He is preparing to stand. His head emerges from out of Ralf's head, a crocodile cracking through an egg. His arms emerge, Shiva-like, from out of Ralf's arms. They wave about, collecting newspaper, satchel, umbrella. For a second the men, virtual Ralf and flesh-and-blood stranger, coexist in mythic form. 'We're bringing some-thing new to life here. It's got integrity. You just have to trust it. You just have to look.'

Ralf fractures, winks, and vanishes. The stranger, obliv-ious, shrugs his coat on.

Leaving the station, I cross the Canal by a footbridge, heading towards the Forum and the quiet, stone-clad purlieus of the Ministry of Trade. As I walk, the bridge's functional iron latticework clads itself in statuary, dust, and a kinder, more southern light. So far, so un-real. I glance twice towards a newspaper icon, blinking tantalisingly close to my focus-point, and it swims into centre-view, unfurling translucent headlines. Another military adventure going sour.

I near the end of the bridge and enter a world of solid hazards, reading as I go. The platform makes an executive decision about the amount of hallucination a body can cope with, and wraps its architectural dreams back into the struts and braces of the actual bridge. I get back the sound of my leather-soled shoes on the walkway's iron grillework.

Still the real eludes me. I enter my meeting in the grips of an awful dream where every solid thing, every brick and kerbstone, has come adrift and floats before me, contingent, weightless and untrustworthy.

AR, like most technology, has bathos at its heart. To survive, it must never quite unveil itself. It must always fall some way short of its promise.

Technology is, in the end, just another species of pornography.

THIRTEEN

A couple of days after I found and hid her corpse, Dad began to worry after Mum. Why hadn't she phoned from the camp?

We knew one other camp regular. Gabby was the daughter of Frankie, the hotel's long-serving day manager. Frankie visited her daughter every weekend, bringing her freshly laundered clothes and a car boot full of fist-sized bottles of supermarket beer. A veteran of the civil protest movement, she spent Saturday afternoons teaching her daughter and her friends rappelling techniques and how to tie figure-eights. Gabby and her friends were building tree houses and walkways. The forest floor was damp and dirty and vulnerable; come winter, they were planning to take to the canopy.

Every few weeks Gabby came home. 'Delousing leave',

Frankie called it, and not without reason, since after a month or so 'embracing the base' Gabby's head was a mass of rat's tails, as though strips of horsehair stuffing from an old armchair had been woven through her hair.

The speed with which Gabby had changed from child to angry young woman was startling. She seemed in one season to have swapped frilly party dresses for fatigues and a webby, moth-holed jumper. She had always been a big girl and after months outdoors her weight had acquired a shape, a purposefulness.

Gabby and Frankie, Dad and I sat in the hotel dining room, around the big table near the fireplace. The mood was sour and frayed. At some point Gabby had decided to meet all Dad's enquiries with a small, confident smile and, under the pressure of Dad's unrelenting questioning, it had become a rictus, a sneer of defiance.

Dad was insistent. 'There has to be some central – some central thing – some centre.'

If the protest movement had had a centre, the gates of the airbase would have been cleared long ago. As it was, the movement pulsed its way around obstacles. When assaulted, it retreated into itself then swelled again, like some science-fiction blob.

'But there are young girls there,' Dad fretted. 'There has to be some protection.'

No one felt they had to point out that Mum had long since ceased to be a young girl.

Gabby was returning at the end of the week and said she would do what she could. All she could really do was pass on our fears. The camp was tenuous and scattered – we were going to have to rely on the gossips to carry the word around the base.

Every day after school I went exploring down by the river. I moved about cautiously, on guard against strangers, soldiers, and above all, Michel. I could not be sure that Michel had abandoned his own fascination with the river. It was Michel, after all, who had invested 'our river' with its meaning. It was Michel who had run it, explored it, who tore his skin on its thorns, and imagined its future, and, for all I knew, still wove millennial dreams round its withered, tilting trees and rusting white goods.

I stayed away from the ring of fridges, afraid I might run into him, though what he'd have found to do here, other than fantasize, I could not imagine. Anyway, I didn't see him.

Four days after she returned to the camp, Gabby phoned Dad. I was making us pasta when the call came through. A tension came over him, hunched there, a reed too brittle to bend. I thought at first it must be the police.

But no. The farce I had made of everything just rolled on and on, a wave too powerful to check.

'Sara never even turned up at the camp.' He came forward and embraced me. I put my arms round him. I felt him shake. I held him, keeping him together. This again. This again, and always – keeping Dad whole against the wrack thrown up by Mum.

The river ran slow and deep along sunken cuttings. The banks were sand, and the river had cut itself a deep bed, but nowhere did it run particularly fast. There were bathing pools, or what would have made bathing pools, but they were very deep. The banks had the consistency of damp sugar, and the water ran milky brown, always.

Something the size and shape of a human corpse could not have floated far downstream. This whole stretch of river was one complex muddy snare. There was too much growth. There were too many pools, and too many reed beds, too many soft, estuarine places, almost-channels, forks. There were too many trees. She must have fetched up somewhere, bloated and bleached, with the plastic bag still wrapped round her head. Once she was found (someone was going to have to find her, eventually) it was going to be obvious to everyone that Mum's was no simple suicide. Suicides do not asphyxiate themselves then leap into millraces. She had had assistance. She had had company. She had had someone get rid of her body. When they found her – and someone was bound to find her – their first thought was not going to be suicide. It was going to be murder.

I had to get the bag off. I had to find her and take the bag from off her head.

The nights were drawing in. When I got home from school, the conservatory was so cold I could see my own breath in the light of the porch lamp. I stepped inside and reached for the wall switch—

No. I drew my hand back, breathing clouds of light into the dark.

I passed through our rooms and out among the halls and landings of the hotel. The empty rooms nagged at me. The place was virtually mothballed now. Wounded servicemen were no longer being billeted with us, and Dad, with all his worries, had neither the time nor the will to spirit up yet another clientele.

Mum's presence had held together, by the weight of its demands, a home that made very little sense now that she was gone. Relieved of the pressure she exerted, the place was flying apart – drawing room and dining room and bar and check-in desk. Our own apartments, too, were getting bigger and colder.

No one vanishes like that. A splash and gone. Not there. Not without help.

Help, then. Since she was not found. Not then. Not later. Helped to die. A fear bred in the dark. Who really has the nerve to tape a bag around their own throat? Who really pulls a boot lid down on themselves. More to the point, *how*?

I answered the last question myself, while Dad was out. The boot lid was double-hulled. There was a cut-out in the plastic, strong enough to haul the lid down, if you lay inside. I lay there in the boot, fingering the hole, horrified at the strength of the temptation that gripped me then, to pull the lid down over me, as she had done.

As for the rest, I had no answers. At night I lay awake, haunted by scraps of memory. A haloed figure. Hair as white as mist. His zipper coming down. Insane. Absurd. But in this season of mists and shadows I could not help remembering that I had left her on the platform with him. His erection white and hard and as long as a dagger. His loamy hands.

Dad kept records of our guests on the laptop behind the check-in desk. The photographs all seemed to have been taken in the same room, against the same wall – as though the country's entire military had climbed one by one out of the same tank, and left by the same magnolia-painted corridor into the bleak, wet light of the same car park.

Everyone sported the same regulation haircut. There were a handful of blonds but none of the ones with the lightest hair – hair that might just be albino-white if they grew it out – looked like the soldier I remembered. Perhaps his hair had turned white after the photograph was taken, bleached by a nameless terror as in a second-rate ghost story.

Face folded into face until I could no longer call to mind what my quarry looked like. So much for that.

FOURTEEN

Dogmen have me surrounded. They yip and slaver, waving crude knock-off AKs, their bandoliers glittering in the Middle's glass reflections of a red and bloated sun. The streets are swimming in their oil-black blood but still they mass, overcoming the city's defences.

'Up here!' A rookie firewoman grabs my hand; a fizzing sensation courses up my arm. 'Come on!' She moves up the stairwell ahead of me with an athletic, pneumatic grace. I struggle to keep up with her. Sweat runs into my eyes. Behind me comes a sick and frantic skittering – engineered claws on polished tile. They're after us.

'In here!' She's found a portal. She pauses, chest heaving, waiting for me to plunge my fist into the fizzing blue-green wall. The amulet on my arm glows dazzling white and the portal shreds itself clear and we find ourselves newly arrived at the municipal command centre, nerve ganglion of the dying city.

The armies of the Augmented are already massing at the gates. The best we can do now is set the place to self-destruct, robbing them of their prize. If they seize control of the city and its weaponry, then there can be no hope for the human diaspora pouring from the gates.

The command centre is built on many levels, balconies and mezzanines. Droids, faceless and beneficent, tend and mend its little fires and short-outs. We move among them as they carry equipment from one place to another.

(The shopping mall, so secure and so surveilled, provided us with countless camera points. Layering real-time AR over its surfaces, tenants and clientele has been a joy. The trouble is the mall itself – it's far too well-designed. People move round this place so calmly, we have had to cast them as faceless 'bots'. Even so, their lack of urgency kicks a sizeable hole in a game that is, after all, about action. We should have gone for our first idea and cast the shoppers as zombies. But we had neither the time nor the resources to engineer how the undead might react to a player's presence. Bared bloody fangs, and flailing arms (barely attached: one falls off and crawls away – a neat sight gag), and the judicious application of projectile vomit – we had all these ideas storyboarded, and abandoned them with reluctance. According to our game bible, the bots – their heads as blank as eggs, their limbs a liquid chrome – are attempting a hopeless repair of the city's failing systems. Frankly they look like what they are: shoppers, laden with bags and pushing prams, all hidden and homogenised under the most cursory AR skinning.)

A scream is cut off mid-flow by a blinding light and glass shatters. The firewoman hesitates, reels, and turns. A shard of blue glass as big as a meat cleaver has pierced her chest. Blood flecks her mouth as she tries to speak. 'Kill the … the city.' (Christ, how did this stunt get through QA?) 'Save … the …'

She falls into me, already rotting and crumbling as nano-engineered bacteria pronounce her clinically dead and therefore ripe for scavenging. Her breadcrumb corpse collides with me – a shivering rain and a little breeze. And on the breeze, a word – 'w-o-r-l-d' – and she is gone. My only helpmate on this level. Dead. Kill the city. Save the world. I am alone.

Scritch scratch.

A dogman has emerged from the portal. Grenades hang from leather belts criss-crossed over its heaving silver chest. Round its middle finger, raised in obscene insult to the human world, the pin, on its little wire ring, still dangles. He shakes it free of its claw and it lands on the floor with a bright sound. The dogman pulls its lips back in a grin and howls. How on earth did this monster get through the portal? The portal's supposed to be locked to everyone but—

The dogman waves a severed human arm above its head. Round its wrist is an amulet. An amulet like mine.

Oh. Nice.

I run.

Criss-crossing the Middle air, policebots swivel to check my progress. Red warning lights checker the ground before me, slowing me up. Any faster, and the police will shoot. (We cooked this gag up to manage the player's behaviour in crowded spaces. We don't want people so taken up by the game that they go rocketing into mothers with prams and old men laden with the week's groceries. Our bible, wrought in Michel's deathless prose, does its best to weave these restrictions into the storyline: 'The city is a strict, borderline-psychotic nanny, and riots and rebellions of the frustrated human populus have brought the predatory dogmen down on the city.'

The policebot is blind to body type. It'll blast a speeding dogman down as cheerfully as it will me. This makes the chase a game of strategy rather than speed. As I weave past bots (well, shoppers) towards the escalator, the dogman (pure avatar) pursues me on a marginally more efficient trajectory, ever nearer, its breath ever hotter as I—

(Stop.)

I pull the wrapshades from my face. The earpieces, cooling, know to close down the rest of the kit. Item: a plastic mesh threaded through my hair. Item: gluey res-idues painted on my hands and face. Item: a thin Lycra top threaded with smart elastic – a slick descendant of the kind of vests my father stitched together for blind servicemen. Item: trainers, their thick soles packed with machinery. For all this, I feel a deal less self-conscious now than I did a year ago. A year is a long time in this business, and every part of Loophole's AR player's kit has been miniaturised to the point where the wearer can be forgiven for forgetting that it's there.

The escalator leads to a cool concrete atrium, an airy space which, in its fidelity to the first-person-shooter aesthetic, looks a deal more gameable than our own, digitally generated AR skinning.

The metro here has a double-door system to prevent people hurling themselves inconsiderately onto the line. There's a man at the end of the platform, in a grey lapel-less suit and smart shoes. He's weaving and bobbing at his own reflection in the glass wall. The other passengers are giving him a wide berth. It's going to take a while for people to habituate to gamer behaviour. After all, it took a little while for us to ignore the way people with handsfree phones talked into the air. AR is much more intrusive, and people's tolerance to its casual public use is far less predictable. The man reaches towards the glass wall, his fingers scrabbling the air. Is he typing? Grappling? I wonder if he's one of our first-adopters, a party guest, in which case he'll be heading where I'm heading now, out of the Middle and on to the outdoor launch event organised by Michel's producer, Bryon Vaux. I should put my glasses back on, go up to the man, test for myself the collaborative side of our game. But I have had enough. I am out of breath, and at the back of my mind hovers the unignorable possibility that the man might not be experiencing an Augmented Reality at all. For all his recent haircut and respectable clothing, he may just be crazy.

The train arrives. I'm finding it hard to shake off the paranoia induced by our game. From where I'm sitting I have a good clear view of six people. A harassed, gimlet-faced woman in a sari. Her bespectacled daughter. A young builder with tattoos who seems determined to sit with his legs as wide apart as possible, as though he were about to give birth. A man whose white facial hair, busy shirt, red-threaded tweed jacket, black boots and expensive retro wristwatch combine in such a messy and confusing way, I'd never be able to identify him in a line-up. Two animated African tourists trying to swap something from one mobile phone to another.

Of these, Glasses Girl, Clown Man and Legs Akimbo have allowed their attention to be snatched away. The girl's glasses are cheap half-silvered jobs, and from the flickering petrol-sheen smothering her eyes I can just about identify which space-opera she's watching. The other two are a scarier proposition, their pupils and irises silvered behind active contact lenses. These lenses are probably not AR-enabled, because the men's heads are too still, absorbed in some reasonably static immersive environment. They're reading, or more likely watching. Legs's thumbs are twitching but they're bare and clean, free of any shiny trail of conductive gel, so his movements are more likely a tic, rather than virtual keypresses.

It shouldn't be such an effort, seeing what strangers are up to on a train. My heart shouldn't still be racing, as it's racing now. The game is over, but it seems to me it's been replaced, not with any sense of the normal, but with another, creepier, more insidious game.

Ten minutes later I change trains for a more direct service, underground at first, then elevated, that stitches a path round suburban hills, up to and through the highest of the city's ring of mountains. The city sprawls here because the valley soil is mostly sand. Any building above four storeys tends to keel over – a fact learned the hard way by ambitious ecclesiastical architects hundreds of years ago. All the really tall buildings – the high-rise blocks and the most ancient cathedrals – are built upon the rock outcrops that rise from the flat valley floor like teeth in a gum. The hills are called islands. Isle of This,

Isle of That. The coincidence wasn't lost on Michel, whose game bible climaxes with the city inundated by a rising flood, skinned with burning petrol. This is pure fantasy. We are too far inland for an inundation.

My phone rings.

'Where are you?'

'I'm running late.'

'Are you on the train?'

'Yes.'

'How far from the stop are you?'

'About a minute.' The train is already throttling down.

'I'll wait for you.'

'Cheers, Ralf.'

This evening – and for the first time ever – Ralf chooses the restaurant. Its walls are hung with antique plates, white with multicoloured designs. The proprietress tells us about them – how all the colours come from a single pigment. How you won't find these plates produced anywhere outside the Levant. It is a quaint assertion, as though her little restaurant could have somehow side-stepped centuries of relentless globalisation.

'Don't knock it till you've tasted the food.'

'I'm not knocking anything.' How strange, though, to be following Ralf's recommendation.

'Is Michel coming to this party, do you know?' Ralf is a fan of Michel's books. He has a full set of slipcased hardbacks, signed. It's one of the reasons Loophole has fallen further and further under the spell of Bryon Vaux. Michel's books are the source material for Vaux's most lucrative film franchise, and Ralf has wanted to apply Loophole's every technical innovation to better realise Michel's world.

When Ralf heard that Michel was going to be writing

our game bible, he was like a kid on his way to see Santa Claus. Sadly, Michel has proved every bit as elusive as the real Father Christmas, communicating with us only by written word. I don't know whether this is just pressure of work, or some personal fall-out from Christmas.

Either way, Ralf is one disappointed fan.

'Vaux will be there, I suppose.'

Ralf puffs himself up at that. Ralf, as Chief Imagineer, has met Bryon Vaux several times now. 'I'll introduce you,' he says, as though this were a favour specially in his gift. There's a pomposity comes over Ralf whenever he talks about Vaux. I used to find it touching, but now it has begun to irritate me. It's not entirely Ralf's fault. He is now, of necessity, one of the great producer's gate-keepers. Every digital entrepreneur and failed screen-writer and wooden drama student wants a piece of him.

Our food arrives. Ralf sits back to make room for the proprietress. He has a paunch now. He's going to have to watch that. I let him order for me, curious to discover what has so excited his retarded palate.

One bite and I'm flailing for the salep jug.

Ralf laughs. 'You see?'

The salep, warm and creamy, gums round the fire in my throat like a retardant foam. My whole mouth sings. 'What is this stuff?'

Ralf shrugs, pleased with himself for so surprising me. 'It's real *çig köfte*. There's this spice in it called isot. A kind of black paprika.'

A minute later I'm recovered enough to dare another mouthful. And another. And another. I wish to God I hadn't eaten earlier, this stuff is delicious. 'How did you find this place?'

'It's one of Vaux's haunts,' Ralf says. 'His local.'

'Yes?'

'He has a house near here.'

The menus come around again. I say, 'They have a milk dessert on here called Chicken Breast. How does that work?' It occurs to me that I have become Ralf.

Ralf pulls out his phone and checks the time. 'We'd better settle up.'

The sun is low in the sky and, in the park, the young spring foliage shines like foil. The party is set up in the ornamental garden. Brick steps climb the hillside. Paths send out branches at precise, perpendicular angles. The effect is softened by all the planting wound round the trellises and gazebos: lilac and clematis, grapevine and rose. Come summer, there will be welcome shade here. This early in the year, it's easy enough to find gaps in the screening foliage to enjoy the view. This evening the city, softened into butter by the sun, puddles around the blue paste jewel of the Middle.

Guests stand chatting in small, nervous groups among the stone seats, ornamental nooks, fountains and artful screens. Waiters in whites move among us with champagne and canapés.

'Glasses on, people!'

And here he comes. Laughing. Glad-handing. Ralf turns and nudges me. I wince against the flashlight spraying and rippling through the leaves and through the crowd that gathers around us as people surge forward to grab their five-second shake-and-grin with our legendary host.

Sunlight catches in his shocked-white hair.

'What's the matter, Connie?'

His hair.

'Bryon!'

Vaux knows Ralf's voice. He turns.

There is something here I am missing. Something obvious and terrible.

'Conrad's here! You haven't met. My business partner. Bryon!'

His face lights up, seeing Ralf among all these anonymous, uplifted faces. Photographers surround him, lighting him up like a poster. No army drab this time. A tux, and wrapround shades so shiny, featureless and deadly black, they might be a single piece of enamel.

Camera flash streaks across the big black lenses of his shades as he reaches out to shake my hand. A beat. 'Conrad?' He hesitates. Bryon Vaux. Producer of Michel's *Shaman* franchise. Majority shareholder in Loophole.

'Connie?'

The crowd carries him on. My hands hang limp and lifeless at my sides.

'Conrad?'

I turn away to face the city, and pulling my wraprounds from my pocket, I let myself slip back into the game.

The city has been rendered down to a jumble of charcoal-grey plinths – stone footprints where building after building has been magicked away. At this distance only the biggest, most rectilinear footprints stand out. Most of the city is reduced to rubble. This is my home with its inner chaos exposed, no more now than a ghastly iteration of the same salt crystal. City as tumour. A spreading circle of dead tissue. City as leprosy. 'Ralf. I've met him.'

'What?'

'Vaux. I've met him.'

'Really? Where?'

I shake my head. I don't want to talk about this, after all. Not here. 'Doesn't matter.' Vaux is older now, of course. Much older. Nonetheless, wealth and the years have been kind to him. There can be no mistake.

Across the horizon, fires leap. Ash drifts in waves. The air shimmers with imagineered heat as bit by bit the city disappears under the pall of its annihilation.

This is the man who accosted me. This is the man who exposed himself to me. This is the man I left Mum standing near, the last day I saw her alive.

A lot of water has passed under the bridge since those days when Gabby used to turn up at our hotel on 'delousing leave'. Whenever she returned from the protest camp for a few days' R&R, you could spot her a mile off from her shag of rat-tailed hair. You could smell her. Nowadays she dresses conservatively, in linen suits and tailored white shirts. She lives abroad, pursuing an academic career. Behind her, fuzzy and foreshortened in the lens of her laptop's camera, her office wall is a mass of sticky notes and dry-marker scribble. 'Is this about your dad?'

When I lost touch with my father finally, in the weeks after the car accident, Gabby did what she could to trace his electronic signature for me. Her academic studies and radical politics have given her some insight into where and how information is actually structured, beneath the reassuring blandishments of clouds and commercial search engines. 'Pretty much nothing is ever lost,' she told me, confidently. But silence is silence, whichever way you cut it, and we never did find my dad.

'Not exactly.' I tell her, wishing I had my story straight. 'It's more to do with the hotel.'

'I knew there'd be something you wanted.'

'Poor Gabby. It's the price you pay for actually knowing how to do stuff.'

'"How are you, Gabriela?" "I'm fine, Conrad. How are you?"'

'I'm crap at keeping in touch, I know.'

'The price of this call is that you come and visit me here. I mean it.'

'Okay.'

'I mean it. Give me a date.'

Eventually she stops twisting my arm, and I can ask her, 'Could our old hotel records still be any place?'

This turns out to be more likely than I expected. There's a regulation says that guesthouses have to maintain their customer records for a couple of years. 'No-one ever gets around to deleting the expired data. Why would they bother?'

This is the kind of digital silt Gabby's undergraduates sieve through in their second semester, hunting for interesting mash-ups. 'I might get one of my students to do the donkey work, so is there anything here we're likely to turn up that should stay confidential?'

'Possibly.'

'Yes?'

I take a deep breath and tell her about Bryon Vaux. Some of it. The barest outline.

'You're kidding.' She is impressed.

'Dad knew him. Treated him. Taught him how to use a visual vest.'

'Bryon Vaux stayed at your hotel? Would I have met him?'

'Almost certainly.'

A pause while she thinks about this. Like most people who navigate data for a living – or who, as in her case, train the navigators – Gabby values her mental privacy, and wears neither wraprounds nor contact lenses. Her eyes are clear. Even over this not especially hi-def video link I can see her scepticism she tries to work out what my real motivation is here. 'You think Vaux can help you find your dad?'

A smart guess, though wrong. 'Possibly,' I say, not wanting to discuss my real suspicions. For a start, they are far too incoherent to share. I can't even convince myself that I'm on to anything important. All I know is – the sight of Bryon Vaux has put the fear in me.

'Your dad never said anything about him?'

'Why would he? To him, back then, Vaux would just have been another serviceman with burnt eyes—'

'But you're sure it's him?'

'I'm sure it's him. I'm positive. Though I can't see how it could be him, logically.'

'Tell me what you need to know.'

'If we can confirm Vaux was billeted at the hotel, I want to find out when and why he discharged himself. What?'

'I thought you told me you were working for Vaux now?'

'Loophole's doing AR work for his production company. Why?'

Gabby folds her arms, examining me through her screen as if I were some particularly knotty firewall. 'Conrad. I don't mean to pry, but why can't you just ask him these things yourself?'

'I don't know him.' It's all I can think of. I can hardly tell her about my mother. 'He's famous, and I don't know him at all.'

In the end, and before I can buck up the courage to contact him myself, Bryon Vaux calls me.

Vaux's production company is buying up immersive technologies. With them, he plans to smear movies across the real. This is where his current creative ambitions lie: in characters who'll share your breakfast coffee. In plot beats played out on your journey to work, and confrontations staged in streets you already know. He imagines dreams woven through the real, and all the dreamers dreaming.

That Vaux now wants to buy Loophole outright comes as no surprise. If the purchase goes through he will almost certainly fold the company into his existing operation, dismantling it in order to get at its motive element. Ralf is Loophole's golden goose, and Vaux is perfectly well aware of the fact. Were it anyone else's commercial manoeuvre, I'd be cracking champagne along with the rest of the management team, glad of a profitable sale. Vaux will pay well for the company and we will all be winners.

But it is not anyone else. It is him. Bryon Vaux.

He invites me to his club. It's very different from the one Ralf and I belong to, and not somewhere I would have associated with Vaux at all, recreating as it does the ambience of certain private schools. It caters to a clientele that has stepped from these schools to exclusive universities to remunerative jobs in the public arts like well-bred children stepping stones across a river. It occurs to me that the club has not been chosen with his comfort in mind at all, but mine.

'How long have you known Michel, then?'

I expected the conversation to centre around Ralf. Our golden goose. Mention of Michel is an unexpected gambit – though of course Michel is the author of the *Shaman* series, source of Vaux's wealth.

'Michel told me about you.'

I'm surprised. 'He did?'

Vaux smiles. 'You grew up together, I understand. And it's the strangest thing. I think I stayed at your hotel a while.'

I feel as though I am falling through a door I thought was locked.

'Conrad, would you walk with me a while?'

A few minutes later, from the balustrade of an industrial museum overlooking the Forum, I weave my fingers before my eyes. The horse and rider rearing up at the centre of the square refuse to appear. They have entirely vanished. They might never have been. There isn't the faintest visual stutter. My God, we're good.

Vaux is sitting beside me on the bench, his hands resting on his knees, big and soft and furred as though they were a couple of pets drowsing on his lap. His feet are small, shod in pale leather handmades. It's an effort for me to maintain my sense of distance, or, indeed, any cautious reflex at all. If it wasn't for the steel sheen in his eyes – contact lenses over eyeballs that are already mostly plastic – I might, God help me, even be returning his smile by now.

Aside from a handful of brute physical details – his

albino-white hair, his height, the cast of his face – little about Vaux meshes with my nightmares. I am finding it impossible to associate his bulk or his bigness with the brutality I remember. His hands, his boots.

'I took Ralf out to dinner last night.'

'Uh-huh.'

His eyes, like mine, are silver-lensed and hard to read. 'I hope you don't mind.'

'Of course I mind, Bryon. But I imagine you, being you, scared the living daylights out of him.' I contemplate the Forum, its soapy white neo-classical columns, its shallow steps and elegant black street furniture and at its centre – an aching absence where its central monument should be. Already I am finding it difficult to remember what the horse and rider looked like. Now that my eyes have registered their absence, the statue is being scrubbed from my memory, washed away as swiftly as a dream.

Loophole's development team, swimming in all the money and resources Vaux has thrown at it, has hit a serious snag. Now Vaux wants to see if I can spot it on my own.

'Hang on.' I study the gap where the monument once stood. 'I think I see it.'

A family of tourists – mum, dad, two children with backpacks – are making their way in front of the arch on the south-eastern corner of the square. As they pass behind the absent column, they stutter and vanish. A second family appears, identical to the first. Mum, Dad and the kids walk across the road, clear the statue's occlusion fan, and disappear, one by one. Another identical family appears, several yards in front of the group that's just vanished. Christ. The glitch. The fault.

'That took you about eight minutes.' Vaux smiles. With silvered lenses in his eyes, the expression is predatory. 'Not bad.'

Vaux has another meeting. I leave him at the mouth of the metro, and walk alone through the Ministries, trying to clear my head.

One by one we are transforming the spaces we have cleared. Here, for example, the ministry buildings have been replaced by paint-blue ponds where no birds swim. Lawns. Forests. We have entirely levelled a square mile south-west of the forum, filling the gap with potato fields that our great-grandparents' generation would recognise. Hedgerows bend and sway.

Walking through this rusticated city, the air tastes fresher, though of course I know it's just as muggy and polluted as always. With grass under my feet – albeit imaginary grass – I have become attuned to subtle gradients. I've learned to navigate, less by what I see, but more by the lie of the land under my feet. I can picture in my mind's eye the organic shapes into which the city has been plugged, and which, after so many centuries, it has still not altogether erased. Little by little, and in unexpected ways, we are rubbing the city away to reveal the pattern of a forgotten land.

The mind juggles maps very poorly. Now that I am growing used to our clarified and minimal city – city as park, as field, as bucolic blank, like something out of one of Michel's later, gentler post-apocalypse tales – I am finding it harder and harder to navigate the city as it really is. The truth is, I don't like going out without my lenses now. An unaugmented walk through the stews of the city, hemmed in by its buildings, assaulted by its aniline palette, my concentration shattered by all its overlapping signage, leaves me feeling increasingly uncomfortable. My heart chatters. My breaths grow short and painful. I need a break.

I need a friend.

Airport security have to let us disembark eventually, and Gabby is at the gate to meet me. 'Looking good,' she smiles. She hefts the bags off my trolley. She wants to show me she's still got her strength.

We climb into a cab.

The altitude here is serious; even in the city centre, there is still snow on the ground. Crowds in expensive coats gather around stalls selling mulled wine and buttered rum. We pull up before the cathedral. Gabby's apartment is high up in a retail and hotel complex nearby. 'Bloody hell, Gabby, what does this cost you?'

'Nothing. I hacked their booking server.'

'What will you do when they find out?'

'Sleep under the desk at work. Busk outside the Cathedral.'

I can't be entirely sure that this is a joke. The apartment is well-appointed, perfect for bringing home women of a certain age – the divorced, the curious, the incorrigible – and ideally suited to ejecting them again in the morning.

'Do you want to freshen up? I've booked us a table for nine.'

The apartment has a wet room. A shower that wraps you up in a warmly scented tropical rain. Towels as big as blankets. Coming out, I find Gabby watching an international news channel. She lifts her hand to grasp mine. 'Good to see you, Connie.'

'And you.'

'You look tired.'

'I look how I feel.'

'Are you up for tonight? Just dinner. Friends. We don't have to stay out late.'

'Of course.'

I slump opposite her in an upholstered chair.

'I dug up what you asked me for about Bryon Vaux. But if you're speaking to him—'

'He spoke to me. Michel told him about me and he put two and two together.'

'So you've talked.'

'Only about work. I haven't asked him anything – important.'

Gabby shoots me a look. She thinks I'm being obscure for the sake of it. That I'm leading her on. She's remembering our childhood games with Dad's tin soldiers; my endlessly changing rules of engagement. 'Look,' I say. 'Tell me what you found. And I'll explain.'

'You promise?'

'Yes.'

'Okay. For a start – and you could have found this out from any celebrity site – Vaux was not a serviceman.'

This draws me up. 'What?'

'Vaux wasn't in the services. He wasn't a soldier. Everyone assumes he's a veteran. He was a *journalist*. Embedded. Good at it, too. It's why the grunts like him. Factually, his films have always been on the button.'

'Now I'm completely at sea. I thought he was a soldier.'

'People do. He plays up to it.'

'But his eyes. He's seen action.'

'Of course he's seen action. He was embedded on the front line. He took a laser in the face.'

'But what was a writer doing among a bunch of army men, getting a vest fitted by my Dad?'

Gabby turns her hands palms up as though to say, where's the problem? 'A battlefield injury, a military hospital, and from there a referral. Wouldn't it make perfect sense, treating Vaux alongside others blinded in the field?'

'Did you find out why he discharged himself from the hotel?'

'Plenty of your dad's guests did.'

'Really?'

'It wasn't strictly a clinic. Some took to the vests, some didn't.'

'And did Vaux?'

'Christ. How am I supposed to find that out?'

'I think maybe Dad would have made a record.'

'Well, I can keep looking.'

'Please.'

'Now. Are you going to tell me what the fuck this is about?'

I take a breath. Another. (The air here is really very thin.) I am going to have to give her something.

In the end it's Gabby who buys me time. 'You can tell me as we go. Come on. We'll walk. It's a nice night.'

She leads me, slipping and sliding ('I told you to bring boots') through the city's pedestrianised centre, from stall to stall, knocking back punch and spiced wine by way of an aperitif. With alcohol inside her, she is a little more forthcoming about what she has discovered. 'The records have Vaux down as twenty-seven when he got his eyes burned out.'

'How long was he at the hotel?'

'A couple of months.'

'Gabby.' No way round this. 'Do you remember – did he have much to do with my mum, do you reckon?'

Gabby is ordering us mugs of rum. She leans against the bar. 'Oh, Conrad,' she sighs, her gaze sliding away from mine to lose itself in the rings and smears on the bartop. 'Who knows what your mum got up to?'

'But you heard something. You know something. Did your mum tell you something? Did Frankie know something?'

She hands me my mug. 'Are you finally going to tell me what this is about?'

'I think Bryon Vaux was the last man to see my mum alive.'

'Oh.' Gabby sips her rum. Again. 'I see.' She sips. 'Well. Fuck.'

'Now, if you can tell me how to broach that particular subject with Bryon Vaux, without landing myself in a world of pain, I'd like to hear it.'

Gabby looks at me. 'From what you've said, he doesn't sound that much of an ogre.'

'Maybe not.'

'And my advice remains what it was.'

'Which was?'

'Just talk to him. Idiot.'

Gabby has gone to bed. On her hotel-room balcony, I sip imported whisky and stare across the skyline, pretending to myself that I'm catching up on my work.

To speed up the due diligence, we have an open audio connection running between the office and my laptop. For my colleagues at home I exist as an oracle, ready with advice, constantly appraised of their slightest doings. At least, that is the idea.

I can just about hear one of our interns making a hash of something over the phone to an old client.

'Hello.'

No-one hears me.

'Hello.'

No-one's paying any attention to the invisible man in the corner. They're just getting on with their jobs. Talking. Laughing. I wonder what they are laughing about. I expected the sound of the office to comfort me, but it hasn't.

'Hello!'

I should go have a shower, get to bed, get a night's sleep like a normal person. Instead I linger here getting steadily more drunk, listening to all the life I have engendered moving around in its nest. This thing I have made. This pattern of people and process and capital: it has its own life now. It no longer needs me.

If I bow out now, gracefully, Vaux can have Loophole and I can be in business again within eighteen months, with fresh capital and an enviable reputation. Ralf will stay where he is, Loophole's newly-fashioned 'creative director'. Naive as he is, he will grow into the role of Bryon Vaux's courtier. It is not what he wants. ('We were having fun, weren't we?') But it is what is best for him.

I down my whisky and stalk back inside, cursing Ralf, cursing the company, cursing myself.

Vaux is a rich man, and rich men will have their toys.

FIFTEEN

Without Mum, Dad and I fell into well-worn routines. We shared the housework. I cooked dinner. Ben washed up. We were adept. This was the life we used to lead whenever Mum was laid up in bed. In many ways life was cleaner and easier now she was gone.

Winter bit down early. From my window the hotel lawn, grey with frost, resembled fur more than grass. I closed my eyes and leant my forehead against the glass, receiving a chill fierce enough to pucker the flesh.

Dad was in the kitchen. The radio was on. Distance robbed the words of sense, though the cadences persevered. Headlines. Seven AM.

I was still wrapped in my duvet, marinating in its smelly warmth. To shed that and slip into a dressing gown and, worse, to swap dressing gown for cold, slippy,

damp-feeling nylon-mix school clothes, was as painful a
prospect, as traumatic, as shedding a skin. Half-naked,
blue and scrunched against the cold, I was fighting with
an overstuffed wardrobe drawer when Dad leaned in.

'Up and at 'em, Connie.'

'Yeah, yeah.'

'What time are you home this afternoon?'

It was a regular day – no clubs, no sports, no events.
'Four.'

'We have someone coming to see us.'

The day passed predictably enough. Mum's disappearance had got fed through the school's rumour mill, but
the story had quickly lost currency, sustained neither
by news nor by credible conjecture. I think my friends,
knowing her politics, quietly assumed that Mum was
leading some debauched existence on the margins, too
loved-up to phone or write.

By the end of the school day, the track by the river
was still set rock-hard – a glassy mass of rills, dents and
patches of dirty ice, buried here and there under mats of
black, congealed leaves. Now the bracken had died back,
Michel's ring of fridges was easy to spot among the trees.

Our hotel had more or less packed in by this point. The
register recorded a few waifs and strays, clueless elderly
couples and a dissatisfied family of five. Still, Dad had
to work, if only to keep up the fabric of the place, so he
doubled as duty manager in a motel nearer the coast. On
the days I arrived home before him, I worked in the conservatory – that loamy, greenish glass monstrosity that
had been tacked onto the back of the house years before,
as though the hotel were not big enough already. In the
burnished light of a setting sun (if I was lucky; otherwise

213

in drizzle and spreading, glaucous grey) I worked on my portfolio, my heads and hands, my architectural projections. I wrote essays, bedding the bald facts of history, geography and the classics with comfortable, indecisive phrases. Notwithstanding. Moreover. Albeit.

This evening, as I negotiated the fence and walked up to the hotel across the lawn, I saw that Dad had come home on time for our meeting. The lights were on in our apartments and, walking into the living room, I saw that our visitor had already wedged herself uncomfortably into the smallest of our wicker bucket chairs.

She had put on a lot of weight since she had bedded me. Such generous breasts, such ungenerous nipples. While she talked, putting my father straight about the wiles of the female psyche, I imagined her great vampire breasts, sucking the lifeblood from the unwary feeder. What on earth was she thinking of, coming here in these circumstances? Well, she was the mouthpiece – this much I knew – of a local outfit which for the most part trawled the hinterland estates, persuading feckless teenagers into a termination. Here though she was purely 'a friend of the family' – this is what she said – someone Mum knew and whose hand she had held (all the while making eyes at Dad and, when that failed, at me). A self-appointed honest broker.

She seemed totally oblivious to me.

'Because, painful as this is,' she said, a dentist preparing a nervous patient, 'I think we have to entertain the possibility that Sara felt threatened here. By you, Ben, I mean.'

Ben collected visits from missing-persons charities the way a lonely pensioner invites builders in to estimate for work he cannot afford. These endless interviews gave Dad the illusion of progress in his search for Mum. He imagined a network of intelligence radiating across the country.

I stayed out of the way of these visits as much as I could.

No one vanishes, a splash, then gone. No one. Impossible.

Mum's rooms. Make-up and dresses and easels and unopened paints. Dad said, 'If you'd rather I did this on my own, I'll understand.'

In the end, after the first shock of her disappearance, Dad had settled in his own mind that Mum had absconded, fleeing the pressures of marriage and family. After so many years with her, I suppose he found it impossible to imagine a world without her in it. He packed Mum's things up in boxes and carried them out to the garage.

Living with Dad, surfing the roll and spin of his moods, his grief, his sense of having been abandoned and his slow-building anger (he was learning, in his nervous, clumsy way, to hate the thing he had loved) I found it difficult to resist his version of events. I didn't forget what had really happened – but it was hard for me to imagine that the episode was ever a part of my waking life. Dad's anxious speculations were so much more believable. I would catch myself, from time to time, imagining what Mum was doing, away from us; among her Wiccan friends, perhaps, or in sheltered accommodation somewhere, free of what she had probably convinced herself by now was an abusive marriage.

I no longer spent all my free time by the river. One lazy weekend afternoon I got Dad's walking maps down from the shelf and, spreading them out on the conservatory tiles, I found the river and I traced it with my finger, through towns and villages, round chalk hills and across reclaimed pasture, out to sea. Impossible.

How much easier to imagine that she was sitting in some B&B somewhere, extemporising her sexual and domestic oppression for the benefit of some credulous social worker.

We were free now, Dad and I. We were weightless. We were falling, and it felt good. I didn't want it to end, and it didn't end, it just went on and on. I no longer seemed to need any sleep. At night I lay awake, listening to the radio under the covers. I was never tired. Things acquired an unnatural clarity. The walk to school. The cool scratchiness of a clean shirt each school-day morning.

But things were flying apart and I could not pick and choose what I held onto and what I lost. Some nights, Dad didn't come home at all. I didn't know who he found to be with. I felt him shucking off shackle after shackle and I waited, with a growing calm, for the moment when he freed himself from me.

At the beginning of the spring term, over dinner, Dad had news. 'There's this new job,' he said.

'Right.'

He looked at me. I watched the anger rising within him: anger from nowhere. 'We have to talk about this.'

'We are talking about this. I'm sitting here. I am talking about this.'

He wanted a fight. After so long at Mum's beck and call, so many years manning the safety valves, watching pressures rise and fall, he imagined that any particle of self-interest was bound to trigger a disaster. He needed the sound of breaking glass to convince him that he was getting what he wanted.

Dad had been invited to work as a technician at a private hospital, crafting new eyes for old. It would not pay well, though it was what he'd been longing to do for years. His hobby, he said finally, had at last thrown up the chance of a modest second career.

'You want to take this job.'

He gaped at me, hopelessly. 'The thing is,' he said.

I said, 'I don't think we can keep living our lives as though Mum's just going to step back through the door. Can we?'

Dad studied me, hunting for a clue, a cue. He was a hair's breadth away from telling me not to speak so heartlessly. My chest was heavy, and heaving with the need to scream my confession in his face.

'Of course,' he said, 'I'll have to sell the hotel.'

I stared at him. 'The hotel?'

'This new job, it's a long way away and it doesn't pay very well.' He made a sound like a laugh. 'It doesn't pay well at all. And to afford it – well ...'

'But my exams—'

'Oh,' he said, 'that's all sorted.'

'It is?'

'You can go stay with Michel,' he said.

SIXTEEN

'**O**f course I remember your mother.'
Bryon Vaux's office is as sumptuous as a living room, with a fire in the grate and a decanter of brandy at my elbow.

'Sara.' He casts his blindsighted eyes into the middle-distance. 'I remember the soap she made. It made us feel so almighty hungry!'

Coconut, honey and beeswax scrub. God help me, it is him. There is no mistake.

Eventually, I find the strength to come out with it. What I saw. The railway station. The platform. The figure there. Albino-white hair. A canvas bag. Gabby found the records. The dates match up. There is no longer any doubt. No wriggle room. No avoidance.

'And you're sure it was me? I did have a canvas bag like

that. A big canvas bag. I remember it. The station, though – I mean I remember the rail station, but heading off on my last day …' He shakes his head. 'Man, it's more than twenty years ago, I can't remember something like that.'

'Of course you can't. Of course. Forget about it.'

He cannot forget about it. 'Sara. I remember her.' He remembers whole conversations with her – conversations I never knew they'd had. Sara wasn't an easy person. Not an outgoing person. Yet Vaux remembers her rooms: the gauzy scarves she'd throw over every surface. Her day-bed, and under it, bag after bag of unopened paints. 'I always thought it was a shame, the way – hell, do you mind me saying this? The way her gears kept slipping.'

Who is he, that he remembers these things? *What was he doing in her rooms?*

When we're done Vaux comes out with me, sees me to the atrium, and there, in time for his next appointment, sits Michel.

He looks different. Bigger. His face is weathered. He sees me and smiles, but it is not an easy smile. He walks over. 'Conrad. Hi.' He shakes my hand – an odd formality, but it's not the gesture that surprises me so much as the feel of Michel's palm. The skin is rough and broken. After ten years tapping and stroking glass, he has once again been working with his hands.

'Well, you know each other,' Vaux exclaims. 'Of course. Mick, you're a dark horse, keeping this guy under your hat.'

'Conrad?' Michel looks at me. 'What's there to hide? He's an idiot.'

'This idiot has built the best damned AR platform my R&R people have ever seen.'

219

There's a deal more of this bullshit to weather before Vaux bears Michel off to his roaring real fire and VSOP hospitality.

Before the week is out, Bryon Vaux calls to tell me he has hired a private detective to gather all surviving records relating to my mother's disappearance. Is this a blind – a means of distracting me from my suspicions about him?

Or is this simply what he does? This is, after all, what makes him who he is, and makes him as successful as he is. He digs and digs and digs, living out the lives of others, so that he can eventually realise them in light and sound.

I am his research project. Perhaps I am his next script.

There are veterans working the city's bars and clubs: soldiers invalided out of the service. Land-mine victims. Purple hearts with missing limbs. Metal hands and carbon fibre feet. Chrome women. Cat women. Upright, tall, fast, oh, so desirable.

She says, 'What do you want me to do?'

I tell her, 'Take your lenses out.'

She smiles as she undresses. 'No.' Small, hard breasts and black plastic straps wound round her legs, and carbon fibre blades for feet. Dead eyes. 'Not that.'

In the clubs, even the dancers have silver eyes. I suppose that for them it is a kind of clothing. What they find to watch behind their lenses I cannot imagine. When I first paid my money and went inside one of these places and saw all those eyeless people, the dead-eyed, the seceded, I couldn't bear it. I walked straight out again.

I've hardened up since.

'Conrad.'

Bryon Vaux is sat at a table near the door. This is not the first time I've run into him in a place like this, and there is no escaping him now. His lead-eyed smile. His teeth. His hands. He hugs me. I know these hands, this pressure, this smell. I have been here before.

He lets me go and his silver lenses glitter in the neon of the bar. He says, 'A funny carry-on, this is.'

Vaux's easiness around sex – his transparent appetite for all this thigh and tit – is faintly clinical. We watch a while as a dancer works the end of the bar. A tall Japanese. Her steel-lensed eyes, so cold, so anonymous, are a protection for her. However exposed she is to our gaze, yet she remains in her private world. What is she watching? What does she know that we don't?

'How did we seem to you?'

Vaux's question takes me by surprise.

'It must have been strange. No? When you were growing up. To be surrounded by the blind?'

Vaux's willingness to discuss the hotel rubs so very badly up against what I remember of him – his bright hair and brute and shuttered face, his fly, his erection. Why can I not simply confront him with what I remember? Even a flat denial would be a relief. As Gabby would say, 'Just talk to him. Idiot.'

But while my mother's death remains a mystery, I cannot talk to him about it. Who wraps a bag around their own head? Who locks themselves in the boot of a car to die? Mum was on her way to the protest camp. She was happy. Vaux was there on the platform with her. The next day she was dead. There is no reason – no reason at all, that I can see – to suspect Vaux of Mum's murder. His present behaviour flatly contradicts the idea. And yet.

I rack my head for anecdotes – anything to defuse this moment. I remember coming home to the hotel with Michel one afternoon and finding the floor of the conservatory strewn with pornography. I can't help but smile, telling Vaux about this. The innocence of it, and the weirdness. My comically eccentric dad and his madcap experiments.

Vaux doesn't laugh. He remembers this. 'We were loudly disappointed,' he says, with a bitterness, an undercurrent of anger I have not heard before. Once again, I am afraid of him. This smiling man. This middle-aged man with his open demeanour and his open chequebook. There is, after all, a darkness here. A core of anger. Not towards me. Not towards Mum.

Towards Dad.

'He pissed us off.' Vaux tries to laugh. He's trapped inside a tale he does not want to tell. It reveals too much of him. But it's too late to back out now. 'We were angry with him.'

'Yes?'

'Well.' He tries to shrug this off. But the memory has come to the surface, and will not be supressed. 'Those vests. Now they seem so crude, of course, but then—' He stares into the distance with his plastic eyes, his man-made retinas. Technology – how it marches on! No one wears a vest these days. 'To read a road sign. To watch TV! Simple stuff, but your dad's vests, his inventions made us feel whole again. We were so pleased to be able to move around a room again and not fall over stuff! And then your dad comes up and rips our balls off.'

'What?'

'Do you know he wrote up that pissy little experiment

of his? I've read it. It's written in this weird, floaty, I'm-not-really-responsible kind of language, but basically it says there's a minimum optical resolution to lust. Pixellate filth too far and the erotic impulse will fail. And you know what?' His hand clamps tight upon my arm. A strong hand. '*Daddy was wrong.*'

He grins. His steel eyes rake the room. 'Look.' Around us table dancers flaunt their curves, their youth, their health, their missing limbs. 'The other guys, the grunts, they'd already had girls. Those poor blind slobs knew what they were no longer seeing. I didn't. When my eyes were stole from me, I'd never even touched a girl. You know that? Never touched one. Never seen.'

'How old were you?'

'Fuck off.' He laughs. 'Fuck off. A virgin, anyway. I was a virgin. A Bible Belt innocent. I hadn't got a clue.'

Of his blinding, he says little. There is little to be said. There are international laws against blinding soldiers on the battlefield, but some armies do not care about such laws. Even those who do care have found ways around the rules of engagement. You can fire a laser at a targeting system – and you can miss.

'So, afterwards,' he says, 'after your dad proved I would never get excited that way, I headed into town. Bought magazines. With the vest I could see well enough to find a newsagent's, but not well enough to see the titties on the covers. I just had to reach for the top shelf and pray.'

A dirty story. He laughs. 'I studied those pictures. I mean, really *studied* them.' He stares into his empty glass. The music dies. The girls retire. The lights come on, flattening everything. Closing time. 'You do that often enough,' he says, 'appetite will do the rest.'

The thing about low-resolution vision, he says, as we climb the stairs back to street level, is that everything looks pretty much like everything else. 'A box is a book is an oil can is a picture in a frame.' He's drunk, and he wants to be understood. 'You see.' He sweeps his hand across the street. 'I see them everywhere now. Everywhere. Always have. Right now. Naked women. Buttocks raised. Cunts dripping. The works.'

'Goodnight, Bryon.'

'Everywhere. Shadows beneath a table. Fuck your AR – my head's got better pictures in it than you'll ever know.'

'Goodnight.'

'Light playing on bathwater.'

'Bryon. Let go.'

'A flag snapping in the wind. This place— Jesus, look around!'

He's hanging off my coat, hardly able to stand. Just how much has he had to drink?

There's the predictable mix of tourists and business people on the pavements, tottering around, blank-eyed, purblind, their movements choreographed by in-eye software that's more conscious of the real world than they are themselves. 'Look at them! Look!'

What is he seeing? This man who has had to assemble his own erotics by himself, from twenty pixels and a prayer? Where is this flesh he sees, this thigh, lip, arse, neck, tit?

'Let me get you a taxi.'

'Fuck you.'

'Come on, Bryon. It's late.'

'Fuck you, I know what you think.' He digs in his pockets suddenly and for a brief moment I have this crazy idea that he's going to pull out a gun. But no, it's his wallet. He waves it open. Jesus.

'Bryon, you're going to get us mugged.'

'Ha!' He pulls out a business card. He shoves it in my face. 'I know what you think, Connie, and fuck you, so I made a mistake. But they're here.' He stinks of whisky and fear. 'They're here if you know how to look.'

I wave down a taxi for him and settle with the driver in advance. God knows, Vaux is hardly capable now. I get him snapped into his seat and swing the door shut on him. The taxi U-turns and disappears. I set off home on foot. In my hand is the card Vaux gave me. I pause under a streetlight to read.

'AMBER' and a number.

Since these silvered contact lenses became the fashion I have been succumbing, more and more often, to a skin-crawling hunger for human contact. With the sale of Loophole, and the contract I have signed, I have the leisure now, as well as the money, to indulge myself. But the act, however well choreographed, cannot assuage this longing I have for someone, anyone, just to look me in the eye.

I wonder: does Amber wear lenses?

They're here if you know where to look.

What the hell did Vaux mean by that? There is only one way to find out. I hold my phone in front of the card, and it reads and dials the number.

Without love, lust blooms. It slides about, fixating on the strange, the wild.

But I am, after all, just like everyone else, wielding my disappointments like a club. I talk and expect her to listen. I grumble and expect her to comfort me.

Amber. Her answering service said, 'Hi, I am a genuine young independent homegrown escort, twenty-nine. Size twelve to fourteen, natural 36F. I can provide a sensuous massage or something more. I'm a normal, everyday, sane kind of person who enjoys a chat to put you at ease – if you want to chat, that is.'

So much for revelation, or a deepening mystery. Though the address, when finally she gave it out, was better than her prices suggested and the house, when the taxi drew up outside, was so big, so white, so ostentatious, I was convinced Vaux had played a joke on me.

A light by the bell said AMBER, so I pressed. And now I'm here. Amber is nice. Not pretty, not passionate, not hardbitten either, not high, not drunk. Not afraid. Just as she described herself, in fact.

The room, though! The room is palatial – but virtually empty. A bed pulled away from the wall. A chair. A mirror. Cameras.

Amber reaches for my hand. I take it and stand close to her. Close enough to smell her hair. Close enough to feel her breathe. She leans back and I kiss her. I take hold of her hair and pull. She arches her back. I run my hand over her breasts and she opens her mouth under mine.

She says, 'Let me do something for you.'

She has a specialism. Well, what the hell.

She takes off all her clothes. Her shoes. Her belt. Her little dress. Her tights. Her strapless bra. Her knickers. She drops them on the floor. She slips her shoes back on. 'Is this all right?'

'Yes,' I tell her. 'It's all right.'

She kneels to fasten the buckles. I stare into the shadows her legs make. She stands and walks around the bed. I come over and sit on the bed and as she passes me I run my hand over her flank. She comes around again. My fingers brush her buttocks. After a while of this, I stop her. She kisses me and I reach between her legs.

'I want to do something for you.'

My fingers come away wet. 'Okay.'

'I want to wear some things.'

'Okay.'

She pulls them out from under the mattress. A baggy long-sleeved sweatshirt in Chroma key green. Gloves and a pillow case the same. The sweatshirt has a cord to tighten it at the waist. She slips it over her head. The gloves are long, velveteen, big enough to hide her wrists, even when she raises her arms above her head. I shake out the pillow case.

'Put it on,' she says. 'Go on.'

I arrange the pillowcase over her head and pull the hood of her sweatshirt over it.

I cross to the chair and sit down, watching her hips, groin and legs move around the bed.

The rest of her has vanished.

The illusion is perfect. The legs step around the bed, deadly and elegant as scissors.

'Wait.'

She stops for me. I get up from my chair and walk towards her, curious. The closer I come to her, the clearer I can see the obvious and unavoidable glitch. The system has somehow to fill in the body cavity where the girl's hips leave off and her sweatshirt begins. The wireframe flickers and bends as she breathes – an irregular ellipsis of gridded grey. I stroke the line of her sex. Her small high buttocks, divorced from the curve of her back, are startling in their roundness and power. Her legs tremble as she balances with feet apart, moving against my hand. I feel for the nub of her anus and push a finger inside her, all the while gazing into the blind grey mathematics of her body cavity.

The standard fills are just a blink away. The girl's body cavity fills with water; instantly I feel my penis engorge. I push my finger deeper into her, stirring the waters there. She groans and bends over, tipping the water away from me. The system isn't encumbered with much in the way of physics – the watery plane simply tips with her hips, held in place by the gravitational pull of her groin.

'Conrad.' The voice comes out of nowhere. It excites me, this disembodied voice so close to my ear, and this extraordinary sexual contraption, at waist-height before me. It stands no higher than my waist. This is what I can't quite get over: how small she is, reduced to arse and hips and legs. No taller than a child. A cunt and its complicated docking mechanism.

'Conrad, I want to do something now.'

'What?'

'I want you to take your clothes off and lie down.'

I undress, and the legs settle on the bed, facing me. They spread apart. 'I'm taking off a glove.'

A hand appears. Disembodied, heartbreakingly small, it settles, fluttering, on her sex. A finger uncurls – the tongue of a humming bird – and seeks her clitoris. Her sex is so wet it shines. Her legs flex, lifting her feet off the mattress, parting to reveal her sex more clearly. Her cunt flexes, ensnaring her fingers, chewing on them. Her legs flail like mouthparts. I close my eyes, afraid, listening to her come.

A disembodied hand. Oh God. The other glove comes off. Now there are two. Two white hands, hanging there in space, working at her flesh, feasting on it. 'God.'

I hunch forward, clamber to my feet.

'Are you all right?'

The legs right themselves. They snap and rise upon their feet and scythe towards me. I stare at them: the swell and tremble of calves and thighs, up and up to their folded junction. I run.

Beyond the room the house is a wreck, all brick and plasterboard. It's deserted. There's usually at least a minder in these places, but there's no-one. I'm alone with her. Alone. I can't remember where she said the bathroom is.

'Hello?' She's coming after me. Poor cow. Still trying to do her job. Probably wondering what shitty review I'm going to give her on what shitty website.

'I'm fine. I just need – I'm fine.'

Very late – stupidly late – it occurs to me to take off my glasses. Without my glasses, the illusion that so frightens me will be broken, and in place of Mandy's white clown hands there will just be some plain, industrious, vulnerable girl in a hoodie chasing after me. Too late, stupidly late, as my fingers brush my face, I remember that I have no spectacles today. I'm wearing lenses now. I can't just pluck them out.

A small, uncertain voice: 'Do you need the bathroom, love?'

If I keep my back to her, I can imagine her as she really is. Whole. Complete. Her voice, after all, is coming from the right height. A normal human voice that says, 'It's the door on your right.'

'I'll be a minute.'

There's a toilet. A bidet. The sink is as big as a shower tray. The mirror, decorated with a cut-glass border, fills the entire wall – how in hell did they ever get it in here? It dawns on me that nothing I am seeing need be real. I blink up the preferences pane on my lenses and hunt for Force Quit but it's buried away in the menus and already Amber's calling through the door. 'Are we done, then?' She tries to sound disappointed but she can't keep the shiver out of her voice. It's freezing out here.

'For God's sake go put something on.'

She stalks off, her absurd heels clattering the tiled hall. What was this place? Some grandee's mansion. What's she doing here?

She's probably taken offence now. They do so easily, these women, their antennae cocked to detect the slightest hint of disrespect. What is it about working in the sex industry makes people want to be taken so bloody seriously?

In the bathroom mirror, my eyes glitter back at me. These lenses strip all the life from them. However did they catch on? I look like a cheap doll. A doll with my mother's face.

Look at my face! It only ever took a little make-up, a few strokes of sponge and brush, and Mum and I looked exactly alike. I was her maquette. In four years I will be forty – the age Sara was when she died. The resemblance has not gone away. If anything, it has grown stronger.

'Fuck you, so I made a mistake.'

He made a mistake, all right. A bloody big mistake.

I lean against the sink, my head buzzing.

I remember Vaux standing before me, his hand on the

230

back of my head, his erection white and hard and as long as a dagger.

Vaux.

Vaux set this up for me. Vaux the rich man, the businessman. Of course the house is big. Why not? *It is his house.*

I bend double over the bowl. Wrong bowl. Bidet. Christ. It's suddenly all so bloody obvious. What, after all, did that young, blindsighted invalid see when he saw me, in the murk and leafy confusion of the lane behind the hotel?

He saw Mum.

'Good afternoon.' And his hand worked at his fly and his erection slid into the light.

Vaux, blindsighted, navigating his crudely pixellated world, had never intended to assault me. It wasn't me he pushed onto his knees, or made obey him in the dirt and weeds of a clearing marked out by rusting white goods. In Vaux's mind it was Mum he forced that day. Or not even forced. Played with. Enjoyed. For all I know, it was a game they had played before. (Gabby said, 'Who knows what your mum got up to?')

Later, of course, the truth must have come out, which is why Vaux quit the hotel.

And on the platform of our quiet railway station, as he waited for his train, who did he see standing beside him?

Mum?

No.

Someone like her, but—

Heavy boots. Shorn hair. ('You feel like a man,' I'd said to her, pulling away for the last time.)

Vaux mistook her for me!

What happened then? At what point did Vaux realise he had mistaken us again – taken mother for son as, weeks earlier, he had taken son for mother?

Was it Vaux watching me that night, as I pushed my mother's corpse into the waters rushing by the mill? Who else could it have been?

Click-clack.

'Are you done in there?'

Abruptly, painfully, I come to. 'Yes, Poppy.'

'What?' Amber rattles the doorknob.

Oh, Jesus Christ. '*Amber.* Yes, Amber. I mean. Yes.'

'Because I need a shit.'

I'm at the flat and half-undressed, shedding my clothes as I go and desperate for sleep, when I hear sounds from the study.

I have a study in my apartment. A glorified name for it. When did I last study? I spend my life answering emails. I swing the door open, fast as I can, less to surprise the intruder as to force my own hand; it would be so easy to bottle it and sneak away.

He is sitting at my desk. Dark suit, dark shirt, no tie. Sandy hair. A smoker's face – a rarity these days. Burst blood vessels in his nose. Kind eyes, and hands like hams. The desk, the floor and every available surface are smothered in papers, scattered folders, spilt plastic wallets, and this is strange, because I don't remember storing so much paper in here. There's more paper thrown about this room than I thought I owned.

He's very confident, whoever the hell he is. He scuds a vast pink hand through the air before him, by way of hello.

'What are you doing?'

'You won't find anything missing.'

'Who are you?'

He stretches his legs, puts his hands behind his head and flexes the knots out of his back. He wants me to see how big he is. 'Cobb. Adam Cobb.'

'You get what you wanted?'

'There was nothing to get.'

I think about this. Once I've got my breath back, it's not hard to figure out the elements of this. 'Vaux sent you.'

Cobb smiles, showing even, yellow teeth. 'Vaux sent me.'

'He should be more careful about how he goes about threatening people.'

'Yes?'

'You're in a world of shit, mate.'

'Why? Are you going to do something?'

'It's already done.'

Cobb's smile widens. 'You mean your cameras?'

I bite my lip.

'It's all right. They're still running. They're still streaming. Do they talk to the police, or to a private security firm? Nice installation, anyway. Can't be too careful, nowadays.'

'Was Amber part of this?'

'Who?'

'Amber. Kept me entertained tonight while you've been smashing up my flat. Vaux's girl. One of many, I'd guess.'

Cobb shrugs. 'I don't doubt that. You want to sit down? I promise you I'm not going to do anything.'

'Get out of my house.'

'In a minute. First, there's something I have to say.'

'Out.'

'Mr Vaux accepts that in the past he was responsible for certain misunderstandings.'

'What?'

'He wants you to know that he regrets any upset following certain compromising episodes. I'm referring here to his stay at your father's hotel. I think we can both agree that these events took place a very long time ago.'

'Are you his thief or his lawyer?'

'I'm his private detective.'

'Tell Vaux I don't know what he's talking about.'

'All that aside, Mr Vaux takes his digital privacy very seriously indeed. You're presumably aware that his medical records, in particular, are off-limits, and attempting to access them is—' At this point Cobb runs out of quasi-legal steam. 'Well, it's illegal, isn't it?'

My blood runs a little colder. 'You want to tell me exactly what I am supposed to have done to deserve this visit?'

Cobb waves the question away. 'You get the visit. Your university friend gets a string of strongly worded emails. She's fine. Her job is fine – if she desists. But you do not set your friends digging around in Vaux's medical files.'

So this is what this is about. Gabby, or Gabby's graduate student, has snapped a tripwire somewhere in their search. 'These misunderstandings—'

Cobb stands. 'You'll be getting a letter in a couple of days setting out the details of Mr Vaux's proposed no-blame settlement. He regrets any upset, he says.'

I don't know what to say to this.

At last Cobb takes pity on me. 'I assume this has to do with his knob. This is what it usually boils down to.'

His knob. Christ. '*So I made a mistake.*' Vaux thinks I'm after him for a spot of rough fellatio on the river path. 'He thinks I'm trying to *sue* him? I'm not trying to *sue* him, for crying out loud. Do I look like a goosed secretary?'

But Cobb is losing interest now I'm up to speed. 'Have your lawyer look over the settlement if you want, but we need your reply and a signed copy of our NDA by noon Monday.'

This is monstrous. 'He's *paying* me?'

'He's trying to swat whatever bee in your bonnet made you think you could dig through his personal medical data. Frankly, it's cheaper to pay you off than have to listen to you. Clear?'

Vaux is afraid of having his dick made a tabloid head-line. It doesn't seem to have entered his head that I am pursuing the mystery of my mother's death.

The thing is, if Vaux really did kill Mum, how did he manage to get her body into the boot of our car?

'So are we clear?'

'You shouldn't have broken in.'

Cobb smiles. I don't know what it is about that smile unlocks the rage in me but suddenly I'm lurching for-ward, fists clenched, furious. 'You want I show you the trouble you're in?'

'Try it.' He sees me hesitate, smiles – and disappears. Vanishes. One moment he is sitting in my living room. The next moment – nothing.

The cameras I have mounted round my flat – my household insurance policy requires them – will reveal nothing, because there is nothing for them to reveal. Cobb, whoever Cobb was, was never here. I have been talking to the air.

The room has flipped back to normal. It is as clean and tidy as I left it. There are no papers anywhere.

Nothing has been touched.

SEVENTEEN

Midway through Easter break, Michel turned up at the hotel to help me carry my bags over to Sand Lane.

I had been living alone since school broke up. Dad was already off working for his private clinic. How typical of Dad that, having invented a way for blind servicemen to see, and all but set up a clinic in his home, he should now be doing the same work, at the other end of the country, at some other person's beck and call, for a pittance.

The sale of the hotel was due to go through any day. How this could even be legal baffled me. It meant that the business, the property, the chattels, everything must have been made out in my father's sole name. Yet it had been Sara's family money that had paid for the place. Perhaps Dad realised from the very beginning that Mum was not to be trusted with the family's finances. And, looking at this the other way, perhaps Sara had been right all along about Dad's oppression of her, and his will to control.

How and when Dad made his arrangements with Poppy, I never knew. The only time I remember him and Poppy ever meeting was when we ran into her in the supermarket, a few days after Sara's disappearance became public knowledge.

She came up to us at the checkout and, in heavy tones, she had said that if ever there was anything she could do for us, we had only to ask. She'd never shown the slightest interest in us before. 'Now call me,' she said.

Now we had this gimcrack arrangement whereby I would stay with Poppy and Michel until the end of the school year. Picture Michel and me, studying for our exams, elbow to elbow in those cupboard-sized rooms, deep in the heart of that housing estate I could not stand. What Poppy made of this arrangement – why she ever suggested it – is a mystery I have never been able to fathom.

Poppy's front garden was even more doll-like than its neighbours. Nothing had been permitted to grow above waist height. It was the garden of someone grown suspicious of life's potential. The back garden was more or less a mirror image of the front: dwarf conifers and heathers, and an anaemic-yellow lawn so close-mown, so fine-bladed, you could see the earth beneath.

The back door was open. The kitchen smelled of detergent. Poppy sat reading a library book – a collection of humorous newspaper columns. She saved her place with a tasselled plastic bookmark and stood to greet me. 'I'll show you the house.' She couldn't have freighted the process with more dignity if she'd been leading me around a stately home.

'This is the master bedroom.'

What was I supposed to say?

'This is the living room.'

When Poppy spoke, it was always at the shrill end of her register, as though she was pleading in her own defence.

'This is the kitchen. And this is where you came in.' Did she imagine the tour had disorientated me?

We ate in the kitchen, squatting on chrome stools upholstered in black vinyl. The stools were old. Their leather-look texture had worn off and they were as slippy to sit on as if they had been oiled. The table was worse – a chipboard thing, laminated in frictionless wood-effect plastic. It was the kind of table you get in caravans. It was attached to the wall. You let it down by pulling a handle.

Poppy laid out matching cutlery. Glasses. Cups. Cake knives. There was barely any room for food. 'I've made you a cream tea.' There was a freezer-cabinet cream cake. Dry, feathery home-made scones with cream. A fruit salad with cream in a jug. Everything in tiny portions.

Poppy had laid out plastic laminated place-mats for us, and our plates moved about on them while we were eating. Watching me, Poppy's anxiety reached fever pitch – she was afraid I might place too much weight on the table's mechanism. 'Please don't lean on the table. Don't put anything heavy on the table. It's a let-down!'

I was more concerned with trying to keep my arse on the stool. I kept slipping off, trying to reach things as they spun away from me across the table's ice-smooth surface.

Afterwards I buzzed from all the sugar I had eaten, and the back of my mouth felt fluey, clotted with uncooked flour.

'We should have eaten outside! In the garden! It's such a nice evening. We could have eaten outside!'

She insisted on washing up. 'I know where everything goes.' Michel and I went into his bedroom and he dug out a cassette tape for us to listen to. We sat on his bed. It was incredibly narrow. 'It's a two-foot six.' Poppy came in to put clothes away.

She gave Michel no privacy at all. How could there have been much privacy, in a space as cramped as this? Michel's room was as long and narrow as the living space on board a yacht. There was a fluorescent tube in the ceiling, and its grey, pitiless light brought the walls in even further. It felt, sitting in that room, like being squashed into a Tupperware box.

I remember there was this weird, wood-effect plastic panel that went around the wall. 'It's to stop the bed from marking the wall,' Michel explained.

'What's the problem with the bed marking the wall?'

'Mum doesn't want it to.'

'The bed's in the way. She's never going to know whether it's marking the wall or not.'

Michel's bed ran lengthways along the left-hand wall. His desk, narrow as a shelf and veneered in wood-effect plastic, ran lengthways along the right-hand wall. There was a cupboard to the right of the door, which, instead of opening normally, slid along metal runners 'to save space'. Michel's bedroom door, the let-down table in the kitchen, the shelf-like desk and the sofa in the living room, its seat so narrow it might have been built for children, were all parts of Poppy's on-going programme to single-handedly 'save space'. (Poppy's talk was modular, a collection of preprocessed jargon phrases strung together. After a few days of this, everything she said began to acquire a meaning beyond itself, like a word repeated so often it turns strange in the mouth.)

Poppy burst into Michel's room whenever she felt like it. Or she tried to. If you leant against Michel's wardrobe, it slipped on the thin nylon carpet (sick-green cobwebs on a ground of darker green) and blocked the door. The bang the door made when it hit the edge of the wardrobe was startlingly loud.

'Oh! Mind the paintwork! Come and move the wardrobe!'

When the wardrobe was in the way the door could only open a couple of inches. Poppy did her best to peer through the gap. Her eye hung in the darkness of the hall, disembodied. An eye without a face. 'Are you all right in there, you two?'

At night I slept in Michel's room, on a camp bed that had once been his dad's. It was made of canvas, stretched over a tubular steel frame. It was comfortable, but if I needed the toilet in the middle of the night, there was no room for me to just roll out of the bed. (I tried it once and cracked my head on the edge of the desk and ended up stuck under the desk, tangled up in the legs of Michel's bright orange tubular steel chair.) Instead I had to shimmy down to the foot of the bed until it tipped up on end.

The sliding door rattled when I opened it.

'Are you all right?'

'I'm fine.'

241

'What's going on out there?'

'I'm going to the toilet, Poppy. I'm fine.'

The lavatory and the bathroom were separate rooms. The lavatory door had a lock and a key, and Poppy kept the key on the outside of the door. Not on the inside, so you could guarantee your privacy, but on the outside, so she could leave the lavatory window open when she went out and still secure the house. Anyway, this is what she said. It's just as likely she locked Michel in the lavatory as a punishment, or used to, before I turned up. Certainly that's what it looked like.

The toilet pan sat under a small, high window. Sitting on the pan, I was just a couple of inches short of being able to lean my head on the door.

'Is everything all right?'

Back in the bedroom, Michel was awake, sitting up in bed, waiting for me. I leant against his wardrobe, slipping it into the path of the door.

We waited, listening for movement. He pulled the sheets away. It took my eyes, still dazzled from the lavatory light, some minutes to adapt. Michel was already hard. His hand was on his prick, moving a little, as he watched me standing there, framed against the white gloss of his little wardrobe, a child's wardrobe – you could still make out the silhouette of the plastic bunnies that once deco-rated its doors. He watched me slip off my T, watched me slip off my pants. I was just as hard as he was. Starlight sheened his thighs, his arms, his prick. Light glistened round the dark bulb of his prick, I wanted to touch it. More. I dared, that night, what I had not dared before. Fingers to my mouth, the salt there, good. I bent my head and felt his hands in my hair, bringing me down, his prick, so beautiful, rigid in the little light – ribbed and veined and very salt.

A bang.

A disembodied eye.

'Is everything all right?'

EIGHTEEN

Ralf, too, has taken to wearing AR-enabled contact lenses. There is something cold, something faintly repulsive about them. They are supposed to make Augmented Reality more appealing. And they do, in a twisted, self-fulfilling way, by making ordinary human communication just a touch less pleasant. It's hard to read a person's face when you can't read the pupils of their eyes.

Eventually it occurs to him to ask, 'So what are you doing, Conrad?'

I have signed an agreement locking me out of Augmented Reality for eighteen months following Loophole's sale. Perhaps I will go back to it. Perhaps not. The whole business has begun to unnerve me. It's not the same now that the old dev crowd has dispersed.

I took Ralf to task over Bryon Vaux's party trick. It didn't even occur to him to apologise. Vaux had given him the impression that the trick was by way of professional joshing. I couldn't make Ralf understand that Cobb – whoever he was, private detective or actor or pure avatar – had frightened me.

Ralf said to me – he actually said this – 'You have to bear in mind the difference the new superconductors have made to how we deploy inductive video.'

What he meant was: there is technology out there now that can hijack the optic nerve. No glasses necessary. No lenses. A strong enough magnetic field, well-shaped, bends a mind to the desired shape. The equipment they'd used to have Cobb 'visit' me that night – I never found it. Either the devices were too small to spot, or more likely their energies had been directed at me from a distance. A van parked in the street. The house opposite. If you can do that, you can warp any part of the real. Reality has been aerosolised, the senses weaponised against us. Every sensation is Muzak now.

'Who was Cobb?'

'Who was who?' Ralf didn't know or care what kind of stunt Vaux had pulled on me. And by then I was fed up. Ralf wasn't curious, and I wasn't in the mood to try to shake his complacency. Moral issues never trouble Ralf's type much – for them, all questions have a technical solution.

Now Ralf is back in the lab where he feels most comfortable: a backroom boy. Beneath the puffery he has acquired – Bryon Vaux's Chief Imagineer – he's still his old self.

He showed me round. Right now he's working on a

full prosthesis platform: a thin exoskeleton that will do you the favour of punching you in the stomach when a villainous avatar takes a swing at you. That will trip you over if you miss that virtual step. That will shake your hand. Kiss you. Slap your back for a level well completed. God knows what.

The metro takes me home. I'm back in the old locomotive factory again – third time lucky, I suppose. I walk past a line of parked cars, studiously ignoring the horn blasts – it's best to keep yourself to yourself on these streets – but the voice is unmistakably Agnes's. 'Connie! Over here!'

Hanna climbs from the driver's seat. She looks exhausted. She shuts her door and leans against it as I approach. Agnes is still strapped into her seat in the back. She waves out her window frantically – a little kidnap victim. 'Conrad! We were waiting for you!'

'How long have you been out here?'

'Not long.'

'We've been *ages*,' Agnes cries. 'Ages and *ages*!'

'Hello, Han.'

'Hello, Connie.' She seizes my fingers and squeezes them, reminding me of the lack of human contact in my life.

'Hanna. You should have phoned.'

'I lost your number.'

'Mick has my number. What?'

Hanna rubs at her temples. 'Can we come in?'

I lead them up to my new apartment on the second storey. It's not ideal here. It's noisy, for a start, though warmer than the rooftop rooms I've had before. 'There's not a lot in here.'

'We've eaten, thanks.'

'I had a kebab! It was disgusting!'

Hanna wants to talk – which is a novelty in itself – but Agnes gets first dibs on my attention. She has lengthened out. She has acquired a whole new set of mannerisms to lay on top of the first set. She is going to be a monster when she's older. Suddenly the mannerisms fall away and she might be years younger as she asks, 'Can I play on your keyboard?'

'Use the headphones.'

'Okay! Where is it?'

'The other room. There's only one other room. If it's not the toilet, then you're in the right room.'

Agnes goes off giggling.

'So?'

Hanna visibly summons up strength and says, 'Michel and I are separating.'

There is nothing I can say to this. I start preparing coffee.

'We've been in a bad place for a long while,' she says.

Strange, the way geography creeps in to these announcements. 'We were in a bad place.' 'I needed my space.' Strange and tiresome. 'What did he do?'

Hanna ignores my attempt to cut through to the blame. 'Michel's very upset about things.'

'I tried telling you that last Christmas.'

Hanna looks at me as though I were speaking a foreign language.

'Remember?'

'No,' she says. 'I don't. Anyway. I don't know whether he told you, but his mum died last week.'

Just dropped in there – another unfortunate event.

'Poppy *died*?'

'He went to sort out the funeral.'

'When is it?'

'It was yesterday.'

'Oh.' The pot starts to hiss and bubble. I lift it off the plate. 'Thanks for telling me.'

'I'm sorry, Connie. It wasn't up to me. I didn't go either. I was looking after Agnes.'

'Agnes didn't go?'

Hanna shakes her head. 'Mick didn't think it was such a good idea.'

'Right. How do you take this?'

'Milk.'

I faff around for a while. 'I would have liked to have been there.'

'Yes?'

'I would have gone.' I never liked Poppy very much but there was something admirable about her. While Dad was tearing himself free and unable to cope with me, she had given me a home. I would have liked to pay my respects.

'Anyway.' Hanna takes a seat at the table. 'He's stayed on in Sand Lane to sort out her things.'

'Right. Jesus, Hanna.'

'I know. It all comes at once, doesn't it?'

I go and glance round the door. Agnes is on the piano stool, earphones cupped round her head like muffs, bopping away to the piano's demo track.

I close the kitchen door behind me and sit down facing Hanna.

'It's about Agnes,' she says.

'I thought it might be.'

'We were trying for a second child.'

'I see.'

'Mick's found out that he's not – he can't have kids. He never could have kids.'

'She's mine.'

Hanna stares at me.

'Yes? Agnes is mine.'

'You knew?'

'Of course I knew. Look at her.'

'Jesus Christ, Conrad, and you never said?'

It's my turn to stare.

'You never said a word!'

'Hanna, I tried. Plus, it's blindingly obvious.'

'I don't believe this.'

'Hanna, I'm not the one keeping secrets.'

'I don't bloody believe you.'

This is probably not the moment to remind Hanna of all the occasions she has slipped from the room, or hung off Michel's arm, or brought Agnes along 'for the ride', or closed the door on me – 'Goodnight, Conrad.' Over the years she has deployed the entire arsenal of avoidance against me.

'You didn't exactly make it easy for me to say anything.'

'Anyway.' She drinks her coffee. 'Obviously we're going to need to be together in some fashion. For Agnes. Mick's a great dad. It's the last thing I want, to keep him from his child.'

'I still don't see why you're both making such a production out of it.'

She stares at me like I've crawled from under a rock. 'Can you not see …?'

'I can see you playing up to every soap cliché, is what I can see. Agnes is nearly in big school, for crying out loud.

Her genes are playing out in the world. They're her genes now. Not yours, not mine. You're not telling me Mick can't see this? I know he has a temper but for Christ's sake.'

'It's not the only problem between us. It's all come together, is the thing. This. Poppy. When did you last see Mick?'

'It's a while.' Was it as long ago as my interview with Bryon Vaux? 'A year, easily. He's always in the summerhouse when I pick Agnes up—'

Catching Hanna's eye, I realise now that this has been a lie. An excuse. He has not wanted to see me. The business of Agnes's parentage has been eating away at them a long time.

'Mick's been going absent a lot lately.'

'Is there anyone?'

'I don't think so.' Hanna sounds almost disappointed. 'I don't think it's that. Anyway, I thought you might know where he went.'

'You don't?'

'He says it's a secret. Something he's working on. A surprise for us. To be honest, Conrad, I'm not sure he's well.'

There's a more practical reason why Hanna has come into town – an appointment at the eye hospital. It's nothing serious; only that, after years of fighting with uncomfortable contact lenses and a constantly changing prescription, Hanna has decided to have her corneas shaved to a better shape. Since she's going in for the op, she figures she will have AR layers annealed in at the same time. It's expensive, but the resolution is very good, far better than anything the unadorned eye can achieve.

'How do you turn it off?'

'Oh, Conrad.'

'How do you turn it off?'

'They teach you all sorts of ways of controlling the layers. Blinks and glances. You know.'

'Okay,' I say, in my most not-okay voice.

'Honestly Conrad,' Hanna laughs, 'I thought this was your kind of thing.'

It was. It really was. First vests, then wraprounds, then lenses, and now this. But there is a difference between a product, something you have to go out and find, and a utility, something sewn in, something so integral to you that you barely notice it unless it goes wrong. AR can only ever work as a utility. Hanna knew this years ago. She teased me about it, practically the day I met her. And she told me that in the end, it was not good, if AR became what it always had to become – a kind of Muzak, smoothing and glamorising the real.

Even as I have come around to her way of thinking, however, she has come around to mine. 'I just don't see the harm in it,' she says.

Agnes is tucked up in my bedroom. Hanna has slipped in beside her. The kitchen-diner's large; there is a pull-out couch.

Click-clack.

I'm sitting up before I'm even awake.

Click-clack.

I know this sound. I swing myself off the couch, tensed against the slightest sound, a thump, a creak, as I lever my weight from the frame. Silence.

Click-clack.

It's coming from the bedroom. A shutter sound. Christ. I take a knife from the magnetic strip on the wall and edge towards the door. I open it, lean round. The bedroom door is open. There is a figure at the window, a box raised to her face.

Click-clack.

'Agnes.'

She turns. She motions, 'Shh.'

I slip past the bed – Hanna is still sleeping – and up to the window. When they refurbished the building they put in soundproof glass. A fancy kind, and very effective. Below us, a car burns in silence. Kids are dancing round it to a music we cannot hear.

Click-clack.

This is her father's camera, the bulky one he got the Christmas I stayed with them.

'Go back to bed.'

'I want to watch.'

'Go on.'

'Is that our car?'

'Of course not.'

'It could be.'

'You're parked on the other side of the building.'

'Agnes?' Hanna's awake.

Agnes puts down the camera and climbs into bed, snuggling down with her mother.

'Why are the curtains open?'

I draw them. 'Goodnight.'

I sit a while with my phone, watching mash-ups, mapping feeds, behaving, in other words, much like every other concerned householder tonight. (The lights are on all over the estate.) The gossip feeds are buzzing, but it looks as though tonight's action is headed west, away from us. Nothing happens. Nothing much. I see some young men wielding bats, crossing the square below my kitchen window. Vigilantes. Good. We look after our own in here, most of the time.

Agnes has settled back to sleep. I'm impressed. I would have thought the big bad city would have given her nightmares.

Their house is enclaved now. I was there last month, picking up Agnes for a date. (It was a kind of date. A meal, a show. It was fun. It was a glimpse of what the future Agnes ought to be like, unless her parents' separation ruins things for her.)

I remember I drove up to the house and there was this flimsy plastic barricade across their road. Pointless. A strong gust of wind would rip it off. That or the bull-bars of a speeding 4by4. There was a gatehouse next to it, and a kid slumped there in the uniform, several sizes too big, of a D-list private security company.

'How long's this been here?' I asked him, jovial enough. Breaking the ice.

'Who was it you wanted?'

There were no special signs of decline there – nothing obvious to explain the barrier. Presumably there are more break-ins there now, but that's true everywhere. The gate is best understood as a gesture – a community's more or less neurotic response to the gathering general threat.

Anyway I parked up below the house. When I first came here the view of the mountains had impressed me into thinking I had fallen into a pocket of genuine countryside, but now I saw that the place was not so very different from the housing estate that had haunted my childhood. It was simply better located, more expansive, its gardens concealed behind high hedges, with lines of mature trees preserved here and there, to hint at woods long since cut down. How many children's memories did this place erase, I wonder?

I sit up in bed again. Spring up, heart hammering.

It's just after dawn – whatever magic there was has gone out of the air, but it's still not properly light. I pad over to the light switch, shivering. It occurs to me that I am naked. Hanna could walk in. Agnes. And the kitchen blinds are open. Fuck it. Snap. And into bed again. Well, couch. Jesus, it's cold.

It's not the light has woken me, or the cold. It's the estate. The memories it has not quite erased. That sound: *Click-clack*.

Was it Michel that night, watching me throw my mother away? Absurd. Taking photographs? No. This is the logic of nightmare – a welling paranoia that, given its head, could swallow everything and everyone.

But even as I'm rejecting the idea – the product of a troubled night, no more, a coincidence – I remember something else.

The riverbank. Michel's ring of fridges. His redoubt. The voyage. 'We're sailing round the world.' Hanna's skin glowing. Michel's lined and weathered face, in the low light of the living room, looking like something made out of wood.

Last year I told Bryon Vaux about my mother. He offered to help me find out about her. He walked me out of his office and Michel was there in the lobby waiting to talk to him. I hadn't seen him in a while. 'Conrad. Hi.' He shook my hand. His skin was rough and broken. He was working with his hands.

I tug my jeans on and go through to the bedroom. Hanna and Agnes are awake, chatting.

'Hanna. I think I know where he goes.'

So, after a gap of twenty years, I find myself going home, back to the town I grew up in.

The weather is getting worse by the hour. The rain comes down in sheets. The radio is a mess of flood warnings and contradictory travel advice. The traffic piles itself upon itself, and all three lanes set solid, trapping me in a tailback that streams up the hill in a red-grey blur. Emergency vehicles shoot past on the hard shoulder, lights showering the rain-mapped glass.

Another 4by4 goes by on the inside. Sod it. I turn the wheel.

The junction is jammed. Three hundred yards from the turn-off I join a line of cars waiting on the hard shoulder. Beside me, virtually the whole slow lane is signalling. It takes me twenty minutes to leave the motorway, and while I'm shunting and braking, the great lid of the sky begins to break up. Its uniform grey clumps into bricks and anvils that catch the late morning light. Sunlight floods the windscreen and the rain comes down harder than ever, the clouds wringing themselves out like rags.

It's mid-afternoon by the time I find a way through the outskirts of town. I park up in a crescent of new houses.

The road into the centre is closed to traffic. I walk along its dotted white line. Even that paltry transgression – stepping where cars would normally run – feels strange to me. I wonder at myself and my own absurdity. I have spent too long in the city, obeying its tight rules of conduct, stepping out its precise, pedestrian dances.

Floodwaters have swept trash in piles against garden walls. Amongst the leaf-litter and twigs are fragments of man-made stuff. Smashed shelving, squares of plywood, lolly sticks, boxes, cartons, pallets. Crisp packets. Styrofoam. Someone is wrestling a sofa chair through their front door. The chair was white once, and from the state of the fabric – the dark line running just below the level of its arms – you can see how high the water came. The sofa falls out into the front garden. A man follows it out. His shirt is smothered in dirt. Perhaps the waters rose around him, too. I imagine him rooted to the spot, vanishing, inch by inch, under a cold, thin slurry.

He drags his sofa chair over and leans it against his garden wall. He kneels, gets his weight under it, and heaves it over the wall onto the pavement. He comes out through the garden gate and drags the chair towards a flatbed truck piled with swollen hardboard and peeling kitchen units. I go to help him.

He waves me away. 'I wouldn't, mate. Your clothes.'

So I stand there, watching him work.

Eventually I come to an area of standing water. It's not deep. I wade through it. My feet are wet through anyway; it doesn't make any difference. There are shops, and a woman in a headscarf is using a broom to sweep water the colour of chocolate out of her front door and onto the pavement. In the road is a pile of ruined stock. Cardboard boxes bursting with rice. Open boxes full of chocolate bars, leaves and toilet tissue. I catch the woman's eye, and look away.

Men in high-vis vests sweep water off the pavements and into the roads. The water spills back behind them as they go. They look absurd, trying to Canute the waves like this, but it's not the water they're trying to sweep away but the filth and fragments the water has deposited everywhere.

A side road rises and turns right, along the river. All along the embankment, people stand watching. The flow, enormously swollen, has swept the bridge away. Two large piles of fallen masonry break the surface of the water, but most of the bridge is hidden beneath the flood. You can tell it's there because of the smooth whale-back shapes the water makes, and the rills of foaming stuff in the lee of each bulge. Here and there, rafts of leaf-litter and rubbish shoot past. They touch and drift apart, touching twiggy arms.

Toward the centre of town, a couple are dumping the contents of their home into a skip. The man comes out with a plastic box piled with toys. A boy runs out after him. He's wearing galoshes and a bright red mackintosh. He wants something from the box. A woman comes out and catches him by the arm.

'Conrad.'

He's by my side.

'Fuck's sake, Michel.'

'I startled you.'

'Fuck's sake.'

We retrace my steps back to the main road. Michel is looking well but weathered. His hair is turning grey – unless, of course, it's dust from the sander (*old gel coat powder tightening across his skin …*). There's a camera around his neck, of course. There usually is. And after all, this is a flood. A real flood. Michel, the bard of apocalypses, has a duty to his readership to get the details right. I ask him, 'Where shall we go?'

'Sand Lane, of course.'

'How are we going to get there?'

'What do you mean, how are we going to get there? We're going there.'

'But it's on the other side of the river.'

Michel frowns at me. 'What are you talking about, Conrad? It's that way.' He points, between buildings I do not recognise, new buildings, new developments, a new town. He's been here more recently than I have, many times, checking in on his mother. He knows this place. His mental maps of it are up to date.

Mine aren't. This may as well be a new town, for all I remember. This is not my birthplace. I was never here.

But the hotel is still standing, my old home, and it's still in good order. It's not a hotel any more. I'm not sure what it is. There is a new fence, and a wrought-iron gate. A sign on the retaining wall sports the logo of a high street bank.

The housing estate has declined. There are a lot of un-roadworthy vehicles hidden under tarpaulins or simply left to rust on the verges and in gardens overgrown with weeds. The gardens have grown up at last, but they are straggly, untidy. The place has reached old age without acquiring maturity. It still looks as though it was thrown together yesterday – then doused in neglect.

Poppy's garden, with its dwarf this and dwarf that and miniature the other, is still the neatest of the lot; she must police it from beyond the grave.

In order to wrap up Poppy's affairs, Michel needs to go

through her papers. First, of course, he has to find them. This is not going to be easy. Poppy was always putting things away in safe places. I remember I ran into her one time she was visiting Michel at university. She said she had some money to give him. Off she went to the toilet. She had it hidden in her knickers. Michel unlocks the front door. 'Check for loose floorboards, for papers stuck in books.' I imagine us dressed in paramilitary black leather, hunting out seditious literature behind skirting boards and inside ceiling lamps.

A local house-clearing firm has been booked for the middle of the week to take away the furniture. Poppy used to make a big production out of it, but all in all it's very poor stuff.

I find instant coffee in the cupboard. The kettle is so clean, so polished, it might have been unboxed yesterday. We stand in the lounge, sipping instant coffee. Neither of us dares to sit on Poppy's sofa.

'Has Hanna told you we're separating?'

'I can't think why.'

'It's not what you think.'

What do I think? What am I supposed to think? 'What about Agnes?'

'I'm doing this for her.'

'Doing what? Quitting? Disappearing? She misses you.'

'I'm around.' He sounds very sure of himself. I know this confidence. I have heard it before, and have fallen under its spell. Michel has a project. 'Let's look at your hands.'

'What?'

'Come on, Mick.' I take his coffee cup off him and set it down in the sink. 'Show me your hands.'

He holds them out for me. He smiles.

'Christ, Michel. What is it? What are you building? A ship?'

'Why build a boat when the sea will come for you?'

'Where is it?'

'Near.'

'Will you show me?'

He hesitates, caught between his self-myth – the brave survivor, girding himself for the war of all against all – and his pride. Even his most committed and literal-minded fans cannot know, as I know, the deep seriousness that underlies Mick's stories of the Fall. At last, he shakes his head. 'Some other time.'

How casually we talk of this! But I have lived with Michel's project all my life. His determination to survive. It's nothing new. Nothing strange. He was always going to do this. He was always going to build this. It was only ever a question of when.

Michel wants to get up in the loft straight away. He finds the garage key in the drawer of the telephone table. He wrestles the ladder out from behind buckets and bags of garden fertiliser and carries it into the house. It's as well that Poppy's not around to see this. *'I'm not having you clambering about the loft. I'm not having you up there stamping about in my things!'*

The loft hatch is in the hall, directly in front of the frosted-glass kitchen door. The hall is only just wide enough for the stepladder. I can't get past. The old claustrophobia grabs me suddenly. It is daunting to think of Michel living out his entire childhood in these few, cell-like rooms. 'How is it up there?'

'There's not much.' Michel is disappointed. He is moving directly over my head and through the ceiling, his shuffling sounds hollow and at the same time oddly intimate – a scratching in the ear.

'Shall I come up?'

'If you like. There's not a lot of room.'

I need the toilet first. I'd forgotten how bloody small the lavatory is – the size of those cells you see in dungeon attractions, meant to contort the body of the inmate before he's hauled off to interrogation.

The toilet roll holder is mounted on the wall on my right. It is a simple chrome bracket. A sprung plastic rod holds the toilet roll in place. On the wall, above and to the left, there is a blemish. I remember it. It is, as far as I know, the only blemish in the whole, seamlessly white house.

It must have come from the rag of the roller. The fleece. I'm not sure, though; it looks more like a piece of paper. It's no bigger than the rim of a baby's fingernail and it's folded over itself at right-angles to make a circumflex or tail-less arrow, pointing towards the corner of the skirting board. I remember, every day, several times a day, I would stare at this blemish as though it were a sign, pointing me the way out of this place.

I get my thumbnail under the blemish and dig in. The fleck slides under my nail, into the quick, hurting me, and a spot of pinkish gray plaster appears on the wall.

Something pops. A loud, hollow sound, followed by a rain of sand. Michel's voice cuts sharply through. '*Fuck.*'

I finish up on the toilet and hurry out. 'Michel?'

A sound of tearing cardboard.

'Shit.'

Michel has knocked a hole in the ceiling of the dining room – not with 'great big feet' after all, but with the corner of a cardboard box. It looks as if the whole thing may fall through. I stand well clear. 'Are you all right?'

'Fucking stupid!'

'What?'

'There are boxes here stuffed so full you can't lift them. What's the point of that?'

'Are you all right.'

'Yes, yes, I'm fine. *Shit.*'

The living room table is smothered in plaster fragments and dust. I run my finger through it. Above me, Michel wrestles the box back through the gap. Dust rains down. I stand back, heels crunching plaster into the dog-hair-thin pile of the floor tiles. 'Do you need a hand?'

He doesn't reply, so I go to the dining room and open the drinks cabinet.

There are bottles in here I remember from my youth. Melon liqueur, blended whisky, various fruit 'creams'. Small, pretty, stemless glasses with coloured bands round the outside. I pour half a glass of sherry, open a bottle of chocolate liqueur, and upend it to see what, if anything, comes out. A brownish syrup winds its way through the sherry.

I knock it back.

I take a second glass out of the cabinet, a half-bottle of coffee liqueur and an unopened schnapps. There's white wine at the back of the cabinet. A corkscrew in the drawer above the cabinet, amongst the cutlery. I press the screw in, and the cork plops into the wine.

Above my head comes a second pop, louder than before. I look up in time to see Michel's foot rise and disappear into the hole he has made. A neat, foot-shaped piece of plaster lies intact under the window. It might have been stamped out by a die. The air is full of dust. Light enters between the room's slatted blinds and cat-cradles the room.

Michel moves from rafter to rafter over my head.

The kitchen ceiling gives way. I go to see. The ribbed plastic shade covering the fluorescent ceiling light has fallen to the floor. The tube has shattered into fragments.

I take the second glass to the foot of the stepladder. 'Michel.'

He's still moving about up there, back and forth, back and forth – a cat trapped in a shed. 'Yeah.'

'I've got you a drink.'

'What?'

'A drink. I've got you a drink. Come over to the ladder.'

He kneels down on the loft hatch and I lift the glass up to him. He says, 'Why did you fuck my wife?'

'What?'

'You heard.'

'She wasn't your wife back then.'

'Did you think I would never find out?'

'You said it was all water under the bridge.'

'I want to know why.'

'We nearly got ourselves killed driving back from that fucking dreadful party you took us to. We took a moment.'

Michel comes down the ladder, very fast. I offer him his drink again. He slaps it out of my hand, but suddenly it all goes out of him. The anger. The frustration. 'Fair enough,' he says.

'Your mum knew.'

'Yes.'

'She told you, that Christmas.'

Michel tries to laugh. 'Not in so many words. She thought I ought to know. Because of your mum. Her depression. The way she vanished. All that.'

'Well. Yes.'

I wish to God I'd said something before. It's too late now.

The Margrave is still trading, in spite of the flood, the broken bridge, and all the petty emergencies snaggling the area. It's a destination restaurant now, with a star. Green eels from the river in dill with a cucumber salad. Somewhere down the lane I dragged my mum's body down, the water must be roiling by. I wonder what it looks like. I wonder if the flood is ploughing under all the changes that have been made since I was here last. I wonder if, unseen by me, it is returning the landscape to something I would recognise. I doubt it. Things do not 'return to nature'. Nature fucks everything up and in the process fashions something new. The mind does not remember old geographies because, at its base, the mind is not nostalgic. It knows how the world is wired.

'You think it's coming, then. The Fall. In spite of this.' I wave the menu – a symbol of human tenacity. It seems to me things are still pretty resilient. They're serving puddings here, for crying out loud.

I tell him, 'It seems to me there's still a lot of rain left to fall before civilisation gives out.'

'The flooding isn't going to bring things down. I'm not talking about disasters.'

'No?'

Michel shoots me a look. 'Since when did disasters have anything to do with the collapse of civilisations? There's always a flood, a drought, a plague of something. Civilisations *deal* with catastrophes. It's why we commit to them.'

'So why choose this moment to go play Noah in the woods? Christ's sake, Michel, Agnes—'

'Thank you for reminding me.'

'Michel.'

'I know I have a daughter. Why do you think I'm doing this?'

I push my plate away. 'Try telling me, Mick. I've been a long time in the real world. It's hard to think my way back into your bullshit.'

'When civilisations collapse, it's because they fall out of joint. They deafen on their own feedback. They can no longer imagine themselves.'

This is an insight Michel has wisely – or at any rate cynically – omitted from his commercial fiction.

He says to me, 'Have you seen what Ralf is doing?'

This I don't expect. But of course, Michel is still writing, and his writing is still grist to Bryon Vaux's production mill. Of course Michel will know what Ralf is up to.

'Broadcast AR.'

Michel's smile is predatory. 'Be careful how you blink.'

'It won't catch on.'

'It won't?' He leans forward. '*How will you know?*'

It's not something I want to think about. But it's another reason, perhaps, why Michel and Hanna have been having such a bad time of it recently. Michel, sneaking off to construct his long-planned redoubt. Hanna with her outpatient's appointment, her simple procedure, her permanently AR-enabled eyes.

On the way back to Poppy's house we detour by the river. Or we try to.

'Where is it?'

Though Michel knows the town better than I do, he's as startled as I am by this change. 'Fucked if I know.'

It's not in flood. It's not in spate. It's not even here. It's been paved over. Canalised. There is no millrace, and no bridge crossing the millrace, just a horseshoe of low stairs and a concrete ramp for prams and wheelchairs, and – where the river used to be – a bicycle lane winds through landscaped parkland. The underbrush and low trees that used to conceal the water have been cleared away and lime-green exercise machines put in their place. It's nothing like I remember. It's devastating. In a way I can't put into words, it's almost the *opposite* of what I remember, and as we walk, I can feel the memories of my youth begin to fizz and react in the solvent of this new real. I stare at my feet, afraid of how much of myself I am losing.

The same high, forbidding fence runs around the hotel garden. The lawn is the same but the beds have matured out of all recognition. They stand like eruptions of wildwood in all that close-cropped green. On the lawn, teams of young executives in branded T-shirts and sloppy pants are attempting to build a bridge from one flowerbed to another without stepping on the lawn. There are wooden poles, large, brightly coloured foam cushions, ropes and buckets. It is some sort of team-building exercise, and it seems to be working. At least, there is a lot of laughter.

'Conrad?'

'I'm okay.'

'Come on, Conrad,' Michel says. 'Let's go home.'

Up in Poppy's loft there's light of sorts – a weak, dusty bulb shining from a socket screwed to a joist. Really the light from the bulb does little more than blend everything into everything else: cardboard, wood, roofing felt. Even the shadows are the colour of dried meat.

Light rises in white columns from the holes Michel has made. These shafts of dusty light do nothing to dispel the darkness; if anything, they make it more intense. I'm trying to orientate myself, but it seems to me that the holes are far too close together. If *this* is a hole in the living room ceiling, how can *that* be a hole in the dining room? The bungalow has always felt small, but this is ridiculous. Up here, you can move from room to room in a single stride.

Because the boxes are so heavy, Michel has been decanting their contents, balancing boxes and plastic-wrapped bundles on the rafters.

There's a box full of toys. A metal dumper truck, heavy as a bastard. A pair of binoculars in a leather case – I suppose they must have been his father's. In a plastic carrier bag I find an old film camera – Michel's, confiscated by his mum when the school discovered him taking photographs of his elderly clients. Bit by bit I bring the stuff down. I try to interest Mick in keeping some of the toys and bits and pieces for Agnes. Agnes. Agnes this and Agnes that. I cannot help myself. I am afraid for her. Michel's redoubt is for her – a bolt-hole for her when the world falls down. The thing is, the Fall will not declare itself. One day, Michel will simply draw a line in the sand and bear her off. 'Does Hanna know what you're planning?'

He says, 'Why don't you keep these at your place for when Agnes visits? We've got enough junk in the house.'

'Michel.'

'What?'

'Does Hanna know?'

He pulls over another box and cuts it open with a knife. 'You would think so by now.'

'What does she say?'

Michel picks at the contents of the box. There's all sorts of stuff in here. Old cigarette cards from the 1950s. Snow domes. Scarves.

'She told me to fuck off, Connie, if you must know.'

I teeter from rafter to rafter, between boxes and tea chests, to where Michel has put his foot through the kitchen ceiling.

Given the wreck it has made of the room, the hole Michel's foot has made is smaller than I expected. He's stamped directly into the light, dislodging and breaking it. To see anything through the hole, though, I have to balance on the joists on my hands and knees. I peer around the metal light housing. It is still just about attached to the ceiling.

Particles of loft insulation are making my eyes smart, but looking through the gap, I see the kitchen laid out below me. The stainless-steel kitchen sink stands directly in front of the window, reflecting light entering from the garden. To the left of the sink is the fridge, and on top of the fridge is a radio. The fridge is next to the back door. The left-hand side of the door frame sits flush with the wall of the pantry.

I thread my way under a support, steadying myself against the A-frame. I kick a hole in the ceiling where the lavatory should be. My foot comes through short of the door, and too much to the left. I'm off by at least a yard.

I move again, hunker down against the frame, and dig through the loft insulation with the toe of my shoe. I find the ceiling and press, steadily and gently. The plasterboard does not crack; instead it crumbles against the retaining pins. The bathroom ceiling gives on one side, and grit and dust falls through the gap. That sound again: a rain of sand.

Light fans obliquely through the loft.

I toe the ceiling again and the whole thing gives way. Michel climbs up the ladder and comes over and together we stare into the bathroom. The ceiling has come down in one piece, shattering against the cabinet, the sink, the bathtub, and the windowsill.

Soon the ceilings are completely destroyed, smothering everything in filth and felt, particles and plaster. We climb down the ladder and explore. Every room looks like every other now – impossible to make out which room is which, or what each room is for. They aren't even rooms any more, just spaces marked out by walls whose tops are just too high for us to touch – the walls of a maze.

Movement is hard because of the amount of felt, plaster and filth we've brought down. We pick our way between the larger pieces and stir the rest with our feet, seeking the familiar terra firma of carpet, floor tile and floorboard. But the mind cannot retain vanished geographies, and we find ourselves adapting to this new terrain. We crush the wood and plaster we've brought down to create narrow paths of pulverised stuff, and bit by bit, as our paths sink below the level of the wreckage, they come to represent a convention as incontrovertible, in its way, as the convention formerly established by walls and doors.

We take off our shoes. We take off our socks. In theory we have the freedom of all the space we have imagineered. Still, we stick obediently to the interlocking trails of our ephemeral redoubt.

We take off our clothes.

We find Poppy's bed and we use it.

On and on like this. We are committed now.

NINETEEN

A year later.

   Picture it: in the hills outside the capital, Ralf is eating *çig köfte* with Bryon Vaux.

Picture it: their favourite eating house. The walls of the dining room are decorated with antique blue tiles depicting water mills and mosques. The table candle casts a greasy sheen over Vaux's almost-convincing eyes.

A while ago, with his purchase and restructuring of Loophole, Vaux threw Ralf a ball. It is doubtful that Vaux has had any idea, until this evening, of just how far Ralf has run with it.

Ralf is mid-pitch, deep in his argument for massively increased funding. He wants Vaux to help him bring to birth the next stage in the evolution of Augmented Reality. He says, 'What makes a sense? What makes sight "sight", smell "smell"?'

He might have handed his employer a package of pornography, the way Vaux's mouth has set. The tension finds its way even to his fingertips; Ralf watches in dismay as Bryon Vaux bends and dents the photographs. Blind dogs, their eye-sockets fibre-opticked into satellite TV. Monkeys flayed and grafted to a newsfeed. Dolphins whose only water is the shipping news.

Entrepreneur, billionaire, icon of the new world order, Vaux has been diversifying his portfolio. He no longer devotes his energies solely to the entertainment business. Entertainment is a spent force, or so he reckons. Enwrapment – that's the next thing. Captivation. Rapture.

Ralf is his pilot through the coming media storm. A good choice – Ralf has always had his eyes on the big picture. ('I have lots of ideas,' he once confessed to me. 'I just don't know how to rate them.' I'd lay money he is not so naive any more.)

'Briefly,' Ralf begins, 'there are three components to any sensory perception. First, a physical phenomenon – electromagnetic radiation, say. Second, a responsive organ, in this case an eye.

'Of course,' he continues, warming to his theme, 'evolution has been pretty parsimonious about what she lets us see of the world. And every sighted animal, according to its specific survival needs, accesses a different portion of the spectrum. None of us – no species – gets the full picture.'

Evolution by natural selection, by Ralf's measure, scrapes barely a couple of stars. Design's the thing. Genius beats genetics hands-down, every time. With Vaux's money at his back and a travel budget that has had him rub shoulders with the best and brightest splicers on the circuit, Ralf has been winning notoriety – the Da Vinci of vivisection.

There is something curious about Ralf's style of delivery tonight – and no wonder, since his late-won eloquence is pulled daily from self-help manuals and crash-courses in public speaking. His pedantry has a saving, surreal quality. 'Every sighted animal' is very good.

But Vaux's plastic eyes give nothing away. 'You said three elements.'

'The third component of sensory perception is the brain. Dedicated areas of the brain take the data received by the organ of sense, and search it for pattern and order. From that comes the model.'

'The model?'

'Your model, my model, of what the world is like. We only have models, Mr Vaux. From the little data granted us, we extrapolate a model of the world. This we call "reality".'

Vaux picks up the photographs again. He imagines, perhaps, that Ralf's explanations may have normalised them. Vain hope – he paws clumsily through the glossies and comes up with a German Shepherd, its eyes wired to a university mainframe.

'We wired him as a pup,' says Ralf, 'before his eyes could see. Dogs are born blind. We gave him other eyes, and he grew into them.'

'The dog adapted to the feed?'

'Quite well.'

'Quite well?'

Ralf shrugs. 'We feed it raw data from the National Weather Centre. Whenever he feels a big storm on the way he starts barking.'

Vaux shakes his head – whether from wonder or confusion or dismay, Ralf (being Ralf) cannot tell. 'A kludge, I admit,' Ralf persists, nervous now. 'The new neuroplastics give better results. With them, we can build new centres in the brain. New optic lobes, for different kinds of eyes.'

Vaux knows nothing of the thefts from Ralf's home, from his car, and from the atelier he maintains in a piece of family property just across the road from Loophole's old club.

Nor is he ever likely to. The thefts are a serious embarrassment for Ralf. That he ever borrowed such valuable and commercially sensitive kit for his own use is obviously a sackable offence. That he left it lying around unsecured for any passing street-thief or housebreaker to steal could well have Vaux suing Ralf for everything he has ever paid him, 'Chief Imagineer' or not.

It is Ralf's own fault. Ever the tinkerer, he has never quite shaken off the feeling that he can achieve more by himself than he can while sitting in state in the bosom of some well-appointed science palace belonging to Vaux.

The thefts were not subtle affairs. Ralf surely guesses that the thieves knew what they were looking for. He surely suspects *us* – but he does not let on.

Meanwhile Michel and I find our own uses for Ralf's aerosolised AR.

We hit the pharmacy without warning: surgical, bloodless and fast.

Wherever the night manager moves, walls tilt, floors vanish, ceilings fall. She comes to rest at last in the corner of the dispensary, barely moaning now, her vestibular system folding up under our psychoelectric assault.

Nausea has overcome her fear. She heaves miserably, spittle dribbling from her chin. She has nothing left to bring up. She has her eyes squeezed shut, but this is no defence against the images being hammered, seventy taps a second, directly against her visual cortex.

And what a cornucopia is here! Medicines and unguents enough to tide us and our loved ones through the Fall. We wander at leisure among the stacks. Pethidine and methadone. Methylphenidate and fentanyl. Oxycodone. While Michel fills the rucksack, I go keep watch by the window. I've repelled one unexpected visitor already. After a few minutes' farcical dancing, trying to open a door that was not there, and falling, repeatedly, through a wall he kept trying to lean upon, our visitor has pretty much given up on reality. He's kneeling now on the lawn outside the clinic, mouth drawn in a scream he will never utter, because it is possible, even at this remove, for me to paralyse precise channels in his vagus nerve. It is daunting that, after years of more or less constructive effort, I should once again be reduced to playing toy soldiers. Making them march. Making them fall. I might be back at the hotel, watching Dad's soldiers picking their way across the back lawn.

Talking of which.

I weave my fingers in the air, tapping unreal keys, extending my field of influence. The authorities cannot be far away; better that I immobilise them while they are still out of pot-shotting range.

We change number plates twice before attempting to leave the city. We encounter no obstacles. The traffic is light. On the motorway, we listen to the radio. There is still no government. Compromise after compromise, pact after pact has collapsed before the region's escalating economic and environmental problems. Tensions are running high and foreign interference is making the problem worse. Last night a dozen election observers found themselves trapped in their hotel by a placard-waving mob.

Still, Michel's millennial interpretations of these events feel excessive to me. For thousands of years, civilisations have dealt with floods and droughts, failed harvests and pests and plagues. Am I so naive to hope that our world might, after all, save itself from itself?

Michel says that collapses happen all at once, and suddenly. I believe this. It does not take long for people to starve.

But when do we start to prepare for the Fall, and how? Michel says we have to become the very thing we fear. That preparing for the Fall brings on the Fall. 'To survive,' he says, 'we may have to hate ourselves.' The boot of our car is a measure of his seriousness. Packed in party bags of ice: paromomycin, ertapenem. Tamiflu. Meropenem, combivir, cefprozil, ceftobiprole. Every stripe of penicillin, polypeptides, quinolones.

I turn us off the motorway, west, towards Michel's redoubt. Soon enough the road dwindles to a single lane over which high hedges impend, the canopies of trees touching here and there to make green tunnels.

The road disappears under pools of standing water. The steering wheel pulls oddly as I gun us through. I find a patch of hard-standing in lee of a barn and park up. 'It's deeper now.'

'Yes.'

'We'll have to walk from here.'

We change our footwear, pull on galoshes and tug thick jumpers over our Ts. While Michel packs stolen medicines into my rucksack, I go around securing the car. Steering lock. Wheel clamp. I check the padlock securing the petrol cap. None of this would deter a determined thief, but hardly anyone lives around here any more and anyway, the fuel crisis is not yet so intense.

It's been raining, and we're still in cloud shadow, though coins of greenish light spin and glimmer over hillsides on the other side of the valley. After ten minutes we come to a home-made barrier – a string of orange plastic tape and a hardboard sign propped against an upturned bucket.

FLOOD

Michel holds the string up for me to duck under. The road lies under six inches of water. A wall has come down and there are stones all over the road.

Turning a corner, everything before us is silver – an inland sea. Birds zig-zag over the vanished land. Otherwise nothing disturbs the stillness. There are no people, no animals, no signs of damage or distress, no abandoned vehicles, no machines listing in the mud. The farmers here are used to floods. They have their routines to save their work and their livestock from the water.

'"The scene was peaceful. Natural. This was the land as it had been, before the improvers and mechanics and engineers got hold of it, turning it to human use. For all the years men had worked and lived here, this landscape had lain in wait, encysted, weathering the drought occasioned by human progress, longing to be remembered."'

'Who's that then?'

'It's you. Twat. Your first book.'

Michel makes a face. 'What can I say? The copy-editor really got her teeth into that one.'

We stand together in silence, watching patches of light and darkness play upon the water. Michel's happiness is palpable. After years of waiting and dreaming, his wish has been granted – the sea has come to him.

Me? I wish I had been braver, all those years ago. Even now Hanna and I might be on a boat together, tacking timidly about the poorer and more broken parts of the earth—

'Help me with the boat.'

The rowboat is hidden under a screen of branches, well away from the waterline. We run the constant risk here of having our kit float off on an unexpected swell. Maps offer only the crudest idea of how the marsh will spread. The neglect and collapse of the old agricultural drainage changes the shape of the shoreline week by week.

The trailer is hidden a short distance away, to discourage thieves. Winching the boat onto the trailer is the hardest part of the job, and the one that takes the most time. Michel frets at this; he fears our exposure here.

'Relax,' I tell him, gluey fingers weaving the air. For the moment, we are ahead of the curve, invisible to all unweaponised eyes.

At the waterline, we take our leave. 'You know how to find me,' he says, hugging me. At the last minute, it has come home to him that he does not want to live alone.

We kiss. I cradle his chin in my hand. 'You said that come the End Times, it would be every man for himself.'

'I did. Give my love to Agnes and Hanna.'

'I will.'

We stow the rucksacks into the bottom of the boat. Michel seats himself in the bows and unships the oars. A subtle current bears him home, away from me, over flooded levels. I follow him along the shoreline a little way, to where the ground grows soft, and rushes grow up to tickle the branches of dying trees.

He will not thank me for this – for attracting attention like this – but I do it anyway. I wave goodbye to him.

Michel still visits his wife and child.

Picture it:

The gate is flimsy, a hollow bar of moulded plastic, and a gust of wind has brought it down, or maybe the bull-bars of a speeding 4by4. The gatehouse, a burned-out ruin, stinks of piss.

He climbs the slippery decking stairs to Hanna and Agnes's door. The door has a new lock. He lets himself in anyway. 'Hello?'

'Michel?'

Hanna comes through from the kitchen.

Michel kisses her cheek.

She says, 'Do you want some tea?'

'Sure,' Michel says.

'Come into the kitchen. You've missed Agnes.'

'I can tell.'

'She's round at Libby's. Do you want me to call her, tell her you're here?'

'No, it's all right.'

Agnes is twelve. She is afraid of Daddy now. Just a little. Just enough to count. Michel says, 'I came to see you're all right.'

Money flows in from his properties and copyrights. Most of it goes to his wife and daughter. Deep into his rehearsal of the Fall, his training, Michel does not need much money.

They live in separate worlds now, Hanna and Michel. Perhaps they always did. Hanna never did credit the sincerity of Michel's dreams of collapse. She has always found them childish.

Once again Michel seeks to persuade her. 'I just want you both to be safe.'

'To survive.'

All their meetings end this way, however light they try to keep things. It is the tenor of the times. Most everyone has an opinion about this now. The coming Fall.

'Yes. To survive.'

'If that is possible.' She tries to meet his eye. Michel believes in survival. It is why he is so strong now, so muscled, so tanned. He looks as though he has toppled out of one of his own book covers.

The redoubt is nearly done, he says. Wood and lathe and stone. A real house, really hidden, against the day the supermarket shelves run empty and civilisation, having cruised along for millennia, collapses in the space of a day. This happens. Cultures do collapse. The Harappans. Egypt's Old Kingdom. The Teotihuacans burned down their city in a ritual fire. The Olmec buried themselves.

Michel has done what he can. He has promised his family rooms in the fortress he is building, half-in, half-out of the earth. When things fail and fall, it will be up to families to survive, he says. Families and clans. Michel is very persuasive. (You don't get sales figures like his, you don't get option deals, unless you have something simple and compelling to say.)

But let's be honest here – Hanna is the tougher of these two. She has to be. She has a daughter to look after. She has no choice but to live in the everyday world, with all its prompts to fear and denial and secession. 'How did you get in, anyway?' she asks, examining the front door.

'You've had trouble?'

'What?'

'To be fitting new locks.'

'No. No trouble.' She studies the mechanism, unnerved by her husband's burglar's skills, and, by extension, all the brutal lore he lives by now, and which she will not learn.

'The thing is, Hanna, it still just about makes sense for people to be kind and decent to each other. But this will change, and it will change on a penny.'

'I know this is what you think, Michel. You have told me this before. You keep saying this.'

'We have to be ready.'

'I know.'

'No. You think you know. You don't know.'

Hanna sighs. She can only stomach so much of this sort of thing. 'I'll give Agnes your love, Mick. Please fuck off now.'

'Hanna.'

'Go back to your boyfriend. Go back to Connie. Go on.'

TWENTY

Whatever this is – ruin or renaissance – the future hurls itself at us piecemeal, raising some of us, hurling others down. The future is not democratic. In cities to the east of the country, people are still living out the kind of lives I remember from my childhood.

It's bloody cold here, but for some reason nobody wears much. I go into a cafeteria to buy a take-out coffee and at the tables sit young builders in plaster-spattered Ts and bare-legged shop assistants. Just looking at them makes me shiver. I try to pay with a card. Stupid of me. The girl behind the counter just stares.

The town, built entirely of brick, is the colour of old blood. I stuff my free hand into the pocket of my puffer jacket and tug its stuffing around my middle. I'm cold to the core. It's not just the weather. The train was a sleeper

in name only, the banquettes were cripplingly uncomfortable and I've slept very badly.

Or maybe it's just that I'm old. Older. Anyway, old
enough for my age to matter: at forty, the age my mother
was when she died. Sara. I drink my coffee, burn my
tongue, don't care.

There is a taxi rank by the station but after two drivers
refuse my fare I haul out a pair of glasses. I blink up a map
and a green arrow unfurls along the pavement before
me. The colour contrast between the map's Caribbean-
coloured 3D rendering and the town's scabby frontages is
so distressing I have to pause to blink up the preferences
pane.

'Got the time, mate?'

I'm equipped for this. Laboriously, I haul on the sleeve
of my puffer and study my cheap plastic watch.

I've been caught out before and mugged. Not today.
This place has a reputation, and I have come forewarned.
Old watch, old shoes, and all I need I'm carrying in a
canvas shopping bag – the paranoid preparedness of the
middle-aged. The kid pulls a face and doesn't even wait
for my reply. As I thought, it's just been a ruse to get me
to haul out my phone. My spectacles he doesn't clock, or
maybe they have no resale value in this place – it lags so
far behind the curve.

The arrow, blue now, leads me to the cliffs. The town,
in the days of its pride, made rigorous, geometric shapes
out of their slopes and hollows, locking everything in
brick. This mathematical neatness makes everything
look smaller and nearer than it is. I'm exhausted by the
time I reach the sea.

Tenements edge the cliff like long brown teeth. It's

as well I have this map running. The road signs have long since been pilfered for their scrap value. Derelict telephone poles, their wires torn away, stand nude and useless on each corner.

Far away a talk-radio station, its volume cranked up and fuzzy with distortion, attempts to comfort the streets. Broken glass shines in the gutters as I cross and climb a stairwell – brick, of course, and even in this biting cold, sharp with old urine.

There is a pile of dog faeces on the external landing. I step around it. Many of the flats are gutted, their doors and windows stoppered with magnolia-painted metal sheeting.

Those still occupied have had their house-numbers wrenched off. The number I'm looking for, 717, has been scratched over the door's paintwork in biro. There is no bell. I bang on the door and wait for an answer. I'm half-expecting him to peer out at me from behind the ash-grey nets, but no, he comes to the door readily enough, no chain, no dog, as if he was expecting me.

'Hello, Dad.'

He stands there, staring at me. It has been a long time since we last saw each other. Most of my life. He's grey now. Not just his hair. His skin is the colour of blurred newsprint. It is smothered in fine lines. 'You'd better come in,' he says, not moving. When I step forward, he steps back.

Perhaps he did expect me. I chose the day carefully, after all – the anniversary of Mum's death. After a lifetime thinking about her, about what she did to herself, I am now, second by second, growing older than her. I have survived her. Every moment now is a bonus. I am going to enjoy myself.

The smell of damp wrestles with the smell of stale cigarettes for domination of the air. Ben has compensated for his circumstances by filling the flat with other, better worlds. There are books everywhere. Travel magazines and Sunday supplements teeter in piles against the walls. There isn't anywhere to sit down beyond a hollow-bottomed leather couch under the lounge window, and Ben paddles his way towards that ahead of me, desperate as a drowning seaman striking out for the lifeboat.

I stay standing.

Ben blinks up at me. 'Well.'

The radio is on. The voice is one I recognise.

'How are you?'

I don't answer. I am listening to the programme. It is. It is Mandy. She's on a review show, discussing some exhibition I'm never going to see. She likes it. She's employing words like 'revenant' and 'spiky'. It's nice to hear her being so positive about something.

'Conrad?'

'Do you mind if we have the radio off?'

One thing about Mandy – she has staying power. Last year you couldn't turn your computer on without there being some banner trailer for her memoir creeping down the side of your screen on creepy, eight-fingered hands. She mentioned me, but glancingly – a minor lover of her early life, before the accident sewed her into her current, compelling form.

Ben snaps the radio off. He sits down. He swallows. He is very thin, strung out on whatever medicines are crowding the table by his side. 'How are you?'

I won't say anything to that. What would be the point? His eyes rove over me, a father's instinct kicking in. Bit by bit, you can see it register with him – my cheap clothing, my cap, my worn boots. The size of me.

Some bit of forgotten etiquette heaves into view behind his eyes. 'Do you want something to drink?'

'It's all right, Ben.'

He looks relieved. I wonder if there's anything at all in his kitchen. I'm tempted to ask him to show me around. 'This is the living room. This is the master bedroom.' I can see well enough how he lives – enough to know that I will never be able to add measurably to his burdens. It is hard for me, and not at all reassuring, to discover that life has exacted its own revenge upon him. I thought that was going to be my job. Now I'm here, there doesn't seem much point.

I tell him what I know. How I tried to contact him, in the weeks after Mandy's accident, but that he had never returned my calls. Even after all this work I cannot pinpoint exactly where his trail of phone numbers and forwarding addresses slid off into fiction.

Ben shakes his head, whether in denial, or because he can't himself remember, hardly matters now. The clinic he worked at, abandoning me to Poppy's care towards the end of my time at school – that was real enough. Even the job checked out. And the one after that. And the one after *that*.

By then, though, Dad had been reduced to some sort of high-grade janitor. After that his work record melted away into casual three-month contracts at this clinic, that care-home, each one further away than the last – he had moved across the public health network like a nomadic fisherman, following the seasons from pond to pond. Even his applications for criminal record checks (spotless, always) petered out in the end. The last six years are completely unaccounted for.

Will I look like this, when I am his age? So small, and, well, *pointed*? Like some small forest mammal, poking its snout up above the leaves. His presence is disturbing. It is so much less powerful than his absence has been.

I am strong now. Michel has toughened me. I could break him across my knee like a twig. I tell him, 'I hired a professional,' and I want to enjoy the way his face quivers, but to be honest all I can feel is a faint and guilty disgust.

I've been paying Cobb for a private investigation. He seemed to me a reasonable man. Vaux, with all the resources at his disposal, had employed him – this was as good as a recommendation.

Cobb, when he wasn't putting the virtual frighteners on me, turned out to be a pleasant, heavy-drinking ex-submariner on his second career and his third divorce. It took him no time at all to track Ben down. He found him managing a state-funded care home, a former B&B on the coast east of here. When Cobb phoned to tell me, he boasted that he hadn't even had to leave his desk. The work had proved so easy for him, he offered me a discount.

By the time I got up the guts to follow Cobb's lead, however, Dad had lost the job, the care home was closed down, and its elderly clientele were dispersed and absorbed. Dad's easy enough to find now that he's drawing his minuscule state pension.

'You know what day it is. Don't you?' I could be harder with him if I wasn't having to stand over him. Looming

like this, everything that comes out of my mouth, however innocuous, acquires the power of a threat. I sit on
one arm of the sofa, and he shifts backwards against
the other arm, edging away from me. I want to shed my
puffer jacket but these kinds of places can't afford heat,
and our breaths are coming out in clouds.

Dad seems to have acquired some of the district's
hardiness, making do in a red lumberjack shirt, the collar
turned up to hide the wattle of his neck. He offers me a
cigarette. Nothing dates him more than this – the genteel
suicide aid of a vanishing generation. 'I know what day it
is.' He takes a lighter from the table. A medicine canister
topples onto its side. He ignores it and inhales, dragging
the flame into his cigarette.

'You knew I found her. In the boot of the car. You knew
I saw her there.'

Ben closes his eyes. Is this suffering, or is he reliving a
painful moment of the past? It could be he's just savour-
ing his cigarette. With a face like his, it's impossible to
tell. Its mask of habitual suffering hides any ephemeral
emotion.

'I can tell you about it if you want.'

The story comes out of him easily, without any kind of
struggle. I don't know whether to believe it or not. There
are details which ring with such a nice irony, I wonder
whether life can really have thrown them up. The bag, he
says, was hers. The plastic bag, wrapped round her head
with packing tape. It's how he found her – after racing to
her aid, frantically trying to make sense of her confused
directions. ('I'm in a phonebox.')

How Sara's bipolar trajectory had kiltered so far off
its usual orbit, driving her to try suicide even before she

made it to the camp, Ben can only speculate. 'I got her to take her pills,' he says. 'Before she went to the camp. It was a deal we had.' Blaming iatrogenic medicine again. Presumably this is a trick he learned off her.

He found her in a motel room, the evening after she left. He knocked on the door and the door was already open. Perhaps she wanted to be found and rescued. Perhaps this was her cry for help.

The bed was a pool of vomit, with here and there frothy little islands of half-dissolved aspirin. Sara had passed out. The bag crackled as it rose and fell against her face. It was torn.

How long he sat there beside her, he cannot now remember. Eventually, borne down by the weight of things, he reached for a pillow and pressed it over her face until she stopped moving.

He picked her up in his arms and carried her down the corridor to the lobby. It was empty. He laid her down on the sofa by the door and went to the desk and rang the bell.

No-one came.

He waited. He doesn't know how long. In the end he picked her up again and carried her out to the car. He laid her on the back seat and looked up the location of the nearest hospital on his phone. He drove there and sat in the hospital car park all night. An edge of blue touched the horizon, and he remembered me. He pulled Sara off the back seat and laid her in the boot of the car. He drove home. He came home in time to see me safely to school.

'Come on, Connie. Up and at 'em.'

'Why didn't you say anything?'

'Oh, Connie.'

'I was fifteen.'

'Conrad.' He squeezes me. He has his arms round me. Strange, that I should be here now, on the sofa, pressed against him, his arms around me as though I was a child. Is this, after everything, what I have come here for? Can the body betray the mind so far? One thing I know – I can no longer bear it. The smell of him. The past. I push away from him, as I have never felt able to push away as a child. I am grown and he is old. At last, and more than twenty years too late, I push away.

'What?' His voice has grown stronger. Having me come here, only to crumble into his arms, has given him back his confidence. He imagines, perhaps, that we are father and son again.

I keep my back to him. I do not want him to see my face. (I don't even look like him. I am my mother's son. I look like her, now more than ever. Put me next to her as she was the year she died, frame us in a white-framed mirror, and you would not be able to tell us apart.)

'You let me hide Mum's body.'

Ben shakes his head. 'It all happened so fast. I was so afraid—'

'*You* were afraid!'

'Please Conrad.'

Bit by bit he grinds it out. His version of events. Frozen with fear, he had not been able to decide what to do with the body in the boot of his car. In the morning, very early – he had not even tried to sleep – he woke me. He knew I'd be expecting a lift to school, so he invented a last-minute conference to keep me from dumping my kit in the car. 'But you opened the boot anyway. You saw.'

'Of course I bloody saw. And you just stood there in the

porch in your stupid apron and you didn't say a thing. Not a thing.'

He palms the table for his cigarettes. Bottles and canisters fall off the table. He cannot find his cigarettes. Where are his cigarettes? Idiot, they're in the breast pocket of your curry-stained lumberjack shirt.

Eventually the penny drops. He draws on his cigarette, shakes out his match. 'When you said nothing, I thought maybe – I thought maybe she wasn't in the boot any more. I thought maybe, in the night, she had ...' He shakes his head. 'Anyway I dropped you off at school and when I got back home I opened the boot and – and I saw. I knew that you knew.'

'And then?'

'I figured, while you were at school, I would, I would have to find somewhere to leave her. I waited till the afternoon, I had appointments, clients to see. And just as I was wrapping things up – do you remember?'

'Remember what?'

'You turned up!' He finds it in himself to laugh. 'You remember that? Outside the conservatory? Tapping on the glass? Three o'clock in the bloody afternoon. Christ.' He sucks flame, desperately. 'I thought you were her.'

'And you still didn't say anything.'

'No.'

'You still didn't do anything. You had until six o'clock and you just carried on sitting there until it was time to pick me up from cricket and when you picked me up you said – this is all you said – "Let's get a drink."'

'Yes.'

'So in the end,' I say, 'you didn't have to worry about anything, did you? You just let me deal with her.'

291

This much he must allow. He coughs, and the cough dislodges something solid-sounding from somewhere in the back of his throat.

'And if she'd been found?'

He coughs some more. A lot more.

'If she had been found and I had been charged—'

'No.'

'You left all of it to me. You let me think you didn't know about her. You carried on for months as though you thought she was still alive.'

'No—'

'You had me carry all that shit. All that guilt. That fear. And even then it got too much for you, so you abandoned me. Left me in fucking Sand Lane. You ran away.'

He fans the table with his hand, feeling for his medicine. He stares at me. His skin is not grey now. It is red.

If I did nothing, what would happen to him now?

He breathes, and then he doesn't, and then he breathes again.

'Oh, for fuck's sake.' I cross the room, heading for what I imagine must be the kitchen. (The only other door smells of drains.) 'Just wait.' Like he is going anywhere.

There are books in the kitchen, too. Cookbooks. There are vegetables in a wire rack by the sink. The room is a mess, but not that much of a mess. It draws me up, to discover that Dad's life is not a complete disaster. He cooks. He eats.

There's a single glass upended on the draining board. I run him some water from the tap. There's no heat in here but at least there is water.

Click-clack.

The water runs over my hand.

Click-clack.

I wrench the tap off so hard, the pipe trembles under my fingers.

Click-clack.

I carry the water into the lounge.

Dad is sitting on the sofa, crouched forward. He's a little recovered by now. He is pressing pills into his hand from a plastic dispenser.

Click-clack.

He looks up, sees me, sees the glass, and extends his hand.

I'd always wanted Mum's body to be found. Ben hadn't. He must have followed me when I left the Margrave. He must have seen me struggling with her. He must have seen me throw her away, like so much garbage, into the water. And when he saw me botch the job, well, he must have finished it.

'Conrad?'

I pour the glass out over his carpet.

'Conrad?' he calls after me. 'Will I see you again?'

He is pathetic. I can't even be angry with him.

I head back to the railway station. The cold calms me down. It occurs to me that Ben was frightened of me today, and that he probably always has been frightened of me. It is strange, to imagine myself as something other than a victim. But picture me the way I must appear to him – the son who silently abetted his father's crime.

By the time I've boarded my train, and too late to make any difference, I feel almost sorry for him. I sit drinking the coffee I bought on the station concourse. It isn't good.

I watch the town's industrial hinterlands fall away.

Goods trains, car transporters, tanker trucks and passenger locomotives weave in and out of sidings and through tunnels, braking and accelerating with an unnatural ease. We stop at red signals, go at green, signals responding to signals, and the scenery flashes by, less a landscape than a series of stills. We enter hilly countryside. The gradient doesn't bother this behemoth at all, and in minutes we have churned along mountainsides and over low saddles to regions so pure and bright, they might be made out of crystal.

The eye hunts for stories. At this speed, it catches only stills. A lorry on a country road, stationary before a flock of sheep crossing a ford. Its livery is in Cyrillic. The trucker has driven a long way – will he fall asleep at the wheel?

A car has come to rest, skewed across both lanes of a mountain road. Its front is stoved in where it pranged the safety barrier. Witnesses are running up the hill, around the blind bend, to warn on-coming drivers and prevent more collisions.

We flash through a small station. On the platform, a couple are embracing a child. Something peeks out of her daypack: a teddy bear, or a rabbit. Her parents have come to wave the child off. Where is she going? To school, perhaps, or to stay with a grumpy lone relative, high in the mountains.

The train is as clean as the landscape beyond. Clean and bright and new. Sweet smelling. Silent. Everyone is smiling. Everyone is like me.

Even the coffee tastes better now. I look out of the window, smiling into the light of the rest of my life. Every moment is a bonus. Every day is an adventure. The view is wonderful. The window is clean, with not a smear or scratch.

Only here and there, where the light hits it at an angle, can you see, printed on the glass, the handprint of a child.